D0940509

EDITOR'S NOTE

I came across the following astonishing chronicle,
purporting to be a record of journeys through time, in
a strange artefact that landed in my garden,
unfortunately roasting my pet tortoise in the process. I
confess I approached the account with extreme caution
and indeed a more than healthy scepticism, but I soon
became convinced that the writer, obnoxious fellow
though he might have been, had not only solved but
actually caused several long-standing historical
enigmas, and had discovered the links between such
seemingly unrelated events as the death of Rasputin,
the marriage of Cain, the drawing of the Nazca Lines,
the Crucifixion, or the Roswell landing.

Sadly, a few backward-thinking historians have
disdainfully rejected the authenticity of the document,
one of them even going so far as to accuse me, in the
august pages of *The Times*, of fabricating the whole
amazing story. I can but wait for posterity and
Boadicea to vindicate me.

Leonardo's *Codex N*, though badly charred in places,
was recently discovered in the burnt-out wreckage of
the time traveller's Dartmoor estate.

– Lemuel Hakluyt

STEVE REDWOOD

WHO NEEDS CLEOPATRA?

reverb

© Steve Redwood 2005

The moral right of the author has been asserted

reverb is an imprint of Osiris Press Ltd

This edition first published 2005 by

Osiris Press Ltd
PO Box 615
Oxford OX1 9AL

www.readreverb.com
www.osirispress.co.uk

A CIP catalogue record for this book is available from the British Library

ISBN 1 905315 03 1

Set in Baskerville 12/14.2pt
Title font Lithos Bold

Printed in Britain by
Lightning Source, Milton Keynes

reverb

For Jenny, the one who got away

Ted Warner 'The Master'

and Angels Barceló

1: A VISIT FROM THE FUTURE

I know it's going to be nice in Paradise.

True, there's a civil war raging among the twenty-one planets, but I'll be on the right side. Boadicea has the Forward Machine, and that makes her practically invulnerable.

And I won't pretend that I won't occasionally miss Maria. She saved my life at Roswell, love at first sight, and I now know it was her presence that saved me after Bertie disappeared. I really had hoped to spend the rest of my life with her. But, still, can't have everything, can we?

And, yes, by the time I arrive, the people I left a couple of days ago will have been dead for tens of millennia, and their planet reduced to a wasteland.

But these are minor matters. Paradise is still Paradise, and I'm on the way there. Recording this account is a rather ridiculous attempt to clear my name, because obviously I can never allow it to be sent Back. Still, it passes the time, and may one day be heard by…well, who knows how many sons and grandsons? A very large number, I suspect.

But where to start that story? At the beginning, of course. But where does a circle begin? When I met Bertie and we made our first journey through time? Or was the real beginning when I stumbled across that astonishing sixteenth-century notebook in an Italian farmhouse? But then long before that, in a way, I had provided a wife for Cain, and so allowed myself to exist in the first place. But it could also be argued it didn't begin in the past at all, but in this far future, when civil war ripped through a whole quadrant of the galaxy, and the enemy thought I had a secret that could help them win it. Or even further forward in time, when a mysterious being called Moroni started – or will start – to become restless.

Wherever I begin, though, Bertie is the key.

Of course, I never knew that until the three Women in Black turned up one day in my front room and began to interrogate me about him.

Indeed, perhaps that's as good a place to start as any. Yes, why not? That, after all, was when things began to turn nasty.

Tuesday 15 June, 2007. That was the day. The late afternoon poorly lit by a resentful sun, a thin haze already approaching over the moors.

The day had begun quite normally, with the unveiling in Bristol of a new monument to Bertie – this time a statue which replaced his habitual bemused look with a stern faraway gaze. I was, of course, required to make the usual tearful speech.

Perhaps you know the story of Henry II and Thomas Beckett? After ordering, or at least inciting, the assassination of the Archbishop in the Cathedral, Henry had to allow himself to be flogged by priests to placate the Church and the people, in order to win support against a rebellion by his son.

My penance for not saving Bertie was to be flogged by countless celebrations of his glory. His tragic adventures, and especially his role in the Crucifixion, had already given him cult status, and his mysterious disappearance so soon after the return from Nazareth added a transcendental element to the story.

My speech was the usual syrupy stuff, and I easily dealt with a heckler.

"How come Bertie is lost for ever, how come he always suffered so horribly, and yet *you* always seemed to get back OK?"

"You forget," I retorted, "I was horribly mutilated at Roswell!"

"Yes, but not as much as Bertie. And he died! As usua!!"

"It is not, unfortunately, given to all of us to achieve such greatness. That's what made Bertie so special: he never shirked the ultimate duty." I wiped an invisible tear from my eye with the knuckle of my little finger, a signal to my security men mingling with the mourners. The heckler found himself knocked like a ball on a bagatelle table to the back of the crowd, where he was righteously stamped on: ours was a peaceful society then, and we wanted to keep it that way.

Such moments were a nuisance, but nothing more. The fact remained that though Bertie might have caught the public imagination right from the very beginning – it was always 'Bertie and N', never 'N and Bertie' – *I* was the one still here to enjoy the considerable rewards. I was now the most sought-after media celebrity in the world. I held twenty-one honorary doctorates. My sperm was selling at five pounds per tail, broken or not.

And yet... I had never been able to completely shake off a feeling that his saga was not really over. Though it was impossible, I found myself imagining that in some distant future, long after the end of our present civilisation, Bertie would somehow still be there, moulding that future as he had moulded, albeit unwittingly, the past. I remembered Moroni's parting words: "Ah, N, my dear chap, not only is Bertie going to change the future, he *is* the future." Mysterious words whose meaning I couldn't fathom.

So when I went back home, and found the three Women in Black waiting for me in my room, calmly sitting on my sofa, I experienced a sick feeling of inevitability.

Home being an old country house on the edge of Dartmoor, set in thirty acres of ground patrolled by two hundred well-trained guards, and protected by a state of the art alarm system, I knew my guests could only have come from one place. As I had recently discovered in Nazareth, the only people who could stop Time Police were other Time Police.

While I stood at the door, wondering how my heart could have passed up through my oesophagus so quickly, one of them executed a smile. Or at least tortured it. Her teeth weren't serrated, but still gave the impression they were.

"Ah, N. What a pleasure to meet you. At last!"

The fact that all three were female didn't give me any comfort. I've been in some tight spots in the past, indeed sometimes in the very distant past, and I had always managed to escape. However, you didn't escape the Time Police, female or not. It was as if they kept part of their consciousness a few seconds in the future, so they could always anticipate your next movement.

I acted, as I always did in such situations, with cool cunning: I threw myself on the ground, swore I had no idea that I had broken any rules, and abjectly pleaded for mercy.

The one with the smile stood up, came across, bent down, yanked me up with one hand, and dropped me in my favourite armchair – did she know that? – then moved back to the sofa with the other two, who were looking at me dispassionately.

"N, please! We are not here on official business. We are just having a short vacation, and only wanted the honour of actually meeting the world's first Time Traveller face to face."

I stared at them.

They were all dressed identically, in a kind of tight black jumpsuit that bulged not only in the right places, but also in quite a few wrong places, presumably indicating communication equipment, disintegration guns, liver extractors…

"My name is Shimmer, and my colleagues are Shade and Shalom."

Long blonde hair that seemed about to burst into solar flares, eyelashes that I could imagine as a row of stakes on which miniature witches burned and writhed, pale blue eyes recalling that of Poe's old man but without a film to soften their intensity, teeth giving off blacksmith's-anvil sparks. Oh yes, and the smile to show she was the Good Cop.

The second woman, black face and black looks. Unblinking yellow eyes that would stare down Sauron himself. Eyebrows like scimitars. Lips suggesting a jilted Venus fly trap. Flared nostrils that would detect the smell of blood a quarter of a mile away. Teeth that preferred uncooked meat. No doubt some shark DNA somewhere, enabling her to detect electric fields around her. Shade. The Bad Cop.

The third one, expression so neutral I wondered if she was an android. Clearly inferior in rank to the other two, brown eyes darting round to whoever was speaking. The obedient Enforcer, the one who held you down, the one who, obeying a quiet nod from one of the other two, would give you the coup de grâce? 'Shalom': the word is a valediction as well as a greeting.

Shimmer, Shade, and Shalom? Well, easier to remember than Tisiphone, Alecto and Megaera, I suppose.

It was only later I realised that, in different circumstances, all three would be considered exceptionally beautiful.

But winsome they were not.

Shimmer continued talking. "We have come to tell you some sad news you may not know. In fact, cannot know. Bertie is dead. The last word on his lips was your name."

This was a shock. Bertie had died before, of course – indeed, nothing in his life quite became him like his frequent leavings of it – but from the way she spoke, it sounded as if being dead in the future was a lot more final than being dead in the past.

Still, it did show two things: that Bertie had in fact reached the future after that fateful day in my garden – and that he'd still managed to cause enough trouble to bring these sleek killers into my cosy sitting room!

Shimmer waited for two seconds – which she clearly considered enough time for me to come to terms with my grief – and then said:

"You have obviously realised – as shown by the … shall we say exaggeratedly respectful way you greeted us – that we are from the Time Police. We are not however from the executive arm; we work in the records department. We've come here on a sort of working holiday, to find out more about your incredible adventures with Bertie. Think of us as historians, trying to sift fact from the legend."

Historians my foot! If these women worked in the records department, then I felt sorry for any filing cabinets which happened to get in their way.

But I was willing enough to pretend to believe the fiction. If they felt they could get out of me whatever it was they wanted without radically altering my external configuration, or the feng shui of my internal organ orientation, then I was all for such an unusually humane approach.

"When we come from, there are now twenty-one inhabited planets, and on all of them the name of your dear friend is spoken by children almost before they say Mummy."

"Or Daddy," added Shade.

"Or Daddy. His exploits are as well-known as those of Dr Watson and Jack Clousseau, or Miss Marlowe and Father Columbo."

Well, perhaps they were from the *very* distant future.

"What we want is to hear the true story, so that his memory can be honoured in a fitting way. A Time Capsule is shortly to be sent into the Andromeda Galaxy, and one of the things we wish to include is the story of Bertie – and yourself, of course – to show any alien civilizations just how indomitable and magnificent is the human spirit.

"We would like to hear from your own lips how Bertie – and you – wrestled the Loch Ness Monster into submission, saved the human race from extinction in the time of Cain, defeated the hordes of invading aliens at Roswell..."

"Excuse me," I said, "I'm sure you're very good historians, but we... um... never went near Loch Ness, and as for Roswell, the aliens weren't exactly invading…"

"There!" said Shimmer triumphantly, "that's exactly why we

decided to come here. So many hundreds of centuries have passed, so many accretions have been made to the original stories, that the truth is in serious danger of being lost."

I didn't have any great objection to *some* of the truth being lost, but I chose not to mention this.

"We have studied all your surviving interviews and speeches (including the one you've just given in Bristol) and, although we admired them greatly, we felt that they were… well, let's say, perhaps tailored for public consumption?"

"You lied," said Shade, with the sort of voice one gravestone would use to another if it were spoiling for a fight.

Shimmer brushed away the stony comment.

"What my colleague means," she said brightly, as if it weren't already quite clear, "is that in your public pronouncements you had to bear in mind that the world is full of different religions, persuasions, preconceptions, and so on, and that, as Bertie was an international hero, you have always had to bear these variations in mind, and have therefore – I suggest – tactfully suppressed or altered certain details which might upset certain susceptibilities."

"Lying, in other words," repeated Shade darkly.

Shalom said nothing, just watched.

Since they wouldn't be here if they didn't already know something – the question was, *how much* did they know? – I made no denial.

"What you say is quite right," I said, with what I believed to be a tone of disarming frankness. "For example, when recounting our adventures with Rasputin, I had to take into account that…"

Shimmer held up a finger, and my words impaled themselves upon it.

"Exactly! That's the sort of thing we're after. Now, there are reports that you did in fact write a full account of Bertie's exploits – and your own, of course – which you never published for the reasons we have mentioned. You called it Bertie's Finest Hours."

And she smiled at me again. Smiling, I have read, involves the use of fifteen facial muscles. I heard every one of them creaking from disuse.

It was enough to warn me that to play dumb would not be a clever thing to do.

"Yes, that's true. I do indeed have my own notes on our

adventures, which I began to write even before Bertie disappeared. I was planning on having them published posthumously."

Like, in about five minutes? I thought gloomily.

"But that's excellent," said Shimmer. "Just what we need. Now, since our… holiday, is rather short, we would be extremely grateful if you could locate those notes. Just to clear up a few minor queries. So that the Andromedans have an accurate picture of Earth's greatest hero. I mean, heroes."

As if to show what extremely *un*grateful might be like, Shade produced a knife that looked sharper than my poor lost wife's tongue, and removed what appeared to be some clots of dried blood from under her fingernails. I consoled myself with the reflection that it didn't *have to* be human.

Shalom sat like a cat, watching.

"Of course," said I, "nothing would give me greater pleasure. But tell me about Bertie. What happened to him?"

"He died with exemplary courage, as you who were closest to him would expect. We will tell you how that came about after hearing what you have to say."

"As we were in the thick of events, we may have sometimes missed the larger picture," I said hesitantly. "I can't guarantee that I've recalled everything exactly as it happened…"

"That doesn't matter." There was a note of impatience in Shimmer's tone, and the muscles holding her smile in place were visibly atrophying.

It was pretty clear they expected me to produce the papers that very minute. Well, maybe that was all for the better. The longer they stayed, the more danger there was that they might decide to explore the house. Thank God I'd been tinkering with the Nazareth adventure only the evening before to try to shed a rosier light on my own role, so that the notes were now lying in a sideboard drawer in this very room. If I'd had to go to the safe, they might have followed me, or used the time to fish around.

I moved across the room, feeling like a gouty rat watched by three cats, and took out the blue folder, which I went to hand over to Shimmer. But she stopped me.

"Oh no, we realise how valuable those notes, your personal record of such a transcendental friendship, must be to you. Careful as we are, even we cannot foresee a fourth-dimensional storm, or a sudden flux in the Chronosphere. It is better that those papers, so dear, I am sure, to your heart, do not leave this house or this epoch. Why not read them to us, and we will take notes, and maybe ask for a few clarifications?"

This good-cop business was getting to her head. Shade was looking disgusted. A fly recklessly flew past, and she skewered it neatly on the end of her knife.

I didn't like the idea of reading in front of them, of course, but perhaps it was better than their taking the notes away, studying them at their leisure, and returning here demanding *too many* clarifications. Also, it might give me the opportunity to omit a few of my more acerbic references to their profession.

I wasn't being given the choice, anyhow.

"Perhaps you'd like a cup of tea first?" I asked. Did they still drink tea when they came from? If I could ring for a servant, I could at least alert other people to the presence of these intruders.

"Read!" Shade snapped. Her patience with her colleague's humane approach had evidently run out.

I rustled through the papers, wondering which Trip to start with.

"Start at the beginning," Shimmer said.

"But there's a lot of stuff that's irrelevant," I protested.

"As you know, we have, in a manner of speaking, all the Time in the world, even though we're in a hurry," said Shimmer, clicking her nails together ominously.

I was in no position to refuse. Hoping to get this over with, I began: *I had never felt so affronted. 'You want me to go Back just to look at a bloody picture?'*

Shade stopped me.

"What's that about a picture? We said start at the beginning."

"But that *was* the beginning. At least, it was the first Trip Bertie and I took together. The Mona Lisa case."

She sprang to her feet. What the hell did she eat? Grasshopper legs garnished with newly-oiled bed springs? "Bloody Mona Lisa! What about the adventure with Cain? That was a long time before."

"In normal chronology, yes, but in terms of our Trips, that came later, when the technology had been improved."

Shimmer said soothingly: "Very well, the picture. We heard about it. As I said, we were listening to some of your old speeches before we came here. You said on the Camilla Parker-Bowles-Windsor Show after you got back from St Petersburg: 'Perhaps the greatest satisfaction I have ever felt was in assisting my friend Bertie to win the hand of the beautiful Mona Lisa, despite the enormous danger I was in from Leonardo da Vinci. Now that she is, sadly, a widow, my sole desire is to alleviate her grief as best I can, and keep alive the flame in her heart for my poor departed friend.'"

"I said that?"

"You said that."

I began again: *I had never felt so affronted. 'You want me to go Back just to look at a bloody picture.?'*

Shade twitched with fury. "Where's the introduction? The background on Bertie? How you invented the Time Machine?"

"That comes later. Look, I can tell you now how I met Bertie, if you insist, but your colleague said you wanted to hear the story as I wrote it."

"So we did," said Shimmer soothingly. "Please continue."

I had never felt so affronted... I glared round, but no one said anything.

I cleared my throat and started again.

The specially-trained and highly-paid guards marched up and down outside, oblivious to my plight.

2: MONA LISA SMILES

In this work of Leonardo's there was a smile so pleasing that it was a thing more divine than human to behold; and it was held to be something marvellous, since the reality was not more alive.
(Giorgio Vasari, 1568)

I had never felt so affronted.

"You want me to go Back just to look at a bloody picture!"

The Chronotech President smiled patiently.

"No, not the picture, the real thing. Mona Lisa herself. For centuries now, the world has wondered who she really was, why she had that mysterious smile, and you're going to solve that mystery."

"But… the first ever journey through Time, and you send me to see a… painting! What about the Pyramids? Or Cleopatra? The Aztec Empire? The Incas? The French Revolution? Maybe Cle…? "

He leaned forward, like the vengeful ghost of a bull who's just spotted the matador waving its severed ear in the air.

"Look, N, I had to sell off five oilfields and a couple of international banking chains to get this thing built. *I* decide where, or when, it goes!"

"Without my design…"

I trailed off. No point. He held the upper hand now. I should have bargained better before handing over the plans. But then, I hadn't wanted too many questions asked. And still didn't.

He graciously acknowledged my surrender by pretending he had a velvet fist in the iron glove.

"Between you and me, it's partly for my son. My Bertie. He's always been taken by that picture, which is why I bought it for him last year. He spends hours in his bedroom just staring at it. It's an obsession, and, frankly, I'm getting worried about him. But I'm sure if he meets the Mona Lisa in the flesh, he'll be cured, and look at porn like normal men his age. Besides, on a more practical level, we mustn't be too ambitious with this first Trip. Something simple and straightforward to test the equipment. Solve the mystery of the smile, bring back some decent film so we can recoup at least part of my investment, and we can go on from there."

The reference to Bertie had caused my heart to stop for a full five seconds while it considered whether it would save a great deal of bother if it just gave up then and there.

I finally managed to speak.

"Are you saying that your son is coming with me?"

"Of course. I thought that was understood from the beginning. Or did I perhaps forget to mention it?"

As I stood there speechless, he added, to aid my understanding:

"You know, this building is a really impressive engineering feat. Two hundred and fifty floors. And to think we're right on the top one." He scratched his chin. "I love my son very much. And my security people are fanatically loyal."

And he gave me one of his special smiles that slithered over me like a jellyfish straight out of the Arctic.

That was how the most famous partnership in history began. Forget that heart-warming story in *Time* magazine about Bertie outclassing every other potential chrononaut in the selection tests, and my tearful insistence that I would not Travel without him. Bertie had never even been near the Training Programme; in fact, I suspected he didn't really know what the word 'chrononaut' meant.

Now, since that time, of course, Bertie and I have shared many adventures, and I have come to understand his… unusual qualities better.

Imagine that every cow in the world has succumbed to Mad Cow Disease. The world is bereft of cows. The daisies in meadows no longer tremble when a ponderous shadow passes over them. But one cow has survived. Untouched by the epidemic. The Omega Cow. This cow, stolidly and stubbornly sane, continues to make its warm circular offerings to the goddess of the soil. Where? It doesn't matter. Let's say in Uzbekistan.

Now imagine that a pungent individual with startlingly green eyes but otherwise not overly favoured by nature ascends in a hot air balloon. Why? It doesn't matter. Perhaps he has been put there by exacerbated acquaintances. Where? Let's say in Chipping Snodbury-on-Wallop.

A storm blows up. A tremendous Odyssean storm. The balloon is blown off course. After many weeks or months or years, it crashes. At the last moment, its occupant leaps out and tumbles head over heels to the ground.

The chances against you or I landing head first in that Uzbekistan cowpat are...well, I leave you to calculate how many heads would be needed to cover the surface of the entire planet.

Here's the amazing thing: the chances against Bertie *not* landing head first in that cowpat are, give or take a few decimal points, the same.

That's the first point. The second is that the chances of Bertie smelling worse after landing head first in that cowpat in Uzbekistan are equally remote.

There are around forty million smell receptors in the human nose. The cilial projection of these receptors offers an effective area of 600 square centimetres. Whereas 200 tastes can be discriminated, that figure becomes a monstrous 2000 when odours are involved. This fact had had no significance for me until I met Bertie.

I do not like to dwell on this. Bertie is, after all, now an international hero, and his experiences have given a new dimension to the word 'suffering'. Even now, as I begin to write these notes, he is being Regenerated yet again in our medical facility after our disastrous Trip to the Middle East. I only mention these unusual qualities to indicate why at the beginning I was not enthusiastic at the idea of sharing the first Time Trip with him.

But two hundred and fifty floors was a long way down.

Everyone has seen the *Mona Lisa*'s smile, of course. But they may not know that Leonardo carried that picture around with him all his life, and even after finally selling it to François 1 of France, he was still allowed to keep it in his studio until the day he died. For some reason, moreover, though he kept meticulous records of all his other commissions and models in his notebooks, he never kept a record of this one. And the picture itself is undated and unsigned. It almost seems as though he was hiding any signs that could point towards the sitter's identity. As if she never existed. Why? Why so devoted to the picture and yet so secretive about the subject?

Of course, there were almost as many theories about her identity as there were bugs in Bertie's beard and they jostled each other like players in a rugby scrum. It was only called the *Mona Lisa*, or *La Gioconda*, half a century after it was painted, on the unsubstantiated word of Vasari that she was Lisa, the third wife of a wealthy Florentine merchant, Francesco del Giocondo. Others believed she was the mistress of one of the Medici; or one of the best known courtesans of the Renaissance, the countess Caterina Sforza; or a fantasy recreation of his mother perhaps; or even a sly portrait of the artist himself.

In other words, the *Mona Lisa* was endless fodder for demented academics and other artistic parasites.

Our other purpose, however, was to discover why the lady was smiling in quite the manner she was.

The theories abounded here, too. For Oscar Wilde, for example, it was a lute-player who had captivated the sitter; Vasari thought a jester was keeping her amused; other people swore it was a Persian cat, and a leading Harvard academic wrote a hundred-page monograph 'proving' she had just farted.

Now don't think I knew all this because of any great interest in the painting. My only concern had been the scientific notebooks. I simply did a bit of research for the Trip. Most unwillingly. Because, like Louis XV of France, who hated the painting so much he had it removed from the Palace of Versailles, I couldn't stand that patronising smile. Frankly, I loathed the *Mona Lisa* – fully in agreement with Somerset Maugham, who spoke of 'the insipid smile of that prim and sex-starved young woman'.

Ah well, we all live and learn!

Well, except Bertie, of course.

Although no one knew for sure, the general consensus was that the picture was painted sometime between 1503 and 1506. So we thought July 1505 would be a nice time to arrive. Summer in Florence without busloads of tourists!

My Time Machine functioned perfectly, and within no time (as it were), and niftily outfitted by our fashion department in the rather sexy garb of the day, we materialised near Florence in the late afternoon sunshine. We left the Machine (and the Spatial Mobility Module) hidden under some trees about a mile out of Florence.

We trudged through the unspoiled countryside, passing a few

luxurious villas and ornate gardens of the wealthy, and dreaming of cornettos. Just after crossing the River Arno via the Ponte Vecchio (to my surprise full of butchers' shops and shoemakers, and not the modern-day goldsmiths) we spotted a couple of scruffy-looking peasants standing on the bank by a stunted tree, and told them we were looking for Mr da Vinci.

"Why, is he waiting for you?"

"Er, no, I somehow doubt it."

"Pity. If he was waiting for you, we might have been able to help you. We know all about waiting. But *looking for* is a bit out of our line, I'm afraid."

"That could be where we've been going wrong," said the other one thoughtfully, scratching his chin with filthy fingers. "Maybe we'd achieve more if we actively looked for him, instead of always waiting."

"I can't agree. These two here are looking, but they haven't found anyone yet."

"That's untrue. They found us."

"Yes, but they weren't *looking* for us."

"How can you be so sure of that? Why are you always so bloody negative? Excuse me, sirs," (turning to us) "were you looking for us?"

"Oh, don't be a fool," snapped his companion, before I could answer. "They already said they were looking for Mr da Vinci."

"*Now*, yes. But what about yesterday? Today they're looking for Mr da Vinci, I won't dispute that (though I certainly could, and maybe later I will) but it could be that yesterday they were looking for us. Or will be tomorrow."

"Why ever would anyone want to look for us?"

"Ah, you've got me there!" Turning to me again: "If you had been looking for us – just suppose – why would you have been doing it?"

"We weren't looking for you, so the question's meaningless," I retorted angrily, fed up with these two.

"There, see what you've gone and done with your stupid questions? Upset these gentlemen."

"Well, all I can say is, if they're not willing to help us, why should we help them?"

"That's a very good point."

"Nothing to be done, then."

"So let's go."

"We can't."

"Why not?"

"I can't remember."

And after giving us a look full of reproach, the two of them turned away and gazed into the distance, one of them shading his eyes with an old boot, the other with a hat. Although the sun was behind them.

We kept on walking, listening to the sweat sizzling at the end of our noses, and very quickly came to the Piazza della Signoria, bustling with noise and people. After passing a troupe of masked singers and lutenists serenading some plump dignitary, we spotted a stern-looking man in his early fifties with a long strong beard and piercing eyes – like the Ancient Mariner might have looked if he'd taken time off to actually eat something at those feasts instead of buttonholing guests outside all the time. I immediately recognised him from the famous self-portrait which he was going to paint eight years later. I approached him with a certain trepidation.

"Excuse me, sir, are you Mr da Vinci?" I asked.

He stared at me angrily. "What sort of question is that? How would you like it if I asked you if you were Mr from Stoke-on-Trent?"

"Sorry. Are you Leonardo the great painter?"

"I don't like your tone!"

"What?"

"Are you implying that all I can do is paint?"

"No, of course not. I…"

"If you'd asked me if I were Leonardo the renowned painter, sculptor, musician, dancer, mathematician, civil engineer, military engineer, hydraulics engineer, naturalist, weapons designer, architect, botanist, anatomist, dentist, bridge-builder, flying machine-, tank-, and submarine-designer, creator of automatons, etc and omitted the rest of my amazing skills, I might have answered yes, because as the quintessential Renaissance Man I am by definition also reasonable, and I don't expect everybody to remember *everything* I do. Indeed, if I have one fault – which, upon profound reflection (for I am also, as must be evident, a Thinker) I doubt – it is that even I can't remember everything I do. That's why I never finish anything. But you didn't even *try* to address me properly."

He gave me a final glare, and was about to stride away when he noticed Bertie.

"*Santo cielo!*" he cried. He stepped up to him, held his jaw one way, then the other, yanked up his beard, turned him round, and in short thoroughly inspected him.

(All our conversations were, of course, in the Italian of the period. As everyone knows, the Chomskyan Universal (or Deep) Grammar Faculty, as well as the UR-language, had finally been located, not, as had been expected, in Broca's or Wernike's areas of the brain, but in the appendix, which finally solved the riddle of the purpose of its existence. With the correct electrochemical stimulation of that organ, plus the injection of stem-cells from addled parrot eggs, it was now possible to learn a complete modern foreign language in less than a week, with a couple of days extra needed for earlier versions, and a couple of days on top of that if you happened to be Bertie. In this account of our adventures, however, I have occasionally retained the original word or phrase to remind readers that they are in fact reading a translation.)

"But this is *perfetto*! Oh if only I'd seen you before! Come with me! I want to do studies of you! I'm going to change my Last Supper! At last I have the perfect Judas!"

He went on stretching Bertie's skin in all directions to savour the Australopithecine bone structure beneath: "*Sì, sì, sì*! As soon as I can get back to Milan! And when I've finished, I can catch two *piccioni* with one fava bean, and use your body in my anatomical studies, though the Pope keeps giving me hassle about that. How can I study anatomy if I'm not allowed to dissect people?"

He turned back to me, much more respectful now. "How much will you take for him, sir?"

I realised that Bertie's... shall we say rugged face had led Leonardo to believe he was my slave, despite the fine clothes.

"I cannot sell him, sir," I replied, "but I would be more than willing to loan him to you so that you may create beauty out of ugliness."

Instead of going along with my brilliant strategy, Bertie was typically selfish.

"You can't dissect me," he said, his lower lip trembling like a raindrop about to fall off a leaf, "or you'll really be in trouble with my dad."

"You allow your slave to speak without permission?" enquired Leonardo.

"He is more a trusted family retainer than a slave," I answered, "and has been with me a long time, so as long as he is obedient I do not object to a certain familiarity."

I turned to Bertie. "Now I would like you to help Leonardo the great art... polymath. He will take you to his studio, and make studies of you. You will meet some very interesting people. Maybe even some of the other models he is painting. This is what your father would have wanted, isn't it?"

"Sir," said Leonardo, "allow me to say I am most impressed with your humane conduct towards your servant. I myself have a servant, Battista, whom I too value greatly."

By now it had sunk into Bertie's head that we had as good as been given an open invitation to meet the Mona Lisa, and his eyes glittered with enthusiasm. It was indeed an amazing stroke of luck. Who would have thought that Bertie's villainous aspect would serve as a passport to artistic society?

We had now reached the front of the Palazzo Vecchio, where there was a huge marble statue. It was Michelangelo's David, finished only the year before. It represents David getting ready to fight Goliath, though I never did understand why he had to fight him in the nude: perhaps the idea was that the shy giant would look away, embarrassed, and then David could take him by surprise with the slingshot. Anyway, our Davie being a good fourteen feet tall, the giant was probably considerably smaller. Unfair fight!

Bertie was impressed.

"*Mamma mia*, that's some statue!" he said. "Did you do that?"

Leonardo's formidable beard bristled, like one of his own paintbrushes that had dried out too quickly. Forgetting his advanced attitude to the lower orders, he strode forward and shook Bertie as briskly as vain and unfairly well-endowed young men shake their members to finish the job in public toilets.

"I certainly did not do it! Anyone can make a sculpture. Sheer brute force. Bang, chop, chip! That monstrosity was done by that little Neoplatonic Medici-bum-licking religious-fanatic ugly gouty upstart of a Michelangelo! What was wrong with Verrochio's David? A disgrace to our public places, that's what this is!"

I got the idea he didn't much like Michelangelo. Well, the latter *was* half his age, and already more famous in certain quarters. And Leonardo hadn't even been invited to work on the Sistine Chapel frescos.

Taking no notice of the people around, Leonardo scooped up a large quantity of recent and unusually pungent pigeon droppings with a piece of parchment, pulled a little mechanical bird from under his robe, loaded it with the droppings, wound it up, and aimed it over the statue, where it circled twice, chirped, dropped its load, and returned to the inventor's pocket with a satisfied whirr.

"And they say my scientific research has no use!" he chuckled, as we moved on.

I found I was beginning to like him.

"I've got a big studio over in the Santa Maria Novella, where I worked on the cartoon for the Anghiari battle screen," Leonardo confided, after his chuckling had died down, "but I keep another *bottega* just round the corner for more personal paintings. I'm working on a rather interesting one right now."

We entered a narrow street – track would be a better word – bordered by dark wooden buildings, and followed him into a studio littered with canvases, panels, and vases for blending paints. Some bored musicians were sitting around. There was also a Persian cat so old and mangy it wouldn't have made anyone smile.

And there it was! The most famous painting in the world! Casually propped up on an easel. I heard Bertie's sudden intake of breath.

You have to remember that these days the painting is covered in masses of gunge – resin, lacquer, and varnish – applied over the years to protect it. More make-up than a drag queen on a Gay Pride day. The sitter now looks a bit yellow and sickly, but then she was quite rosy-cheeked, and the skies behind were more blue than green.

And that famous smile was already there! Only…

It wasn't quite right. If lips possessed skeletons, I would have said this was only the skeleton of the smile. A skeleton, moreover, in discomfort. There was still something missing, that pinch of triumph, that 'if you knew what I knew!' glance. Clearly, Leonardo hadn't finished the painting yet – in fact, he never did get round to giving the girl eyebrows.

But I had no time to confirm these first impressions, because we were immediately led through to a small recess at the back of the studio…

Where Mona Lisa herself was sitting painting her toenails!

She actually had a rather nice tan, and her figure was nowhere near as dumpy as the artist made it out to be. Instead of that schoolmistress parting in the middle, her hair, a rich brown, was flung sensuously over to one side. Her feet were bare.

A pleasant surprise, I must admit. But there was still something odd about her lips, even in the flesh…

"This is Wenefride, though she likes to be called Winnie," said Leonardo. "She's from England, a place called Torky or Porky, something like that, but she's pretty much assimilated into Florentine society now."

Torquay! But that was my home town! The most famous face in the world – from Torquay! Possibly even my street! If it existed then.

I desperately hid my astonishment.

"Winnie? That's an unusual name, I'm honoured to meet you," I stuttered, my head reeling. "I'm Ennio, an Unreliable Narrator, and this is Bertrando, a good-natured idiot."

Leonardo put a far-from-avuncular arm round her shoulder, while Bertie twitched and gazed at her with perfect adoration, muttering '*mamma mias*' with the regularity of a dripping tap. Smitten to the quick, no doubt about it. His breathing increased, which caused Winnie to move back slightly.

Leonardo misunderstood the reason for my astonishment.

"The unique curve of her lips, I see, has not escaped your acute attention. This is the temporary effect of a teeth brace I invented and fitted a few weeks ago. Show them, Winnie."

Winnie didn't seem too happy with this, but obediently opened her mouth, and we saw what looked like a guitar string running along her gums and in and out of her teeth like a DNA double helix. She closed her mouth again. She was obviously suffering some discomfort.

"You'll notice," went on the painter proudly, "this by chance gives her a rather unique expression, a hint of lasciviousness, a mocking reproof, a come-hither-but-don't-expect-to-get-what-you-want look, plus a tinge of sadness, and profound awareness of the cruel mortality of humankind, don't you think? That's why I decided to paint her. It will, I think, be my greatest painting. And that's saying something!"

And he smiled at her with every sign of deep affection.

Bertie finally managed to speak. "My goddess!" he murmured.

Winnie looked puzzled, and Leonardo frowned. The avuncular arm became more possessive.

"Don't you get too *fresco* with her, exaggeratedly aromatic creature, or you'll be out of a job again. I can remember your face well enough to paint it without you. *Capisci?*"

At that point, for the first time, I noticed an extremely handsome young man standing in the corner, and looking most unhappy. This disquiet might have been because he was rather close to a half-dissected body, but I sensed that it was more to do with the lovely Winnie.

"This," said Leo, moving across and putting another more-than-avuncular arm round the young man's shoulders, "is Salai, my assistant."

Ah, Gian Giacomo Caprotti, whom Leonardo had brought back from Milan fifteen years before, when he was only ten: "a graceful and beautiful youth… in which Leonardo greatly delighted," as Vasari bluntly put it. 'Salai', 'little demon', was the painter's nickname for him.

I caught Winnie's expression. It was not friendly. We had stumbled on an interesting domestic scene. It seemed to me that Leonardo was more than fond of both Winnie and Salai, and that these two regarded each other as rivals.

Well, Salai glared at Winnie, and Winnie glared at Salai, and Leonardo glared at Bertie, and I thought I might as well do the same. Despite our amazing luck – or rather, in order not to waste it – I wanted to leave immediately. I didn't trust Bertie's self-control. This was his idol, the woman he had worshipped since he was a boy. I needed to get him alone, give him time to cool down.

But before I could drag him away, there was a dramatic interruption. It appeared someone had spotted the mechanical bird's unnatural call of nature, and told the irascible Michelangelo, because a brick came hurtling through the open door, followed by a voice from outside: "Since you couldn't produce that bronze horse and rider for the Sforzas in ten whole years, see if you can manage something out of this! And, by the way, another lump of your *Last Supper* fresco has just peeled off, *pazzo!*"

Leonardo gave a roar, and headed out that door and was out of sight faster than a quark in a particle accelerator.

Bertie is nothing if not romantic and impetuous, as I was to find out (to his cost more than mine, thank the lord!) through many an adventure. During these few minutes, his already limited self-control had drained away from him like the bonhomie from an unsuspecting lobster plunged in boiling water. No sooner was Leonardo out of the studio than he was already declaring his undying passion to a startled Winnie.

"I adore you and worship you and want to shield you from a cruel pitiless world," he informed her, his green eyes glistening with ardour and sincerity.

But Winnie wasn't interested.

"Look," she said, "nothing personal – well, apart from the fact you stink and are ugly even for a Brit – " (our Italian obviously hadn't fooled her) "but I came backpacking to Italy for a bit of sun, sea, sex, and grappa, to find a few Latin lovers, so why should I waste my time on you? Coals to Manchester." This was remarkably prophetic, if not quite geographically accurate.

"But I can spoil you and look after you, and I'll never ask you to do any ironing," protested the ardent suitor.

"Think I haven't heard all that sort of stuff before? Then when they find out I haven't got a bloody dowry, that's the end of their honourable intentions! So I'm sticking with Leo, despite his… catholic tastes. He's going up in the world; I heard the King of France is interested in giving him a court job in Milan again. What I'm trying to say, nicely, is, stop panting and sod off!"

She later confided to me that she wasn't usually so blunt, but that her period had started that day. Leonardo had promised to invent a tampon for her, but, as with so many other projects, he hadn't yet got round to doing it.

Bertie ignored the 'stink' and 'ugly' bit, and fastened on the dowry problem.

"But I wouldn't want a dowry. My dad's the richest man in the world."

Well, let me tell you, I moved faster than that mouse who spotted the farmer's wife with a carving knife in an untimely place. I had Bertie in an inverted reinforced triple nelson and out in the street before Winnie had even started to laugh in disbelief.

"Tell Leonardo we'll be back tomorrow morning!" I yelled back.

I blocked Bertie's windpipe for a few minutes, which calmed him down. I made it clear to him that if his father found out about this he wouldn't even be allowed to keep the painting in his room any more. He eventually saw sense (at least I thought he did: I should have known better) and we spent the rest of the day sight seeing before finding a little inn for the night. After ordering supper we settled down with a bottle of the local wine.

I had already decided that we would leave as soon as possible the next day after getting some film. I couldn't risk Leonardo of all people finding out we were from the future, though I would have liked to get to know Winnie a bit better myself. My wife Mabel, of course, had her good qualities, but I could no longer remember what they were. Besides, when you're five hundred years away from home, it's comforting to find a home town girl. And as I said, she was much more beautiful than the picture suggests.

After our food was served I discovered that there was a slight problem with my plan – that idiot Bertie wanted us to take Winnie back with us!

"Are you mad? She'd never agree to it! And even if she did, I wouldn't!"

"My dad's your boss!" said Bertie sulkily.

"Who gave me the strictest instructions to do nothing in the past that might alter future history. Haven't you ever read Bradbury or Moorcock or Redwood or Silverberg? Watched *Star Trek* or *Back to the Future*? And you want to take the Mona Lisa back!"

"I've already got the *Mona Lisa*. I want Winnie!"

"But she *is* the Mona Lisa!"

"But the picture's done. If Winnie comes back, who'll notice? In history, no one ever heard of her."

I realised I had been unlucky enough to be present at the unveiling of Bertie's maiden thought. Others were occasionally to follow, often at the most inconvenient times. In the same way that a drunk man, told to walk along a straight chalk line, will inevitably step right on the line now and then as he staggers from side to side, so Bertie would occasionally surprise me by stumbling into the path of logic.

As I bit into what the innkeeper had the effrontery to call venison, I tried to make Bertie understand the butterfly effect, to see that some insignificant change now might have enormous repercussions after the passage of five hundred years. In vain. In the end, I pulled rank, refused to discuss the matter any more, and sent him off to fetch more drinks.

If I'd known Bertie then as well as I do now, I'd have fetched the drinks myself.

When I woke up, with the sort of headache that only Humpty Dumpty would have fully understood, I sensed something was wrong even before I painfully opened my eyes. It took me some moments to realise what it was.

Bertie's natural odour was being besieged by more pleasant perfumes!

And there he was, wearing a snazzy new cloak of silver brocade, trimmed with blue velvet, and a pair of pink tights. Combing his hair and beard! And whistling.

I muttered weakly, "Bertie, what's happening?"

He faced me with a cheerful expression. "I didn't want to disturb you," he said, "but it's gone eleven, and we promised to be at the studio."

"Gone eleven! But how…?"

"The drink," he replied. "We both collapsed last night, apparently, and they had to carry us upstairs."

Well, that explained why I'd shared a room with him. A small undamaged part of my brain reflected it must have been a combination of drink and Timewarp Lag. Odd that he seemed to have recovered more quickly than me.

The Venetians were the first people to import sizeable quantities of coffee into Europe, but unfortunately they didn't do it till a century later, so we had to make do with cold water and a meagre breakfast of bread, cheese, and olives.

I made Bertie promise not to make any more passes at Winnie – he consented more readily than I expected – and then we set off for Leonardo's studio. On the way, I purchased a small ornamental dagger, and stuck my miniature digital video camera onto the pommel. I reflected that if only I'd been better prepared to film the day before, we could have been safely back in our own time by now.

When we got there, however, Salai stopped us outside the door.

"Please wait, if you don't mind," he said politely. "I think the master's on the point of finally finishing the portrait. I've never seen him so excited."

I thought I saw him and Bertie exchange a secret smile. Was Bertie getting corrupted by the artistic ambience so soon?

We peered in, and saw Winnie sitting there, her back towards us, and Leonardo beside his easel, a frown of furious concentration on his face.

Salai had been right. Within a few minutes, the artist gave a joyous exclamation, flung his brushes aside, and stepped forward to give Winnie an enormous hug. He then spotted us, and said, "Come on in, just take a look at this, and be humble!"

We went in, and I saw the difference at once.

The painting now had the famous *Mona Lisa* smile!

As did the sitter! Exactly!

There was no doubt about it. The basis of the smile was still the teeth brace, but now there was an added quality to it: that sense of having secrets not to be shared. I positioned myself so that I could secretly film Leonardo, Winnie, and the painting all in the same shot.

We had been unbelievably successful. Within less than twenty-four hours, we had the film, we knew the identity of the sitter, we knew that the smile was at least partly the effect of a prototype teeth brace, and we even had a pretty good idea why Leonardo treasured the picture so much.

So why did a nasty feeling of foreboding stalk me during the following minutes of congratulations all round?

The answer, in one word, was smiles. There was something wrong with all of them. And they all seemed to be related somehow to Bertie.

Winnie. Not just the smile, with that new mysterious hint of sardonic triumph. But also, in contrast with the day before, she now smiled at Bertie whenever she caught his eye. I even thought I caught her winking once.

Leonardo. Beneath his expression of artistic triumph, a most sinister smile crossed his face when he intercepted one of those glances.

Salai. Gone was the rancour of the previous afternoon, replaced instead by a smile of quiet confidence, almost of smugness.

As for Bertie himself, his smile was floating somewhere in the wake of an enormous grin, like a rubber duck following a whale.

I was not amused.

Even less so when Leonardo finally turned to me and said:

"As you see, today I am at the top of my form! And that, let me tell you, is higher than Michelangelo could even dream of! I shall at once begin my study to replace the head of my already marvellous Judas in the *Last Supper* with this even more villainous one of your servant! You will understand, Signore, that I need to work alone, so I would be grateful if you could leave your man here, as we agreed. Perhaps we could meet tomorrow for a stroll around this beautiful city… "

Something was going on, I knew it. Even Bertie's grin floundered a bit at this request. But as I could hardly say, "Sorry about that, but we were just about to pop off to the future", I joined in the smiles, though mine was through gritted teeth.

Deeply troubled, I left the studio, only too aware of Salai's mocking glance as I passed him. 'Alone' seemed to include everyone but myself.

I spent the whole of the afternoon and early evening trying in vain to shake off this feeling of impending disaster, before returning to the inn, where I nervously threw myself upon my bed to await Bertie's arrival. I suspected that Europe's brightest and dimmest both had their own opposing agendas, and fate had cruelly cast me on the side of the dimmest.

The ominous black cloud hanging above me opened its bowels at around eight o'clock, when Salai came bursting into our room.

"Come quickly," he cried, "Bertrando's been poisoned!"

"What!"

"There's no time for questions! *Fai presto!*"

We ran towards Leonardo's studio, Salai muttering something about "Why couldn't that stupid woman keep her mouth shut?", and found Bertie lying on a bench, watched over by Leonardo. His face was a mixture of overripe mulberry and egg-yolk yellow, his bulging eyes flecked with red. He was foaming profusely at the mouth, and his skin was peeling off.

Yes, he looked even worse than usual.

"Who," I cried, "has done this dastardly deed?"

"Oh dear sir, it was I, all unwitting!" lamented Leonardo, turning round. "A terrible accident!"

Cantarella. The Borgias' favourite drink – for their guests, that is. Nice slow-acting poison. Cesare Borgia's dad, Pope Alexander VI (there was a time when popes were *fun*), used it regularly to bump off cardinals irritatingly afflicted with longevity, so that he could then seize their property. Cesare, a man of action, preferred stilettos and strangulation, but kept a few bottles of laced wine for when he was feeling lazy.

As I checked Bertie's pulse, Leonardo told me that when he had resigned his job as military engineer for him in the spring of 1503, Cesare had given him, as leaving presents, the warm corpses of two of his close relatives (for his anatomical studies), a pair of hose, and a bottle of wine. The corpses and the hose had long since been unravelled, but being a teetotaller, he hadn't got round to drinking the wine, and had indeed forgotten all about it. But today, after finishing a couple of very successful sketches of Bertie's head, he had, to celebrate, fished out the wine, and offered him a glass as a toast to the 'new Judas'. Almost at once, Bertie had complained of stomach pains, and had begun to retch and writhe in agony.

"At this point," said Leonardo, wringing his hands, "I remembered that a bridge I had once constructed for Cesare had collapsed while his army was passing underneath it."

I didn't believe a word of this story. You didn't just 'forget' a bottle of Borgian wine unless you had already drunk it! Jealousy, that's what it was. He must have found out Bertie's too-honourable intentions towards Winnie, and had dealt with the matter in a typically Renaissance way. I could see his point of view: to have someone chatting up your favourite model was bad enough, but when that someone was Bertie...

Mind you, such a feeble, blatantly contrived story was a bit surprising, coming as it did from perhaps the cleverest man in Italy, whose best friend was a certain Niccoló Machiavelli…

Having said that, Leonardo didn't strike me as a murderer. I had the hope that he would have given Bertie just enough poison to make him sick, not to kill him. As a warning, *a la Firenze*, to him to keep away from Winnie. His next words disabused me of this ingenuous optimism.

"As soon as I realised the wine had been poisoned, I dispatched Salai to inform you. I wanted to speak to you first before moving your retainer to the hospital. Doctors are butchers these days. They know nothing. They still follow the antiquated ideas of Celsus and Galen. Your slave didn't drink that much. Out of the hospital, he just might not die; inside it, he certainly will! Perhaps you would prefer him, faithful family retainer that he is, to stay with you, spend his last few hours, if such they are, with someone who obviously cares for him."

I desperately searched my mind for anything I knew about arsenic. I was vaguely aware that in my time there was a kind of antidote to arsenic poisoning, only I had no idea what that antidote was.

But they would have even less idea in the hospital, even though the Ospedale di Santa Maria Nuova was one of the best of its time. No one had been able to help even someone as important as Pope Alexander VI when he somehow swallowed one of his own concoctions.

The only chance was to get Bertie back to the future without delay. But in his present condition he would be quite unable to walk to where we had left the Time Machine outside the city. I would therefore have to summon the (as yet untested) Spatial Mobility Module to fly to us on remote and then take us back there. But this was risky – there was always the danger that it might inadvertently plough through the odd building or two and leave fewer sights to be sightseen. Only in the most extreme emergency should this kind of manoeuvre be attempted. After several seconds of deep deliberation, I decided that the poisoning of half the crew (who also happened to be the only-begotten son of the President of the Company) could be considered just such an emergency.

But it was vital that nobody should see the SMM, especially Leonardo, the one man in the world with enough scientific genius to be able to recognise it for what it was. Luckily, the light was already beginning to fade, a Tuscan sunset waving one of its ridiculously ostentatious goodbyes. In half an hour, an hour at most, darkness would cover the flight of the SMM from the Time Machine into the city. If I landed it on the roof of the inn it should be invisible to anyone still on the streets.

But would Bertie survive that extra hour?

I believed he would. Surely, if Leonardo had really intended to murder him, he wouldn't have called me. I simply didn't believe he was going to die. Suffer horribly, yes, but that was another matter. The security of our mission, and its secrecy, was more important than a bit of minor discomfort, especially since that discomfort would all be borne by Bertie.

So I told Leonardo that anyone could make a mistake, admitted that I didn't trust the hospital either, and that I was sure Bertie, a man with a deceptively strong constitution, would stand a better chance if he was able to simply rest at the inn, where, by chance, I had some very powerful medicines which would surely help him.

Leonardo offered to help me carry him there, and didn't even ask why I would happen to have possession of such medicines. We got Bertie back quickly – Leonardo was surprisingly strong for his age – and then the artist left. He didn't hang around, saying he would call later, and that in the meantime he would see if he could concoct something to save Bertie.

"Naturally," he said, "I have more medical knowledge than anyone else in Florence, so I'm sure that if I flip through my notes…"

The next hour was nerve-racking. I kept telling myself that a humanist and humanitarian like Leonardo wouldn't have given Bertie enough poison to kill him. And indeed Bertie's mulberry-and-egg-yolk complexion didn't seem to be getting any worse (though to tell the truth it was difficult to see in the gathering dark), or his groans any more piteous.

And as if I didn't already have enough problems, there were clear signs that our room had been ransacked in our absence! Just how many enemies had Bertie managed to make? Luckily, I'd had the forethought to hide the SMM remote control in my codpiece. For once, I was pleased that nature hadn't been ostentatiously bountiful with my privy accoutrements.

I'd just decided it was now dark enough, and that I could risk summoning the SMM, when a hideously deformed and sickeningly repulsive hunchback in a dark hooded cloak burst into the room!

Before I could reach a corner to cower in, the creature threw off the hood, ripped off the beard, and revealed itself as Winnie! She was in a terrible state.

"He knows!" she said.

"Who knows? Knows what?"

"Leonardo. He knows or at least he suspects about your Time Machine! In the studio late this afternoon he warned Bertie to stop feeling my tits (as if I hadn't had to tell him a dozen times myself!) or he'd have him thrown off Giotto's Bell Tower and Bertie got all uppity and said he'd feel my tits whenever he wanted to because we were going to get married and that was one of the perks of marriage and he was going to take me somewhere where no one from this century would ever find me again and then he realised he'd said too much and shut up but Leonardo didn't seem to have noticed anything but he quickly calmed down and said it was silly arguing and offered him a glass of wine but Bertie began to change colour almost immediately so I ran out of the studio and came here looking for you but you weren't here and when I tried again a bit later I noticed a lot of Machiavelli's men were watching the place and that's why I came back disguised as a hideously deformed and sickeningly repulsive hunchback in a dark hooded cloak to warn you."

This wasn't quite the version Leonardo himself had given me, but that was hardly important. Machiavelli's men watching the place?

"What's this nonsense about a time machine?" I blustered. "Come to your senses, girl!"

"Oh God!" she cried, "you're so bloody English! You really think I don't know who you really are?"

Within five minutes I had learned what had happened the night before.

Bertie's flashes of intelligence, like four-leaved clovers or returned golden handshakes, were rare, but they did exist. I myself had pointed out to him over dinner that Salai seemed furious at the attention that Leonardo paid to Winnie, and that must have given him the idea. He'd bribed the innkeeper to drug my wine (ha, hoist with your own petard, you conniving little bastard!) and while I was immersed in a recurring dream of Cleopatra in which I was a two-headed asp, he sneaked out to go to Salai for help. It was common practice for the assistants and the apprentices to sleep in the *bottegas*, so he knew where to find him. He convinced Salai he'd take Winnie away if he helped him, and then Leonardo's heart would be free for him. Salai knew where Winnie was staying, and somehow arranged for Bertie to spend time alone with her. How he persuaded her that we really were from the future I still don't know. She said that she just *knew* he was telling the truth. The cunning little bastard promised her he'd take her into this marvellous future (hidden in the Time Machine so that I couldn't stop him), and she'd become the daughter-in-law of the richest man on the planet.

Perhaps he also promised to wash and shave. I wouldn't put it past him. The promise, I mean, not the action.

Now the poisoning made sense. I'd been right, in a way. It hadn't been for something as silly as jealousy. Leonardo never let his feelings get the better of him, except when it came to Michelangelo. In the thousands of pages of his notebooks, there is almost nothing personal.

More than an artist, Leonardo was a scientist. Bertie had hinted at some kind of time machine. Of all the people living at that time, as I very well knew, Leonardo was the one least likely to laugh his head off at such a concept.

By poisoning Bertie, he had intended to force us to return to the Time Machine (if it existed), because he made the reasonable assumption that in the future we would have better medical facilities, and that we would return there as quickly as possible in order to save Bertie's life.

His whole purpose had been to follow us to the Machine, or to keep watch on me if I had some way of summoning it. Teaching Bertie a lesson for daring to make a pass at Winnie was simply a pleasurable bonus.

He had us! The only way to save Bertie was indeed to return to the future at once. But, if what Winnie said was true, I was trapped in the inn. If I brought the SMM here, Machiavelli's men would see it, and capture it. If I tried to make it to the Time Machine by some other means, they would follow me.

The only tiny thing in my favour was that they didn't know that I knew that they knew.

I ferociously furrowed my fairly noble brow until I suddenly had an idea, as most self-respecting heroes tend to do in these circumstances. I remembered from my reading that Leonardo's first officially-sanctioned dissection wasn't till late 1507, when a very old man died peacefully in the hospital. But we were in 1505 – and I had seen a half-dissected body in the studio only hours earlier!

"Ah ha!" said I.

Winnie looked at me hopefully.

"Have you suddenly had an idea, as heroes tend to do in these circumstances?" she asked

"I have indeed! Is that body still in the studio?"

"Yes, the master was using it to study the function of the heart. It was going to be thrown out tomorrow: it was starting to go off."

"Perfect! Now, do you know where Michelangelo lives?"

I have to admit, Winnie was awfully sharp. Well, she *was* from Torquay. She looked at me questioningly for a moment, snapped her fingers, stuck the beard back on, threw on the hooded cloak, and then, bent double, stumbled out of the door, saying: "Be ready to move in half an hour, I'll be back by then."

Of course, Winnie knew even better than me that at that time dissection of the human body was taboo; it smacked too much of necromancy. Only a very few specially licensed doctors were allowed to conduct dissections as teaching practice. True, this was a period of relative religious tolerance (the Popes were too busy assassinating and guzzling to waste time persecuting heretics) but Michelangelo was a religious fanatic. That was why he put so much effort into his art, which was all for the glory of God.

And he'd just had his statue shat on!

Winnie must have moved fast. Within fifteen minutes, there was a great uproar in the streets, the gleam of burning torches, and the tall lean figure of Michelangelo, his broken nose clearly silhouetted, led the way towards Leonardo's studio, screaming, "Now we know why he never finishes a painting – he's too busy necromancing!"

To my great satisfaction, I also noticed dark figures detaching themselves from hiding places around the inn, and setting off in pursuit of Michelangelo's mob: Machiavelli's men, moving to protect Leonardo and his studio.

It was my chance. I brought out the remote control, and within minutes, the SMM was hovering just outside the window, a transparent sphere against the darkness behind it. I leant out and slid open the entry hatch. At the same moment, Winnie rushed back into the room. Between us we were able to shove Bertie through the window and into the machine.

I spotted Leonardo running across the square like a man a third his age. I don't think I've ever seen such fury. He scrambled on to the roof of the stable that lay beneath our window. Winnie hauled herself into the SMM after me, as I started to lift the craft into the air. We took off only just in time – with a despairing roar, Leonardo leapt up at us knife in hand. I heard the sound of the knife gouging the hull as the hatch closed on him, and he fell back onto the roof.

"That was a close call," Winnie said.

I didn't answer until we reached the Time Machine. What I had to do next wasn't going to be easy.

"You've probably saved our lives, and I'll always be grateful, but you know you can't come with us," I said, as I docked the Module onto the Time Machine, and opened the airlock between the two.

The biggest tears I've ever seen sprang to her eyes. She begged me not to leave her in Florence. Salai, she said, had threatened to kill her if she stayed there. He had enjoyed his master's undivided affection for fifteen years, and had no intention of letting a mere woman come between him and his great love. There was no telling what he might be capable of.

"Not only that," she said, clutching my hands. "Imagine what Leonardo might do to me now he knows I've helped you."

"I'm sorry," I said, "you don't understand. If you'd read your Bradbury…"

"I saved you! Without me, you'd never have escaped! And anyway," she added, sobbing onto my strong manly chest, "we've never had sex. Leonardo loves me, but not in that way. He has about as much sex drive as a panda. I must be the most frustrated English backpacker in Florence! So much for the brochures!"

Her arms went round my neck, and she lowered her voice, though Bertie was in no condition to be listening. "I'm going to marry Bertie, of course, for the money – that's what small town girls do – but… well, you're an extremely attractive man, and I'm so frustrated that I doubt, I really do doubt, that poor Bertie will be enough to satisfy me, especially as my hormones are now at their most uncontrollable."

She knew about hormones at the start of the sixteenth century? More lost knowledge?

Of course, these final words had no effect on me whatsoever. As if I would take advantage of a woman in distress, even if her bodice was becoming undone, and I was realising that Leonardo had prudishly or prudently disguised her true voluptuousness!

Nor would I ever consider being unfaithful to my dear sweet wife Mabel.

But I couldn't leave her behind – Leonardo and Salai were Italian, for God's sake, I'd seen *The Godfather*! And I had to think of my dear friend Bertie, my loyal Time Travelling companion. I suddenly became aware how unjust I had been to him, reminded myself how he had gallantly risked all for the woman he loved. How could I ever look him in the face again if I left the woman he had promised to marry to what would surely be a cruel and bloody destiny?

We made it back just in time to save Bertie. He was desperately ill for a couple of weeks, but he pulled through. We couldn't know it at the time, but this first Trip would turn out, in fact, to be his least painful one.

Of course, I nearly got thrown off that top floor by Bertie Senior, not only for having left his son alone with Leonardo, but for allowing Winnie to return with us: the point of the trip had been to cure Bertie of his infatuation. But as soon as he met her, he was enchanted by her down-to-earth charm, and quickly decided not to worry about whether or not we had altered history by bringing her back.

"We'd never know, anyway," he said cheerfully.

The film I'd taken was an instant hit, especially the shots of Bertie and Winnie exchanging smiles behind Leonardo's back. Bertie Senior had thought about hushing up the real identity of the Mona Lisa, but soon realised that there was money to be made through interviews and photo shoots with Winnie, though she herself didn't seem too happy with the idea. Most of the world was delighted. Yes, the truth led to the sacking and/or suicide of several hundred art critics (and, in five cases, murder), but this only improved the human gene pool, and though it ruined relations with Italy, it vastly improved tourist figures in Britain.

I admit I did feel a bit guilty about Leonardo. It seemed that in the pain of his loss he at once expunged every reference to her in his notebooks, and yet he could never bring himself to let her portrait go. I told myself that it wasn't my fault, that at the end I'd really had no choice.

Bertie and Winnie got married a few weeks later. They'd planned to have their honeymoon in Florence, for old times' (very old times') sake, but when they learned that the entire populace, their amour-propre mortally wounded, had armed themselves with tomatoes, they went to Disneyland instead. They then returned to live in a beautiful castle near Exeter, bought and renovated by Bertie's dad as a wedding gift. He'd wanted to buy Windsor Castle for them, but Winnie had insisted on being close to 'her dear husband's dearest friend'.

For a short time, I was foolish enough to believe that I, as well as the happy couple, might be destined to live happily ever after.

3: WHAT THE LADY SAW

I stopped reading, and looked across at my visitors. I didn't think I had anything to fear so far – whilst I had had to miss out a few damning details, what I had said had been more or less the truth. However, when I found myself suddenly lifted two feet into the air and shaken by a furious Shade, I painfully reflected that truth sometimes hurts.

"This can't be true! Where's the near-invincibility? The secret training regime that turned Bertie into a deadly fighting machine and military strategist? Are you trying to take the piss? How dare you lie to us?"

Shimmer came to my rescue, gently prized Shade's fingers from my neck, and deposited me back in my chair.

"What my colleague is trying to say is that we know it was you who insisted that Bertie be your travelling companion."

"I insisted? Are you crazy?"

This was pretty reckless considering my position, but to be accused of that…

"We've seen the evidence, N, we've seen all the videos of your press conferences where you state time and time again that you realise the entire success of any Trip will depend on him."

"Look, Bertie's father is the richest man in the world. A day's interest on the small change in his pocket could build a nuclear reactor. The whole Chronotrek programme was funded by him – the facilities, the Time Machine itself, the engineers… Either I took Bertie along with me, or I didn't get to go at all."

"But *you* invented the Time Machine!"

"Yes, but I didn't have the funds to build it."

Shade, her fingers thwarted, now returned to the attack with her tongue.

"You expect us to believe that you were the leader in these Expeditions? Or that Bertie would allow himself to be treated as a slave by some primitive paintmonger?"

Shimmer touched her arm, to placate her.

"I'm sure N is telling the truth. It just goes to prove that Bertie was even more astute than we had been led to believe. Deliberately hiding his light in a barrel under a bush. Or perhaps his powers were only latent at first. And even so there are already hints of what was to come: Bertie goes five hundred years into the past, and rescues the woman he loves, happily willing to sacrifice his own life in the process. Exactly what we would expect from him."

That wasn't quite how I had seen it; in this case, the woman had rescued Bertie and not the other way round. And I strongly doubted that his light was bright enough to attract attention, even on top of a bushel. But I had to tread carefully. If by some miracle he had become some sort of folk hero for these visitors, it would be wise to keep my opinions to myself.

"I still think he's lying," said Shade doggedly.

"We mustn't judge too soon. Remember, that's why we're here, to separate the legend from fact. N is very kindly helping us to do this, and we already have some interesting sidelights on Bertie that we didn't have before."

Shade bit off a wart from her right hand, and spat it at the wall, where it bored a noticeable hole. "The two peasants by the river, did they say what they were waiting for?"

"No, they didn't," I replied, surprised she would remember that detail.

Shimmer gestured impatiently. "Just a coincidence, there's no way..." She stopped herself. "But what about the Time Machine itself? You've said absolutely nothing about its construction. How you had the genius to simply leap over the then-fashionable but completely erroneous ideas about wormholes and negative density and exotic matter, and hit on the Egg-Timer Principle. Were you sitting under a pineapple tree beside the Yureka River?"

I wasn't ready to face that question yet. "Remember, I haven't yet put these notes in their final order. There's more about the Machine later."

Then, to divert their attention, I gave what was meant to be seen as an embarrassed smile.

"If you would excuse me, ladies, I need to go to the bathroom."

"Why?" snarled Shade. "What are you hiding in there?"

"Of course," said Shimmer. "Agen... our colleague Shalom will accompany you."

"I do happen to know where the bathroom is. It's been in the same place for some time." I instantly regretted my instinctive retort.

Shade seemed to stare at my tongue, as if wondering whether that ought to stay in the same place any longer.

"It's for your own protection," said Shimmer. "Bertie has – had – many enemies in the future, who might try to take vengeance on his friends."

There was no point in arguing. I left the room, turned right, followed by the still silent Shalom, and moved along the passage to the nearest bathroom. I did wonder briefly whether to try to make a run for it – surely I'd come across one of the guards within seconds – but something about the way Shalom moved told me I would never have those few seconds. Although I didn't detect in her the simmering hostility of Shade or the smiling menace of Shimmer, I figured she would be all the more efficient for being impersonal.

When I reached the bathroom, I opened the door, and then turned round to face her.

"Do you mind?" I said.

She looked surprised, then seemed to realize what I meant, and nodded. She stuck her head inside, checking to see that the window was too small for anyone to escape through, then stepped back. I thought she was going to speak, but she must have changed her mind. I went in and closed the door behind me, cursing myself for not having chosen one of the upstairs bathrooms with bigger windows. But then I doubt if she would have left me alone in that case.

I stood dejectedly over the pan while my earlier coffees began to trickle slowly and reluctantly out.

That's what fear does for you.

But then I noticed an odd thing. The toilet is beside the wash basin, and over the basin is a small ornate mirror. As I stood there, cursing the undignified reluctance of my urethra to relax, I happened to glance into it.

And there I glimpsed, or thought I did, the door slightly open, and an eye applied to the crack! And was that an intake of breath I heard?

If I'd had the presence of mind to feign having noticed nothing, I might have been able to glance again, and find out whether it was just my nervous imagination or not, but I made the mistake of swinging round. No eye, door completely shut. But then I already knew how quickly these women could move.

The shock led to an instant escalation from a go-slow to a complete stoppage in the waterworks department. I shook the tubular interface between bladder and outside world with the desperation of an alcoholic expecting miracles from an empty whisky bottle, but with no better result. So the little devil now couldn't even manage this simplest of tasks! "Get out of my sight, you wimp!" I muttered, and stuffed it back where it came from, pulling up my zip furiously, half hoping to inflict deserved injury on it.

I stepped out of the bathroom, scowled at Shalom who was waiting a few feet away, and returned to the sitting room, where I immediately picked up my folder and started to read out the second adventure. I wanted to avoid any more questions as long as possible. With luck I could finish the reading and get rid of these unwelcome visitors before they realised something didn't quite add up.

4: CAIN AND MABEL

Clarence Darrow: Did you ever discover where Cain got his wife?
William Jennings Bryan: No, sir; I leave the agnostics to hunt for her…
Darrow: The Bible says he got one, doesn't it? Were there other people on the earth at that time?
Bryan: I cannot say…
Darrow: There were no others recorded, but Cain got a wife.
Bryan: That is what the Bible says.
(The Scopes Trial, 1925)

There were a number of reasons why, a month later, after Bertie had recovered, the next mystery we were sent to solve was that of Cain's wife, and not that of Cleopatra's amazing sexual attraction. Firstly, Bertie Senior told me to go to hell; and secondly, he wanted to really test the range of the Chronoporter, to see just how far back it would go. Moreover, after our unfortunate experiences in sixteenth-century Florence, it was felt that it would be safer, with far fewer people there to harm us – four, to be precise: Adam, Eve, Cain, and the mysterious wife who came from nowhere.

More important than all of these, I suspect, was the financial consideration. The International Society of Creationists had put up a lot of the money, so sure were they that the trip would prove their beliefs true. The previous President of the United States, before his assassination, had himself become a Creationist, as this was a concept far easier for him to understand than evolution, genetics, or politics, and had donated the vast sums he had made from the Arabic-speaking fifty-first State to the cause. Bertie Senior, a man with strong religious leanings himself, had no objection to getting back some of his investment.

There was, nonetheless, quite a bit of dissension over this Trip.

Some of our backers wanted us to go to Eden itself, and film the actual creation of Adam or Eve, or both. Tempting as it may have seemed, it was far too risky. If we disturbed God on the job, startled him, his hands might jerk at a delicate moment, leaving Adam with an ingrowing member, or Eve with her nose balanced on the end of her breast. Besides, God in those days was someone better avoided, like a scorned red-haired woman. I mean, all Adam did was eat one

47

measly apple, for Christ's sake! And you just ask someone from Sodom or Gomorrah what God was like in those days – you can't: he wiped out the lot!

Others were happy with the Cain idea but wanted us to film the murder of Abel as well. This too was an attractive idea, but the power supplies of the Time Machine were limited. At most, we believed, it could stay in the past for three days. Given this time window, we couldn't film the murder of Abel in Eden and nab Cain with his wife in the Land of Nod. Safer to restrict ourselves to the latter, and solve the age-old mystery of just who this wife was. After all, that was the fundamental purpose of our Trips – to finally provide answers to unsolved mysteries.

Our backers, of course, were convinced they already knew the answer. They simply wanted to prove it to everyone else. But whilst they were all convinced that everybody was indeed descended from Adam and Eve, they had differing views on who exactly Cain's wife had been. For the majority of them it was obvious that Cain married one of his younger sisters (Genesis tells us Adam and Eve 'begat sons and daughters' after Seth). Incest would have been no problem in those days because the children of Adam and Eve would have inherited the perfect gene structures of their parents. Nasty mutations only set in after people started being naughty.

A minority thought God might have created a wife specially for Cain, or that he had created other tribes, an even smaller minority proposed that Cain entered holy matrimony with a passing demon, and a further minority so small that it could only be found on the Internet was convinced that Cain had shacked up with a visiting alien, thus giving rise to the infamous Nephilim.

Our job was to find out which, if any, of these theories was the truth.

However, this Trip was going to be a bit different in another way, too – there would be four of us going. Bertie insisted on taking Winnie with us. (We still called her Winnie, though she insisted that other people call her Mona Lisa.) Or rather, Bertie confided to me, Winnie insisted on coming.

"I don't like the idea too much," he said. "Didn't that Cain chap murder his father or something? But Win's got it into her head she wants to come, and says if I don't let her…"

The forlorn way he glanced downwards told me precisely what threat Winnie was holding over him (or withholding from him). I had never seen him so subdued. His marriage wasn't turning out quite so well after all. Presumably, it had been his father's concern over this which had moved him to decree that Winnie would be coming with us.

To tell the truth, I was quite pleased. Very pleased, in fact. Almost enough to make me forget that my dream of visiting Cleopatra had been thwarted once again.

No longer constrained in fashionable Florentine clothes, Winnie was a stunner. She had at once gone on a diet, and now had a lithe slim body quite unlike that suggested by her portrait. Her hair, her eyes… well, everyone's seen her on television a hundred times, so you'll understand when I say she only had to smile at me for my scrotum to swell like a frog.

She had one single imperfection. She had married Bertie, not me.

Despite this, however, she had given me numerous subtle indications that I was not unpleasing in her sight. I also remembered what she'd said in Florence about her frolicking hormones. I confess I was rather excited by the prospect of her joining us in Nod.

This excitement I carefully hid from my darling wife.

But dear Mabel was such a suspicious creature. Just because of an inconsequential peccadillo a few months earlier – or was it that ridiculously minor indiscretion just before that? – the dear woman had taken it into her head not to trust me. This I found very hurtful, but I bore it with the stoicism traditional in one who marries into a rich family.

My stoicism was truly tested when I discovered that Mabel trusted me so little that she went to Bertie Senior behind my back, and threatened to kick up a stink about Winnie unless she was allowed to come along too! She had connections – indeed, certain calumniators have disgracefully accused me of marrying her for that very reason – and he acceded to her request. Perhaps he imagined he was doing me a favour, thinking that the newly-weds might make me feel *de trop*.

The odd thing was, Winnie apparently backed her up, and told Bertie and his dad that it was only fair that if she, as Bertie's wife, could come along, so should *my* wife.

I am a man long inured to life's cruel blows, and you will notice, if you look closely, that in the film taken as we entered the Chronoporter, I am managing a diluted homeopathic smile.

⊕

Since we didn't know exactly how far back to go (Bishop Ussher's claim that God created the world in 4004 BC, later refined by Dr John Lightfoot, Vice-Chancellor of Cambridge University no less, to 9.00 am, 23 October, and initially accepted even by Darwin, was by now a bit suspect), we didn't get it right first time. We began to materialise over a boisterous city that reminded me a bit of Las Vegas, and spotted a procession of ten righteous-looking men carrying placards protesting against the rampant debauchery there. Our sudden semi-arrival scared them, and they ran screaming into the wilderness. We later found out that the city was called Sodom. Apparently, had those good citizens stayed, or even only half of them, things might have turned out differently, some sort of gentleman's agreement between God and Abraham. Just goes to show how tricky this time travel business really is.

Then we over-compensated, and caught Adam enthusiastically masturbating beside a tree, egged on by a sardonic-looking serpent. We gave him the benefit of the doubt and assumed that Eve hadn't yet been created. And indeed, as we were blinking out of existence again, I could have sworn I glimpsed an enormous figure with a vicious-looking bistoury, and Adam making a desperate bolt for it.

(I should mention here that we could 'hop' to secure fine adjustments. In physical terms, it was like landing on the wrong side of a lake and trying to cross it by leaping from one giant water lily to another: you couldn't rest your feet more than a second or two on each one without it sinking into the water. Once that happened, we were trapped; the only time jump we could then make would be back to our starting point.)

Next time we touched down amidst vast stretches of sand bordered on one side by bare jagged hills. Compared to this, the Sahara was a rain forest. It must have been just after noon.

"Are you sure this is the Land of Nod?" my wife asked.

Even Bertie was looking at me a bit doubtfully.

"Of course," said I. "We're east of Eden, aren't we?"

"Well, let's ask someone, just to make sure."

"Who?" I said. My innate good breeding stopped me adding that any fool could see the place was deserted.

Mabel gave me one of her special sweet smiles oozing with that mixture of honey, triumph, and superiority which had many a time made me contemplate the ecstasies of murder.

"What about *them*?" she said.

Never trust the Bible! Less than twenty yards away two dirty-looking characters in loin-cloths were scuffing their toes in the sand.

We approached them, and I asked politely: "Excuse me, dirty-looking characters, is this the Land of Nod?"

"Could be," said one.

"But then again, might not be," said the other helpfully.

"Why do you want to know?" asked the first one.

"We're looking for Cain."

"Well, we haven't seen him. And we've been here since… how long *have* we been here?"

"Don't you know?" snapped his companion.

"Well, we were here yesterday, I think… Yes, we must have been."

"Why?"

"I don't remember being anywhere else."

"That doesn't prove anything. There's a fifty-fifty chance we were somewhere else."

"You're right, I'm not ashamed to admit it. We could have been in a lot of other places, too."

"No, we couldn't."

"Why not?"

"There aren't any other places, except Adam's. So it's fifty-fifty, as I said before you began to waste my time arguing."

"But what if we were nowhere?"

"Ah, now there I grant that you have a good point. And I'm not one to argue for nothing. So that makes three possible places – Adam's patch, nowhere, and here. Thirty-three percent probability. Approximately."

They turned towards us.

"We definitely haven't seen Cain, but as there's a sixty-six percent probability (approximately) that we weren't even here, don't let this discourage you. But have you seen… what was his name?"

"Can't you even remember that?"

"If I could, I wouldn't need to ask you, would I?"

"You wouldn't *need* to, but you might do it all the same, just to annoy me. You like annoying me. Anyway, I don't remember, either."

"So we could be waiting in vain, then?"

"It's a possibility not to be dismissed lightly."

The two scruffs looked glumly at each other.

"So what do we do now then?" asked one.

"There's nothing we *can* do except wait."

"We could go home."

"Where's home?"

"I don't know. A long way away, that's for sure."

"So we have to wait then."

"For what's-his-name, you mean?"

"Of course."

"You're right. Let's wait for him."

"We might see this Cain character, too, while we're waiting."

"Yes, that would relieve the monotony."

Whereupon, they turned their backs on us as if we no longer existed, and stared into the distance.

As we walked away (Winnie especially seemed anxious to get away) we heard one muttering to the other: "But what if we were meant to meet him somewhere else?"

We wandered on, and soon came across a tent and, lounging outside it, prodding disconsolately at his macrophallus, Cain.

We knew it was him, first of all, because the big scarlet UR-mark branded on his forehead was a dead give-away. Secondly, as soon as he saw us, his ruddy countenance fell and he looked extremely wroth. He stormed up to us, his eyes wild, wielding in his big farmer's hands what looked like a human thigh bone. Abel's? I wondered. Family keepsake?

"Fuck off!" he screamed. "Can't touch me, God said so, look, I've got this frigging Mark, you dare touch me and you get what for! In the bollocks! Bam!"

I should point out here that my translations of Cain's proto-expletives are very approximate, striving to capture the *physicality* of the words rather than their pure semantic or semiological value. Indeed, as Isabel Iglesias and other scholars have observed, the UR-language lodged in our appendixes was disconcertingly fluid, with nuances, appoggiaturas, and even new meanings, being created by the minute, almost as if it already sensed the coming of the Tower that was to splinter it into a million dialects.

If you're wondering what Cain looked like, just stop off at Easter Island, and take a look – real close – at those statues. Only Cain was bigger and uglier.

We backed away a little bit. Except Bertie, of course.

"Yes, what does that mark stand for?" he asked casually.

"This?"

"Yes."

"God fucking put it there. Stands for 'Pitiless Murderer', I think."

I didn't like the pride in his voice when he said this.

Bertie had broken the ice, but it might have been better not to. For now Cain's bloodshot eyes noisily swivelled round to land on Winnie. Perhaps I should mention she was wearing a very fetching mini-skirt.

"You married?" he asked with a most unpleasant leer.

"That's my business!" she replied archly.

"Well, so happens I'm looking for a wife, 'cause I fancy being fruitful and multiplying, since there's fuck all else to do these days. At least when Abel was alive, I had someone to knock around. And bloody short of pussy round here. There's some skinny bint God or some other fucker dropped outside my tent last week, supposed to be my wife, but she won't let me near her! So you'll have to do." One of his eyes then squelched round to my wife. "Or you, at a pinch." He fingered his pizzle, which now reflected both his growing optimism and his growing ambitions. "Nah, I'll have you both."

Mabel looked rather smug, no doubt convincing herself she'd come out equal with the Mona Lisa herself. Not such a big compliment, I thought, when you considered that Cain had never had his end away. And he was already probably a hundred years old or more (his father lived to 930). If I ever went without sex for a hundred years, I imagine my sweet wife would start to appear attractive to me, too.

Well, maybe.

"I think we might have to make a run for it," I whispered to Bertie.

Bertie planted himself firmly in front of Winnie, in the same pose as the *David* we'd recently seen in Florence, or Popeye facing Bluto. I had to admire his courage. I promised myself right there and then I would look after his widow, see to her every need.

"Stick to your own wife, you great dollop!" said he. A bantam cock couldn't have shown more spirit.

Cain raised the thigh bone menacingly, but the sight of it must have reminded him of what had happened last time he'd spilled some blood: it had at once proceeded to cry unto the Lord from the ground. He lowered the bone, and answered dejectedly:

"I *have* tried to stick it to my own wife, but she keeps her legs so close together it just gets sore!"

"Perhaps if you tried asking her nicely..." suggested Mabel sweetly. Did I imagine the humming of bees?

"I have! I've told her I need a fuck – *need* one! – but she still gets her legs tighter than a mermaid's."

So much for mermaids simply being folklore!

I thought rather bitterly that Cain had no right to complain. The girl had only been there a week! Mabel had made me wait for months! And then had the cheek to criticise me afterwards!

"Have you ever thought of marrying one of your sisters?" I asked.

Cain wasn't too impressed with my suggestion.

"Have you seen them? I'd rather fuck my mother! Only she wouldn't let me either, after the first time!"

All this was being secretly filmed, but I guessed our sponsors might be doing a bit of censoring.

Bertie cunningly and diplomatically tried to deflect the conversation, calling on an ill-remembered item from his wasted schooldays.

"Why did God spit in your face when you offered him a birthday present?"

The wrath at once began to wax again, so I hastily interposed:

"What my friend meant was we frankly are on your side – as were Lord Byron and Baudelaire, in case you're interested though I guess maybe you aren't – and simply don't understand why your offering wasn't considered as good as Abel's."

Cain reluctantly (and, I was sure, temporarily) took his eyes off the two women.

"It was that little snotfuck Abel!" he said.

"Eh?"

"Little cunt peed on the fruit I was offering, but I didn't know, did I, so God got a whiff of it and blew his bloody top!"

"But that's terrible!" said Mabel, a tender-hearted woman except when it concerned me.

"But didn't you explain to him?" I asked.

"Nah, I just killed him instead. Anyway, he deserved it for the barbaric way he sacrificed those poor sheep."

"To God, I mean."

"Wouldn't listen to me, would he? Just ranted on about he was a god, and wasn't going to put up with piss-poor food!"

"But why didn't you talk to your father before taking such a drastic step? He could have explained to God…"

"Fuck Dad!" roared Cain. "Look how he grassed on Mum! 'The woman whom thou gavest to be with me, she gave me of the tree, and I did eat!' Snivelling snitch! Think I'd take advice from *him*?"

For the first time, I saw Winnie look at him with something less than loathing. Considering his earlier revelation, I figured a Freudian interpretation might have been in order here.

"But why did Abel do it?"

"Fucked if I know! Maybe 'cause I shagged a few of his blessed sheep, who knows? Kinder to shag 'em than to cut their throats."

He had a point. For some reason, I was reminded of St Paul's little dictum about marrying and burning. But Mabel winced, Winnie looked disgusted, and Bertie simply opened his eyes wider.

We were saved from any more embarrassing disclosures when Cain suddenly gave a roar, dashed behind his tent, and a few seconds later reappeared, dragging by the arm a naked young woman, scarcely into puberty but with a surprisingly well-muscled body.

"See, filches my food, and doesn't even give me a blow-job back!" said Cain, much aggrieved.

The girl was clutching a fistful of dates, grapes, olives, and eggplants.

For all his fallen countenance, Cain clearly wasn't really hurting her, and although she was twisting and struggling, neither did she seem genuinely afraid.

Then she saw us.

Within a very short time, we all knew why Cain's pubic tumescences remained untreated.

Now I'm not one to knock God. With a whole Universe to create and manage, plus one hell of a rebellion in Heaven, you couldn't expect him to remember every blessed little detail. But considering the whole human race (at this time) depended on a bit of fourth-base nookie, you really would have expected him to make sure Cain's wife was of the appropriate persuasion.

That little minx, the moment she spotted Winnie's legs, a potent combination of silk and velvet with a touch of kitten fur, broke away from Cain's grip, dashed forward, and had her hand inside her knickers quicker than a politician's reply. Winnie was so surprised she hardly reacted, and it was left to my sweet Mabel to put an end to this shocking scene.

"Remove those fumbling fingers of infamy!" she ordered, stepping forward, and giving the girl a smart smack. Mabel had come from a good family.

The girl looked up at her with frightened eyes, then darted away, disappearing over the nearest dune in no time.

Cain had witnessed this open-mouthed, and expressed his amazement in the following Ur-manner:

"What the fuck?" he said.

We tried to explain to him that sometimes women prefer women, but he wasn't civilised enough to grasp the concept.

"So what the fuck's this for, then?" he shouted, outraged, slapping his member down on a nearby rock, flattening a somnolent lizard in the process.

We realised it wouldn't take him long to answer this highly rhetorical question, so I hastily summoned the Spatial Mobility Module (the emergency remote control mechanism yet again proving its worth). Whilst he was occupied picking hastily shed lizard skin off his manhood, we took the opportunity to skedaddle out of there while we could.

Once we were a safe distance away I guided the Module to the ground for an impromptu council of war.

"It's not safe to stay here longer," I said. "If Cain takes it into his head to grab you two girls…"

"…then we use those," said Winnie, pointing to the two laser pistols beside the console.

"Don't touch them! They're only for the most desperate emergency. If we harm Cain, we may destroy the future human race!"

"So you're going to leave that poor innocent girl at his mercy? Yet another helpless female used and abused by yet another brutal male?"

"Yes, we must stop him!" said Bertie, whose blood was still up.

Also wanted to ingratiate himself with Winnie no doubt.

"We can't!" I said. "We can't just come back, and alter history like that! The Bible says: 'Cain knew his wife; and she conceived.'"

Well, we argued and argued, but finally they came to accept my point of view. We simply couldn't interfere here without the direst consequences.

"Besides," I said, "you saw yourselves that the girl wasn't really afraid of Cain. She may grow fond of him in time, notice his good qualities."

I have to hand it to Mabel and Winnie: they didn't ask the obvious question.

We were preparing to leave, when Winnie made a most unsettling comment.

"You realise," she said slowly, "we may already have changed history."

"What do you mean?"

"Cain's wife is clearly lesbian, *non è certo*?"

"So?"

"But she didn't know it before."

"Eh?"

"All she knew was that she didn't fancy Cain. She didn't know she liked women. Because she had never even seen a woman before! Cain said she was dropped outside his tent last week. As she wasn't one of his sisters, that means God made her especially for him. So she'd never seen another woman!"

It took some time to sink in, but of course it was true. I said, uneasily: "But this doesn't alter anything. Cain may not have had his way yet, but that must be going to change, because the Bible says they did have a child."

"And why? Because she isn't much more than a child herself. Cain must be twenty times her age. It's not surprising she didn't fancy him, whatever her sexual orientation. But she would one day be a woman, with a woman's needs. As she got older, and those needs increased, she might well have turned to Cain. Since there was no known alternative."

"So what you're saying is…?"

"She may now always reject Cain! She knows there is a better alternative, a much better alternative! She may spend her whole life

STEVE REDWOOD

seeking it. Instead of a hairy, selfish, sweating brute, she is now aware of the possibility of a warm, caring, considerate, infinitely more sensual and satisfying kind of partner. Another warm breast with…"

She noticed our expressions, especially Bertie's, stopped, and then laughed.

"I'm just saying how she *might* feel, of course. Look at the mate the poor girl has! Now, if it were my darling Bertie…"

I noticed hesitation even in Bertie's answering smile. And what had she said about Leonardo?

But this was not the time to wonder about Winnie's predilections.

"In other words, by letting her come into contact with other women, we may have guaranteed that she never sleeps with Cain!"

"And if that happens…"

"We may have no future to return to!"

Winnie's bloody mini-skirt!

When push comes to almighty shove, there's no one harder than a righteous woman. My sweet Mabel, grim churchgoer, assiduous giver to charity, frequent mourner at funerals, now spoke up.

"That girl is Cain's God-given wife. It is her duty to satisfy his marital needs. He is much too soft with her, as we have seen. We must make her perform the duties of a faithful and obedient wife."

I caught Bertie's eye. We looked away from each other.

"Exactly!" said Winnie, who a moment before had been extolling the Sapphic alternative. "And we must do it soon, before we run out of time. How much longer do we have?"

I was acutely aware that our wives, our passengers, were making our decisions for us, but, then, wasn't that usually the case?

"Two days, I should think, though I can't be certain."

"We'd better go back and look for her right away then. If we leave it till tomorrow, and then can't find her, we'll really be in trouble."

So we set out to find Cain's wife.

We could probably have found her very quickly if we had used the Spatial Mobility Module, but we didn't dare expend any more energy. She couldn't be far away – she couldn't survive for long without Cain's supply of food.

Cain's tent was in a small wadi, surrounded on one side by flat desert that seemed to roll on to infinity as if it had nothing better to do, but on the other were rocky outcroppings, cracked arid hillsides studded with tiny caves. And that was the direction Cain's wife had gone in. We spread out to begin searching.

It was Winnie who found her, less than an hour later, lying at the base of a large rock, blood still oozing from a wound in her head. She had clearly slipped, and cracked her skull.

Winnie called us, and we stood in a frightened circle around the body.

Wondering how soon it would be before Time adjusted to what had happened, and flicked us out of existence.

Half the human race was gone. We knew Adam and Eve were later going to produce Seth, and other children, but without the strong blood of Cain we'd never make it to the twenty-first century.

Perhaps because none of us knew what to say, we didn't speak, but buried the body under a mound of rocks. But finally, we had to look each other in the eyes, and face up to this new reality.

It was Winnie who spoke first, pale but determined.

"Our duty is clear," she declared. "Mabel will have to stay here, and mother half of the human race. She was the one who struck that poor innocent child and caused her to flee, thus leading directly to her tragic death."

"You can't leave me here!" screamed Mabel.

I looked at her sadly. I tried to keep my voice from trembling.

"We have to, my one and only. Winnie is right. There'll be no human race – or at least not the one we're used to – if we don't leave a wife for Cain."

"Leave Winnie!"

"We have to be fair, my cherished one, we mustn't allow personal considerations to influence such a vital decision. So we'll vote on it. Who says leave Mabel?"

"Me," said Bertie.

"Me," said Winnie.

I turned to my wife sorrowfully.

"That's it, I'm afraid. Two votes to one."

"What! Are you voting against me?"

"Of course not! I am your ever-loving husband."

"But my vote and your vote makes two!"

I held her tenderly by the hand.

"Ah, if only it could be so! But, as the interested party, you clearly

59

can't be allowed to vote. You couldn't be impartial. So, heartbreaking though it is, my sweet, I'm afraid it is, as I said, two to one."

"But Winnie voted!"

"So?"

"She's an interested party!"

"Ah, my treasure," cried I, bravely suppressing my tears, "let not jealousy and feminine illogic cloud your judgement. The vote was about you, not about her. I love you beyond all reason, as you know, but your implied suggestion that Winnie, the Mona Lisa herself, the wife of my good friend Bertie, would let self-interest influence her vote, is unworthy of you."

It grieves me to report it, but my sweet wife was only human, after all. She refused to do the honourable thing, and instead tried to make a run for it. My heart almost bursting with grief, I brought her down with a flying tackle.

We took her back to Cain.

He was fingering his member impatiently.

"When can I wham it in?" he demanded.

"Never!" screamed Mabel with such fury in her eyes that Cain almost flinched. "You are an uncouth and uncivilised brute!"

I noticed, however, with a tinge of annoyance, that she kept peeping, with unrighteous fascination, at the splendid object of Cain's obsession.

Winnie pulled me and Bertie to one side.

"We'd better let him get on with it quickly," she said, "and we'd better stay here until we know the deed is done."

"Just a minute!" I protested. "She *is* my wife. I understand that for the good of mankind, she must stay here, and I am willing to sacrifice married bliss, and even the pitter patter of tiny feet, for the greater good, but I really would prefer not to be present."

All right, call me old-fashioned, even sentimental, if you like; I'm not ashamed of my human weakness.

"But we have to be sure he does in fact perform. If we return to the future, and for some reason or other Cain and Mabel haven't produced any babies, there won't be any future! We may return to a planet without a single human being."

That sounded rather nice for a moment. No more queues, taxmen, reality television, celebrities, drug addicts, lawyers, people wearing baseball caps back to front… Then I reflected that there might not be any more us, either, since the people who built the Chronoporter would never have lived.

"Very well," I said, "that is, I admit, not a trivial consideration. But remember, our Machine has to return very soon."

She must have noticed I was a bit downcast, because she whispered in my ear, "I promise you I won't forget your unselfishness in sacrificing your wife for the greater good. I'll make it up to you in a way I know will please you."

I smiled gratefully at her. Such sensitivity! Such a generous spirit!

Even so, as we wandered back to the TM, my heart was heavy. I had been with dear Mabel for more than ten years, and though, of course, no marriage can be entirely perfect, I could still recall moments verging on happiness in the first month or so.

It is so hard sometimes to do the honourable thing.

Everything should have ended there. My selfless donation of my dear wife had probably saved the human race from extinction, and this thought served to mitigate my profound grief. I didn't expect, or even desire, praise for my fortitude in bearing this terrible loss with such courageous equanimity.

We decided to spend the night in the TM, and check the following day to see how the happy couple were getting on. But within a couple of hours, while it was still only mid-afternoon, Cain came stumbling towards us. And Winnie, with Bertie sprawled asleep beside her, was lying in her bra and panties just outside the TM!

Bertie had tried to dissuade her from sunbathing, but she'd pointed out that she'd given up the bright sun of Italy in July for the pale impostor taking the mickey out of England in March, all for him, so how could he be so mean as to even think of depriving her of this chance to get a bit of a tan? I knew Bertie was right – Cain was after all a known murderer and obviously as lecherous as they come – but I'd felt compelled to side with Winnie.

If a beautiful woman wanted to relax in front of me in tiny light blue panties and transparent bra, I would have been churlish indeed to forbid it.

I was inside the TM, keeping an eye on her through the view port – no wonder the Marquis de Sade had called her 'the very essence of femininity'! – and now I frantically searched round for one of the stun pistols, convinced that Cain would now become a raging monster. In my mind, I could already see the tabloid headlines: *He came; he saw; he bonkered.*

But instead of hurling himself upon her, he threw himself down before her.

"Please don't leave her here!" he pleaded. "I just can't do it any longer! Please, I beg you! Take her away! Or take *me* away!" He grabbed her hands in supplication.

Winnie, who must have dozed off, looked up and misunderstood Cain's intentions.

"Bertie, save me!" she screamed.

Bertie woke up instantly and, plucky little fellow that he was, hurled himself at Cain, who at first simply parried his blows with one hand, while with the other he clutched pathetically at Winnie. But then Bertie, realising his blows were having no effect, kicked him in the groin. I now noticed how subdued his member was, its earlier panache and cocksure confidence completely gone. Cain's patience snapped, and within a second Bertie was lying flat, his nose protruding through the back of his head, a clear example of Hooke's Law stating that the deformation of a body is proportional to the magnitude of the deforming force.

By now I had found the pistol, and brought Cain down with a well-placed shot in the buttock.

I scrambled out, held Winnie tightly to calm her down for a few minutes, and then between us we lifted poor Bertie into the TM.

He wasn't quite gone.

"Look after Winnie!" he whispered before the rictus of death set upon him.

I promised, of course. What else could I do? We looked down at brave foolish Bertie, and comforted each other in our loss.

$\oplus$

As the whole world knows, Bertie didn't really die. Well, he did. But he was resurrected. No, that's not quite it, either.

You'll all have seen the 'experts' on television claiming to reveal how it was done. Most of what they say is utter drivel. But even now, when poor Bertie really is gone for ever, I am not at liberty to give too many details about our medical breakthrough. It is dangerous knowledge.

But I see no harm in revealing that the technique was suggested by unpublished stanzas of the *Book of Dzyan*, revealed to Madame Blavatsky by the Masters of Wisdom when she was in Wurzburg in 1886, working on *The Secret Doctrine*. Stanzas which gave vital information about the astral 'Silver Cord', which was mentioned as long ago as *Ecclesiastes*.

Just as the revolutionary hour-glass concept of my Time Machine allowed for the 'spilling' of our Machine and ourselves into the past, so it was our understanding and utilisation of the Silver Cord which gave us a safety net. We projected our Astral Bodies – but at once captured and retained them in an electromagnetic force field. There was therefore a constant 'tug' on the Silver Cord.

Otherwise impossible restorative surgery now worked on Bertie because the Astral Body (or a copy of the Vital Force, if you like) was already present! It was as if someone's will to live were multiplied by a thousand.

The process was still long and painful, of course. The passage of Bertie's nose through his head had left an ominous tunnel. Even with the Astral Body present, a more intelligent person might have been beyond recall. In Bertie's case, however, the relative emptiness of his head had minimized the damage. Nonetheless, he wasn't able to move for nearly a month.

One of the medical technicians revealed to me an odd fact: when he was dead, Bertie's odour had diminished so much that it was no worse than that of any other decaying corpse; but as soon as the Regeneration process began, the old familiar odour had also been resurrected. This perhaps explained why the millions his father had spent over the years seeking a cure had been in vain – Bertie's aroma was somehow tied to his Astral Body, perhaps even had its origin in another dimension. I resolved to try to be more understanding in future – from a distance.

There had probably been more than physical damage, as well. Bertie began to have what he swore were 'memories'.

"What kind of memories?" I asked.

"Well, I know this will seem odd, but I'm surrounded by women who all seem to worship me!"

I kept my face straight and considerate, for the benefit of the other people present.

"And me?" I asked. "What am I doing?"

"Well, that's the other odd thing: you aren't there!"

Oh yeah, great! When Cain's on the rampage, I'm there: when there's crumpet all round, I'm not. I dismissed it all as trauma-induced hallucination.

Meanwhile, I did my best to fulfil my promise to look after Winnie. A promise made to a dying man is no light thing. Even if he didn't die in the end.

Oh yes, I saw the scurrilous stories written about us, the vile insinuations inspired by Mabel's rich relatives that we had planned everything just to get both Bertie and my sweet wife out of the way. I ignored them. Such accusations were beneath contempt.

As were the smirks and giggles, and that disgraceful article in *Private Eye* wilfully misrepresenting the significance of Cain's words, 'I just can't do it any longer.' The writer depicted me as an unloving inadequate husband who had left poor Mabel so frustrated that even Cain couldn't fulfil her accumulated needs. This was an unforgivable insult, not so much to me as to my darling Mabel, who had understood the importance of her role in human history, and, always a deeply moral woman, had spared no effort to perform her duty and give us all a future.

There is a small plaque above the console in the TM which I insisted on having. It says simply:

In gratitude to Mabel, who gave her all for the human race.

5: THE SANDS OF TIME

When I stopped reading, there was a few moments' silence while I struggled to overcome my emotion, as I remembered my dear sweet wife.

Shimmer's eyes were shining.

"What women! Winnie, able instantaneously to comprehend the gravity of the situation and to come up with a solution! Mabel, giving up on the spot all her past life, her friends, her comforts, her beloved husband, and enduring the odious embrace of a lascivious monster in order to fulfil her duty! And yet there are still those who question the Great Unclutt…"

Once again she cut herself short.

"Brave women indeed," she went on, "but that's nothing to the way Bertie, unarmed, stood up to Cain to defend the honour of his wife! Prepared to die for her without a second's thought! No wonder he later gathered such a following!

"And you, N," she continued, turning to me with a smile that for some reason reminded me of an alligator having an orgasm, "were perhaps the noblest of them all. Giving up your beloved wife, willingly risking all the inevitable misunderstanding and gossip because you knew that what you were doing was the right, the *allamerican* thing to do!"

"Er, I'm English," I said.

She gave me a puzzled look. "We know that," she said.

I left that mystery for a moment, and tried to recall what she had been saying before stopping herself. Something about some kind of Great…what? But I had no time to think because Shade, whose heel, I noticed, had worn a hole in my carpet, and whose hands all the time had been curling into the oddest shapes, demanded: "How did you know your Time Machine could only remain in the past for a limited period?"

This was the kind of question I always dreaded, even from my own colleagues.

"It was clear from the equations," I answered, as if it was so obvious I couldn't believe I'd even been asked.

"What equations?"

I gave what I hoped would pass for a patient smile.

"Time has a 'gravitational' pull, the Tug, we call it. Analogous, in a way, to the Astral Cord I mentioned. When something goes into the past, it is inevitably drawn back to the present, since the 'present' is its natural place. The hour-glass shape of my Machine was designed to utilise this universal 'spring' effect. Sooner or later, the 'sands of time' have to pour back. Or, if time is a river – which, of course, it isn't – you can only swim against the current for so long. The everyday pull of gravitation is in fact simply a limited manifestation of the much more fundamental Temporal Tug, as Einstein almost realised in his theories of curved space. But surely you must know all this?"

I asked the last question with the hope of distracting her from the original question. Shade took the bait.

"Of course we know it – and a whole lot more!" she snapped. "A little girl could have explained it better than that!"

Shimmer held up a placating hand.

"I can understand you must be a bit tired of having to explain your brilliant invention time after time. But how truly exciting that must have been, the 'hop' from the time of Adam to that of Cain. The hop forward! Did you realise the significance of that at the time?"

I wasn't quite sure where the question was leading, so I tried to stall for time.

"I don't think I quite understand what..."

"Of course, it wasn't really moving forward, since you hadn't completely materialised in the time of Adam, it was more like a ball being thrown in the air and bouncing in different directions until it finally comes to a stop. Nonetheless, I'm almost willing to bet that's when your brilliant mind first glimpsed the theoretical possibilities, aren't I right?"

"Um, yes, I suppose so."

Shimmer leaned forward excitedly, and I feared the questioning was going to become even more dangerous, but at that moment the telephone rang.

It was the fixed line, so I began to rise in order to answer it. What luck! Surely, whoever it was, I would be able to give them some clue that my security system had been breached.

But, at a sign from Shimmer, Shalom was suddenly in front of me, holding me back with a hand that made diamond seem like a marshmallow that even other marshmallows would pick on in the school playground. I knew she'd moved, because a second before, she'd been sitting opposite me, a few feet away. However, I didn't really see her move. All I saw was the after-image of where she'd been.

Her expression was as neutral as ever.

Who the hell were these people really? I'd had dealings with Time Police before – indeed, one had once saved my life – but they hadn't appeared anywhere near as deadly as these visitors of mine.

The phone rang until the answering machine clicked on, and then came Maria's voice:

"So you're still out speechifying, eh? Anyway, something's come up. Let's just say I bumped into someone... interesting... while I was getting stuff for our guest. So may not be coming back tonight. I'll be quite safe, don't worry, a secure compound. Anderson can bring the stuff, anyway, should be there by eight, eight-thirty. Call you later, when I'm sure. Bye!"

The machine clicked off.

No 'kisses as big as a pregnant elephant'?

Just as suddenly as she had crossed the room, Shalom was back opposite me, sitting on the sofa, giving almost no indication of having moved in the first place.

I knew I ought to protest and expostulate and say things like, "What the deuce...!" and "By gad, Madam!", but I was still in a state of minor shock. Behind the shock, though, was now a tiny hope: it was true that Maria might not be coming (bumped into who?) but Anderson and the escort would be. Twice Maria had been involved in near-fatal accidents, which I feared weren't accidents at all, although I had no idea who might want to harm her. That partly explained the security measures around my house. When they arrived, it would then surely be possible to warn Anderson. I simply had to hold out till then.

Shimmer smoothed back her blonde hair, and struggled to re-establish the smile.

"I must apologise on behalf of my colleague Shalom. Before she joined the History Faculty she used to be a bodyguard, and even now, when taken by surprise, she still sometimes lapses into her old ways. You see, in her job, one never knows whether a telephone may be booby-trapped."

"I understand," I said.

67

Her voice became as smooth as a post-coital caress.

"Your caller mentioned a guest. We weren't aware… I mean, I do hope we aren't interrupting…?

"Oh no," I said, "it's just a friend – Tom – who's coming tomorrow. Maria likes to plan ahead."

To my intense relief, she seemed to accept that. Thank God they didn't have built-in lie-detectors! If they knew who my 'guest' really was…!

"Maria? Is that the army nurse you met at Roswell?"

They really did know a lot about me!

"Yes, we became good friends." *Much more than that!*

"And Anderson is…?"

"Oh, Captain Anderson, Head of Security."

I'd hoped that would worry them a bit, but Shimmer passed it off as lightly as if I'd told her aunt Matilda was coming for tea.

In order to prevent her from returning to her questioning about the Time Machine, I added: "Shall I continue recounting our – Bertie's – adventures? So that I can finish before the Captain returns?"

Shimmer and Shade exchanged glances, and seemed to come to an agreement.

"Of course," said Shimmer. "The Trotsky case, wasn't it?"

"Not quite," I said, "but historically quite near."

6: HOSPITALITY RUSSIAN STYLE

Grigori had an unusual aversion to cakes and other sweetened foods.
  (Aron Simanovich, Rasputin's secretary,1924)

Well, our film of Cain upset a lot of people, though not the Creationists, of course, who were cock-a-hoop and pranced down the streets wearing fig leaves and munching apples. A hundred evolutionary scientists, led by Richard Dawkins, leapt off the Millennium Wheel in a bizarre ritual of atonement. The Galapagos Islands were blown up, and the name of Darwin execrated. Apes and monkeys beat their chests in relief: the one-hundred-and-fifty-year-old slander had been avenged.

But the average viewer lapped it all up, sighed to Cain's tender courtship of the two women, felt a naughty frisson when he hinted at his intimate relations with his mother and his sheep, cheered when Mabel so nobly offered herself to mother the human race, thrilled to the sight of Winnie in her underwear, and shivered and shuddered as Bertie's nose made that fatal last journey.

Blood and sex: that's what they really loved. Unlike Bertie's father, they didn't want answers to life's Big Questions, since that might make them think, and the whole purpose of television was to do the opposite. The most popular current programme was *Big Baby*, in which millions were glued to their seats watching the gladiatorial crawlings in a specially designed crèche hidden in an old nuclear bunker. The day Baby C did her first poo in Baby D's cot, with Baby D still inside it, half the western world leapt excitedly to their feet, or at least tried to, held down only by the sheer weight of their enormous buttocks.

(I had once believed, before meeting Cain, that, obeying the law of the survival of the unfittest, mankind would evolve to have armchair shapes, that eventually babies would be born, extremely painfully, already in a TV-compliant sitting-down posture.)

Bertie's dad was canny. Yes, he was still filthy rich, but, as John Stuart Mill remarked, 'men do not desire to be rich, but to be richer than other men'. Besides, the Time Machine was costing as much to maintain as a whole fleet of Polaris submarines or an ageing film star.

He needed to claw back some of his investment, and pay-by-view was the way to do it.

But at the same time, Chronotech's motto was 'We Solve the Unsolved', and despite pressure to have us go back and film, say, one of Caligula's orgies, or Custer's Last Stand, Bertie Senior refused, and remained true to his original vision of only using the Time Machine to solve genuine mysteries. But this didn't always have to be incompatible with the loftiest traditions of gutter journalism.

"Blood and guts," he pronounced, "that's what we need."

"And sex," I added hopefully. "Plenty of that in ancient Egypt. In Cleopatra's Court, for example…"

"No mystery there. We need something bloody and mysterious."

"We could try to solve the Jack the Ripper mystery," I suggested. "If Bertie were to dress in drag, and act as bait…"

I was, of course, only joking, but this quip was later to be held against me.

"No, we don't want English (or even Irish) blood and guts, too near home, especially with that terrible case last year." He was referring to the Catholic priest who had assaulted five nonagenarian female parishioners in the confessional and hung their knickers over the crucifix, 'to prove,' as he later declared, 'that we're not all fixated on small boys'. The Vatican, of course, had sacked him, angry at this deviation from a sacrosanct tradition. "No, I want you to film Rasputin's death."

Rasputin?

I glanced quickly at Bertie (now fully recovered), who put on his pugnacious expression and stared right back at me. So it had already been decided!

Bertie, I knew, was a great admirer of Rasputin. Well, they were similarly unkempt and dirty, though Bertie's body, beard and brain stem were all a good foot shorter than Rasputin's, and his eyes narcotic rather than hypnotic. What appealed to Bertie was the idea of a man who almost never washed either himself or his clothes going to tea parties with the (somewhat curdled) cream of St Petersburg society, and persuading high class ladies that they had to experience sin (with him) in order to learn to fight it. His very nickname 'Rasputin' meant 'licentious' (his real name was Grigori Efimovich Novykh). It was even rumoured that he was bedding the

Tsaritsa herself while Nicholas was at the Front gallantly chain-smoking and nobly overseeing the massacre of his troops by the Germans. Serious historians dismiss these tales as gross exaggeration by his enemies, but Bertie lapped them all up.

So when Bertie Senior went on to tell us to go to Russia slam bang in the winter of 1916, I guessed it was because papa was once again pleasing his baby boy.

Still, whatever the reason, there was certainly a genuine mystery to be solved, and it was a bloody enough one to ensure the highest ratings.

There are various, and conflicting, accounts of Rasputin's death, but the most famous of these was by the chief assassin himself, Prince Felix Yusupov.

His version was that he induced Rasputin to come to his palace in St Petersburg in the middle of the night by saying that his wife Irina, a renowned beauty, wanted to meet him, and that there, in a basement done up to look like a dining room, Rasputin devoured cakes and wine laced with potassium cyanide enough to kill a dozen men, but was still chatting away two hours later. So Yusupov then shot him at point-blank range, and Doctor Lazavert, the conspirator who had prepared the poisoned victuals, declared him dead. They left him there on the blood-stained bearskin rug. An hour later, Yusupov came back down into the cellar, where Rasputin still lay, until he suddenly leapt to his feet and, 'his green eyes, like those of a viper, bursting from his head', attacked his host: it would appear that he was miffed by the Prince's lukewarm hospitality. Yusupov managed to stagger away, while Rasputin escaped into the courtyard, where another conspirator, Purishkevich, shot at him four times, hitting him twice, once in the head. Then, being a gentleman, and a respected member of the State Duma, Purishkevich, in his own proud words, 'ran up and kicked him as hard as I could with my boot in the temple'. Yusupov, possibly annoyed that Rasputin had, like the uncouth peasant he was, allowed his blood to ruin his nice bearskin rug, then came and beat him with a club for some time. The inert body was rolled into a blue curtain and bound with a rope, taken to the Petrovsky Bridge and hurled into the Neva River, cracking the ice and disappearing beneath it. Two days later it was recovered, and water in the lungs showed Rasputin had still been alive in the water, and had only finally died from drowning. His daughter Marya later said that one eye was almost out of its socket, and that there were deep marks on the wrists left by the bonds that Rasputin had managed to break while under the freezing water.

If the story was true, how had Rasputin been able to survive so long? If untrue, what was the purpose? To justify Rasputin's murder by implying that he had diabolical powers? Very well, but why would Yusupov make up a story in which he himself doesn't come across in the most flattering light? Inviting a supposed friend to supper, poisoning him, shooting him in the back, and then beating him to a pulp when he's already half dead, is specifically frowned upon in *Debrett's Guide to Etiquette*. Of course, he *had* studied at Oxford University, which might have developed (apart from his latent homosexuality) his propensity to tell whopping great fibs. But even so...

I must admit I was quite excited by the Trip ahead.

How was I to know this would be my first brush with the Time Police?

We got to St Petersburg (then called Petrograd) at around nine o'clock on December 29 (the 16th by the old Julian calendar) 1916. Even though we had prepared for the cold by donning thermal underwear as well as special protective suits, I still felt my testicles cringe in protest as we stepped out of the Machine. It seemed that the air was full of meteorites, but they turned out to be simply the congealed coughs of passers-by.

No wonder Winnie had declined to come this time!

This Trip had presented us with an enormous technical difficulty. On our two previous Journeys we had simply left the Time Machine somewhere safe, and then either walked or used the Spatial Mobility Module to get around. But this time we had to film a murder in a basement cellar in a palace. We could hardly walk in with our camera and say: 'Do you mind if we film the five of you viciously murdering a monk whom the Tsar and Tsaritsa regard as the only person capable of healing their son? We promise we won't tell anybody about this extraordinarily botched-up and quite unbelievably cowardly murder.' Something told me that they wouldn't be amenable to this suggestion. We would end up in the Neva beside Rasputin.

Nor could we materialise earlier in the cellar and install hidden cameras, since the TM could well be bigger, or at least higher, than the cellar itself. Knocking down the walls and ceiling was not really compatible with discretion. Apart from which, with a century to Travel, we couldn't time our arrival with the necessary precision.

The technical people had come up with a clever, if risky, solution: the TM would take with it a much smaller version of itself.

But we couldn't just arrive after the murder, and then use the smaller machine (nicknamed Baby) to go Back, for two reasons. One was that we wouldn't know exactly when to enter the cellar: it would have to be just before Yusupov arrived there with Rasputin; but after the servants, fellow conspirators, and so on, had left it empty for the intended victim. Secondly, in order for Baby to be as good as invisible in the cellar, it would have to be phasing in and out of time. This uses a tremendous amount of energy: vital energy which would have to be drained from the main TM. Thus, once again, we needed to know exactly when to enter and when to leave the palace.

So we would have to arrive *before* the murder, to calibrate times and distances (from the main TM) for Baby. Then we would wait until after the murder had taken place and make a short hop Back in Baby and film it from inside the fateful cellar.

That was why we had chosen to arrive late in the evening. From the information we had, we believed we could stay for up to ten hours, so we would have time to make our measurements, and maybe film a bit of the city, even though it would be dark. Plenty of time.

If nothing went wrong.

As soon as we arrived on the outskirts of the city, we used the SMM to check the distance between the TM and Yusupov's Palace on the Moika Kanal. This information we dialled into Baby (which for some reason the engineers had fashioned from a 1960s Police Phone Box, though twisted into the necessary egg-timer shape) and then, as we had time to spare, after a look at the Romanov Palace, Tsarskoe Selo, we came back into St Petersburg and decided to film Rasputin's residence and the people going in and out as filler material for the pay-per-view.

I say 'we'. In fact, Bertie decided. As punishment for not having helped him against Cain, I had been demoted. He was now Captain! Bertie! Although it made my hackles rise to take orders from him, the alternative was not to go at all, and I had become rather accustomed to being an internationally famous time traveller.

Leaving the SMM on some nearby wasteland, we began to video the front of 64 Gorokhovaya Ulitza, the apartment block where Rasputin had been living since 1912. Bertie suddenly grabbed my arm in excitement.

"Look!" he said, "look, that's Rasputin!"

And indeed it was. I never did find out what made him step out into the courtyard behind the narrow, badly-paved, poorly-lit street. I suppose he could have been expecting someone, his best friend Anna Vyroubova, perhaps.

Or was it his renowned clairvoyance and it was us he was expecting?

We knew it was Rasputin, not only from his appearance, but from the fact that as he gazed slowly round, even the rats and pigeons paused until his gaze had moved on. The rats seemed to suffer no ill effects, but a lot of the pigeons just fell onto their backs, twitching feebly on the ice. They reminded me of Mabel in seductive mood.

Although we were keeping well back, and our cameras were obviously too small to be seen, the tall figure suddenly stiffened and stared directly at us. A cold chill began to run up my spine, but got frozen between the second and third lumbar discs.

For Bertie, though, it was love at first sight. Don't misunderstand me. Despite gossip that in his religious frenzies Rasputin might occasionally show a man what sin was, Bertie himself was quite strict on these matters. I'd been told by a fellow pupil of his that when they were going through their de rigueur homosexual phase at school, Bertie's lasted roughly a minute – the time it took him to look at the other willies that were being proudly pulled out for mutual inspection. Then, 'Mine's much bigger', he had said, proved it, and then walked off. That was it. His phase was over.

My mistake was not to move away the moment I noticed Rasputin looking at us. And then I found I couldn't. Time seemed to stop. When it started again, Bertie was running forward to greet his hero.

And by the time my head was completely clear, he had, on behalf of both of us, accepted an invitation to tea and vodka with a man destined to die horribly within hours!

⊕

Rasputin lived on the third floor. Nothing luxurious, despite his connections. He cared nothing for money, giving away the many bribes he received. We passed through a poorly furnished antechamber into the visitors' room, chock-a-block with chairs for the many people who came to see him. At this time, there was only a bright-eyed young woman nervously fingering a cross. Rasputin introduced us to his two teenage daughters, Marya and Varvara. The former was to write a book sixty years later, claiming that her father was a misunderstood angel.

We'd only been chatting for a few minutes, about the War (I pretended we had just come back from the Front) when Rasputin suddenly broke off, rubbed his crotch, excused himself, made the sign of the cross from right to left, in the eastern Orthodox fashion, belched, and took the bright-eyed woman into the back room, righteously removing her worldly apparel as he did so, although she religiously clung on to her cross.

Bertie gazed after him in admiration, clearly besotted with him and with his direct approach to the complexities of human relationships. This, no doubt, was how Bertie had always secretly wanted to behave. With Winnie apparently he was still having a tough time, as I had deduced from a few morose comments.

Frightened as to what would happen if we didn't get out soon, I grabbed Bertie and forced him into the small antechamber, where we had a tremendous, if whispered, argument.

You know what the little idiot wanted to do?

Warn Rasputin not to go to Yusupov's Palace that night!

Now even Bertie should have had enough Regenerated brains to know that preventing Rasputin's death was out of the question. He was too pivotal a figure in history. We'd probably caused quite a few minor Temporal Paradoxes in our Trips already, but most of them had been ironed out, presumably by that excellent housekeeper Entropy. But had Rasputin continued to live, world history would almost certainly have been changed.

But did this bear weight with Bertie? He showed alarming signs of reasoning power, and said history round about this time was bloody awful anyway, with thousands of Russians dying daily in a disastrous war, and that perhaps by saving Rasputin we might get the war stopped (the monk was known to be against it), and maybe even avert the Bolshevik Revolution, and the Stalinist evil that subsequently came of it. I pointed out that if you changed Russian history you changed all history, meaning ours too, and that among other possible devastating effects, some of the top brands of deodorants for small hairy men might never come into being.

Irony was as much wasted on Bertie as a delicate haiku or a comb.

Usually pretty malleable, this time he was really sticking his heels in. He was enjoying being Captain. I suspect also that he was somewhat under Rasputin's potent influence. In the end, however, by threatening to tell his father, I managed to make him promise not to reveal anything to our host.

In return, he insisted on staying a bit longer at Rasputin's – or as he put it with a slight blush, Greg's place.

What could I do? He was technically my superior. As I may have mentioned before. Besides, from past experience, I had a feeling you couldn't change history anyway. The most he could do was get himself killed again. I considered staying with him, but Rasputin made me feel uneasy, so I muttered something about having to check the TM settings and left.

Outside, the secret police who were supposedly guarding Rasputin (but in fact spying on him) looked hard at me as secret policemen are wont to do, but didn't challenge me: perhaps they feared their saliva would freeze if they opened their mouths. I turned the corner and summoned the SMM to take me to the TM, where I spent an hour thawing out and worrying.

Bertie had promised to be back in the TM by eleven o'clock, but the hour came, and he still hadn't called the SMM. I now felt much more than nervous. The secret police might have arrested him, and be torturing him at that very moment. That wasn't why I was nervous: I am valiant and strong-minded enough to endure any amount of torture inflicted on Bertie. No, I was nervous in case he had after all, despite his promise, warned Rasputin of what lay in store for him.

By eleven-thirty I was near panic. I had no choice. I went to Rasputin's apartment again.

The *starets* himself answered the door. At first he appeared a bit agitated, but then recognised me. It seemed that Bertie had gone with his daughter Marya to visit a friend of hers in a block a bit farther along the street. He said that he would send Katya, the maid, to fetch him, and meanwhile insisted that I enter. I had to comply to avoid seeming rude, and he bade me sit down on one of the chairs opposite him. I felt uncomfortable as we waited in silence. In between constantly looking at his watch, Rasputin stared at me with those penetrating deep blue eyes. For a moment I felt my mind wandering, then pulled myself together and stared straight back. Particularly strong-minded people are naturally impervious to hypnotism.

I heard the sound of splashing water coming from the bathroom, and also, I thought, a strange moaning sound, like an animal in pain. No wonder, I thought, the water was probably one degree above freezing.

"Varvara always spends hours in the bathroom, what girls will do to make themselves pretty!" Rasputin smiled, referring to his other daughter, and once again I was forced to remind myself that, whatever the dark legend, Rasputin was in many ways just like any normal father.

A few minutes later, Katya reappeared. Rasputin spoke quietly to her, then turned to me.

"I must apologise for keeping you waiting in vain," he said, "but it appears your friend left my daughter and her friend half an hour ago. He said he had some urgent business to attend to. And that time was of the essence." (Here he smiled fleetingly.) "And now, if you will excuse me, I too have to get spruced up a little, for, just between ourselves, this is a rather special night for me."

And he gave me the most lascivious wink I have ever seen.

"*Proshchaitye*, goodbye," he called after me as I left.

I was glad to escape from the apartment. Not from fear this time. Rasputin had been nothing but courteous, and I caught him secretly smiling now and again, no doubt imagining the forthcoming tryst with the beautiful Princess Irina. No, I wanted to get away because I found myself wanting to warn him myself, but I steeled myself not to.

As I came out of the courtyard, I saw a black limousine gliding along the street. Yusupov and Lazavert come to collect their victim!

I would have to worry about Bertie later. I ran for the SMM. I had to get to the Yusupov Palace before the limousine did, to check exactly when they arrived. I would then have to hang around outside until they left again with Rasputin's body. That way I would know

77

exactly how long Baby would have to be in the cellar. The temporal phasing in and out would use a lot of energy, and the more energy used then, the less there would be to keep the main TM in the past.

I reached the Palace in less than five minutes, and it wasn't till seven minutes after midnight that the limousine arrived. I watched anxiously as three men got out. It was all right: Rasputin was one of them. I recognised his face clearly as they passed under a lamp over the Palace entrance. So Bertie had kept his promise, and not warned him about the plot.

If Yusupov had told the truth, it would now be two hours before the murder was completed. But I didn't dare leave in case the cakes and wine story had been a mere invention: I couldn't be completely sure that the body wouldn't be driven out within a few minutes.

So, reluctantly, I had to abandon the idea of scouring the deserted streets looking for Bertie. I wondered whether he might not have got drunk at Rasputin's place, and then continued drinking with Maria. Could he even be trying to seduce her? That was unlikely, since I knew he was as besotted with his new wife as I was. Perhaps he had lost the other SMM remote control, and was passing the night in a club and was planning to find his way to the TM with the dawn.

There was no way of telling, and I didn't dare leave my lookout post a few yards from the gates of the Palace. To fill in the time, I composed a few emotional sonnets to Winnie. I'd never been interested in poetry before; it must have been the ice all around me that reminded me of *Doctor Zhivago*.

At exactly two twenty-four, I heard four shots ring out, and twelve minutes later the limousine swept out of the Palace en route for the Petrovsky Bridge. I followed in the SMM, filming all the time. The ferocity of the conspirators was amazing. Even though they believed their victim was dead, they still all kicked the body for five minutes before finally hurling it into the river.

I went back to the TM, hoping that Bertie would be there, but there was still no sign of him. I had no choice. I would proceed as planned, but without him. I transferred to Baby, and dematerialised at three-fifteen, having set it to go Back to the Palace at four minutes past midnight, thus allowing three minutes to 'hop' to locate the cellar itself.

My timing was perfect. There was nobody in the cellar when I materialised there, and the corners were so dark Baby probably wouldn't have been seen even without the Temporal Phasing in and out.

At twelve-nine, Rasputin and Yusupov came in, the former revealing, after doffing his beaver greatcoat, a sexy blue satin shirt embroidered with cornflowers, with a golden sash round his waist, and even sexier blue velvet breeches. His previously matted hair was brushed back, and it was clear from the shine on his cheeks that water, and maybe even soap, had been in contact with them.

I chided myself for not having had more faith in Bertie. He had obviously revealed nothing to Rasputin. Perhaps he had been so upset by the thought of his new friend's forthcoming murder that he preferred not to have to witness it. Occasionally, he revealed residues of fine sensibilities. I could understand his reluctance. Indeed, I was grateful for it. It saved me from being stuck in a very tiny confined space with him for two hours. Despite my discreet nasal filters, I hadn't been looking forward to a prolonged onslaught of gregarious pheromones.

Everyone knows the terrible events that took place there. The cakes laced with potassium cyanide. The poisoned Madeira wine. The sounds of a make-believe party upstairs to make Rasputin believe that the Princess Irina was there waiting for other guests to leave. Rasputin at first not eating the cakes, then changing his mind. The downing of the Madeira wine. Yusupov having to play the guitar and sing gipsy songs for hours. His nerve finally cracking as Rasputin showed no signs of collapsing. Rasputin being led to the crucifix, and being shot as he gazed at it. The pronouncement of death. The shocking return to life half an hour later.

I filmed everything, amazed how close Yusupov had kept to the truth. I saw Rasputin eat the cakes, and with evident relish, just as Yusupov had stated. He did often seem confused – the poison must have been having some effect, or else it was excitement at the thought of possessing Princess Irina – and would sometimes stop mid-sentence, as if trying to remember something. I suspected that Bertie had inadvertently let out a couple of uncomprehended warnings, which were now nagging at his mind.

I was even able to film the final shooting in the courtyard by leaping out of Baby, and filming from the doorway that Rasputin escaped through. He staggered through the courtyard, and was indeed finally brought down by Purishkevich's third bullet. I filmed the fourth bullet being put in his head, and then the frenzied bludgeoning and kicking of the conspirators. I filmed the snow around his body as it rapidly turned red. I filmed the body being tied and then bundled in a blue curtain, with Felix Yusupov still hacking away at it. I filmed until the car was driven out of sight. I filmed everything.

Even though I had known exactly what to expect, and even though I told myself that what I was seeing had really happened nearly a hundred years ago (as well as two hours ago), I was still stunned, almost sickened, by the ferocity of the murderers.

But I pulled myself together. It would have been impossible to stop the assassination anyway, and I had some of the most dramatic film in history, that would make the Company a fortune. And almost certainly make me Captain again, since I alone had done all the filming.

There was no point remaining any longer in the past so I threw the Return switch, and Baby arrived back inside the TM at three-fifteen again.

I then checked to see how long I had before the TM would be Tugged back to the future. Two hours only! Our calculations had been a bit out. Two hours to find Bertie in the middle of a St Petersburg night at minus twenty-three degrees!

I flew around in the SMM for an hour or more, wondering if maybe Bertie had slipped and fallen in the street. Nothing. I then decided to find out whether there were any drinking clubs, or even brothels, open. Bertie might have gone in for warmth or comfort. The problem was, at this time of night, with snow falling as thick as Bertie's dandruff, the streets weren't exactly packed with strollers whom I could ask.

In the end I did spot a couple of scruffy-looking men loafing around beneath a bridge. I ran up to them.

"Hey, *muzhiks*," I said, "have you seen a small, dirty and amazingly smelly bearded man?"

"Don't you go calling us peasants!" growled one. "We're tramps, not peasants."

"I wouldn't say we're exactly tramps, either," his companion countered. "We do a lot of tramping, it's true, but a person who tramps isn't necessarily a tramp, any more than a person who flies is a fly, a person who watches is a watch, or a person who prunes is a prune."

"That's true. And anyway we do much more than tramp. We wander and wait as well." A pause. "Have you ever wondered why we wait so much?"

"I may have."

"What do you mean, you may have?"

"I may have. But if I did it must have been yesterday, or even before yesterday."

"Why?"

"Because if it had been today, I would have remembered."

"What, you can't even remember what you did yesterday/"

"No, can you?"

"No."

"I bet we were waiting."

"Why do you say that?"

"Well, what else do we do?"

"We tramp sometimes."

"Ah yes, of course. But that still doesn't make us peasants."

"Unless we're peasants who tramp."

"We're more likely to be city folk. We're in a city now."

"So we are. And it's bloody cold. Why in God's name did he tell us to wait here?"

"Maybe he didn't."

"He must have. We wouldn't have come here today, otherwise."

"Perhaps we came yesterday, and forgot to leave."

At this point, I gave up and moved on, reminding myself to avoid scruffy-looking tramps in future. Or in past.

I thought of returning to Gorokhovaya Ulitza, to ask Maria if Bertie had said where he was going, but decency forbade me. 'Excuse me for waking you up in the middle of the night, but I've just finished filming your father's gruesome murder so we can make a fortune in the future, and I wonder if you know where my friend got to?' It would sound bad if I ever came to write my memoirs

I found a few more people lying in doorways, and I shook them to ask them where a mentally-challenged tourist might go for entertainment, but they simply disintegrated into shards of ice.

In the end I had no choice but to return home without him.

Bertie Senior would be broken-hearted to lose his son: but he'd be even more broken-hearted if he lost the Time Machine as well. Our orders were very clear on that point.

And someone ought to be there to comfort the widow.

I don't wish to remember the first few hours of my return. Although the logic of my painful decision was unassailable, my body wasn't. Bertie's dad made what was for me an even more painful decision, and expressed his grief, not in tears, but in blows. However, he finally agreed that I had done the right thing in retrieving the Time Machine. Perhaps Bertie was not totally lost – it might be possible to send the TM back in a few days to the exact moment at which I had left the past, so that I could resume my search for him. This remote possibility cheered everybody up, and they at once forgot Bertie and turned their attention to the film. We would finally put the competition out of business!

They all stood excitedly round the screen while I put in the cassette. Feeling proud, and thinking that the loss of Bertie and the loss of my blood to his father's grief was a small thing compared with this fantastic exclusive, I stood back.

We all watched Yusupov enter the cellar.

With Bertie!

As they were putting me together in the company's medical facility (Bertie's dad had remarkably strong paternal feelings) I had time to figure out how this could have happened.

Bertie must have broken his promise to me, and told Rasputin just what lay in store for him that night. It wouldn't have been too difficult to convince his idol that he was telling the truth: by forecasting, for example, exactly what he had been planning to wear that night, or who he had been hoping to meet. So Rasputin had decided it would be a good idea to 'die' (long before *The Third Man*), since the plots against him were growing faster than the fungus in his beard. He now had a wonderful opportunity to slip away into safety.

And to do it he hypnotised Bertie into believing he was Rasputin himself. That wouldn't have been difficult, as the scarcity of ideas in Bertie's mind left vast empty spaces like the Russian steppes for planting suggestions, and in his fantasies he already half equated himself with the monk. What would have been difficult was persuading Bertie to wash himself a bit, and to put on some elegant clothing. Good God, that person I'd heard in the bathroom must have been Bertie! And the sounds of pain the direct result of his flesh being seared with soap and water! The story about Marya and her friend had been a lie.

Rasputin would then have hypnotised Yusupov (and Dr Lazavert, the driver of the limousine) into also believing Bertie was the *starets*. It was dark, and Bertie already bore a strong resemblance to him. It wasn't possible, of course, to hypnotise the other conspirators, but neither was it necessary, because they only saw Bertie when he had already been shot in the head and was covered in blood. In any case, they were too busy beating him to borscht to take a close look at his face.

And then? I was only guessing, but if Bertie had already told him when and where the body was going to be thrown in the river, all he had to do was go along some time after the conspirators had left, and fish Bertie's body out before anyone else found it and was able to see that it wasn't Rasputin.

But the body *had* been found, and even identified by Marya! Had she too been hypnotised? Or was she in on the plan? Yes, that must have been it.

Then all he had to do was disappear. Shave, maybe. Set up a charity stall for dancing bears in some lost village. Make a living by hypnotising people into stopping smoking. He'd be safe. His face is better known in our own day than it was then, when it would hardly have been recognised outside the capital.

Imagine his shock when I arrived, before Yusupov did!

With his quick Siberian wits, Rasputin had invited me in, and hypnotised me, too. Bertie would already have told him about our plans to film the murder. Looking back, I seemed to recollect that he had not merely looked at his watch, but had been swinging it too. He must have left me with the post-hypnotic suggestion that when I saw Bertie later, I also would believe I was seeing him, Rasputin.

The spell must only have ended with the mental dislocation of the TM wrenching me back to the present.

With hindsight, it was easy enough now to spot certain inconsistencies. For instance, Yusupov later wrote that Rasputin had had an unusually gentle and submissive expression, and hadn't seemed to sense any danger, 'as though fate had clouded his mind', and that after the murder Rasputin had stared at him with a look of 'diabolical hatred' in those 'green eyes of a viper'. Green? Rasputin's eyes were famously a deep blue. Also, Marya later claimed – and his friend and secretary Simanovich bore this out - that Rasputin never ate cakes, whereas I witnessed 'him' gobbling them down just as Bertie enjoyed doing.

And there was only one person in the world who would be so daft as to sit listening to gipsy songs for two hours when he was supposed to be having a secret tryst with a beautiful princess!

Unfortunately, my colleagues took it badly, too, refusing to understand that it wasn't my fault. Rasputin had hypnotised Bertie into having a wash and dressing up, for God's sake! No one could have resisted such incredible power!

It didn't help when they found my sonnets to Winnie in my Travelling Suit.

"So you stood by twice while poor Bertie was being tortured!" they exclaimed, looking at me with loathing. "First, you sit snugly in the Mobility Module writing astonishingly bad love poems to the man's wife, for Christ's sake, while he's being tortured, and then, as if he hasn't suffered enough, you go Back and callously film every detail of his murder, without lifting a finger to help him!"

I was deeply hurt.

"Look," I said, "I'd never written poetry before. You can't expect Petrarch or Emily Dickinson first time round!"

"Yes, but to rhyme 'Mona Lisa' with 'Phone 'n tease 'er', 'Gonna please 'er', 'Groan 'n squeeze 'er'…"

Uncultured pigs! "We can still show the film," I said. "After all, Bertie's not dressed as Bertie, and we can fudge the close-ups a bit. It will still bring in a mint."

They declared I was an unfeeling monster, and agreed to work on bringing Bertie's dad round to the idea.

Strangely enough, Winnie was the most understanding of all. I'd been terrified of meeting her after this disaster. But she was unselfish enough to see beyond her own grief.

"Oh, how you must be suffering, too," she declared, "to have lost your dear friend in such a terrible way! And I widowed at such a young and tender age, the flower of my beauty still in full and almost embarrassingly sensuous bloom! You have lost Mabel, and I Bertie. Now more than ever we must share each other's sorrow." She held my hand earnestly, and, smiling bravely through her tears, said: "Tell me that poem again; it somehow makes me feel better."

What a woman! What courage! For, unlike his previous death in the Land of Nod, this time there could be no reprieve for Bertie. To Regenerate him, we had to have the body, and that body had been burnt a hundred years ago. The Silver Cord had been snapped. As I had stepped out of the TM, Bertie's Astral Projection, kept safe between powerful magnets, had given a tremendous banshee wail, turned a pale sickly colour, and begun to slide slimily down the walls of the tank.

⊕

Enter the Time Police. They brought Bertie's body back and put things right again.

Not without giving us all a good bollocking, though.

"We can't shut you amateurs down," roared one of them, "because you're indispensable to the early history of Time Travel. But be more bloody careful, or we'll find a way past that Paradox – don't think we can't! Cock up again, and we'll take you Back and dump you in the middle of a bunch of rutting dinosaurs!"

The Time Police. TPs. Teepees.

Not entirely unexpected.

Even a Claude Van Damme could grasp that if our Time Machine turned out to be the first of many, the temporal equivalent of the Wright Brothers' aeroplane, then sooner or later some trans-temporal Force would be necessary to prevent space-time-continuum crime or interference. Indeed, I half suspected that the two irritating men we kept coming across on our Trips might be plain-clothes Teepees, though having seen the real thing I doubted it.

Because these Teepees certainly weren't people to mess around with. Yes, they brought Bertie's body back to us, but replaced him with the real Rasputin who was later fished out of the Neva, full of bullet holes and in even worse shape than Bertie. They certainly had a Licence to Kill and Mutilate. They probably caught the poor bastard as he was trying to fish out Bertie's body himself.

It appeared that Rasputin's mistake was to have chosen Bertie. After he'd been warned of the fate awaiting him, if he'd shown a speck of gratitude, let Bertie go, and chosen any other dirty unkempt individual to hypnotise, he might have got away with it, since the probability of the body floating to the surface of the frozen Neva was very remote. The Teepees might not have been particularly interested. But Bertie was, with me, the first Time Traveller ever.

And, for the time being at least, it seemed they were looking after their own.

When Bertie came to life again – it took nine weeks this time because of all the damage to the body – he was a bit upset with me himself. But when he saw the film, saw himself acting as if he were indeed Rasputin, he accepted that I too had been hypnotised.

In return, I forgave him for having broken his promise to me.

I'm not the sort of person to hold a grudge.

7: THE TIME POLICE WHO WEREN'T

All through the latter part of my narrative Shade had been getting more and more agitated, her fingers forming a kaleidoscope of distorted shapes, but she had just managed to refrain from interrupting me. Now she jumped to her feet, quivering with fury.

"Bloody Teepees! Why couldn't they ever let sleeping dogs lie?"

Shimmer pulled her down again, trying to soothe her.

"It doesn't matter," she said, "we knew this already. It doesn't change anything."

Shade subsided, while I was uncomfortably aware I'd been labouring under a false assumption.

But if my visitors weren't Time Police, what were they?

And since the sleeping dog in question was Bertie, why should they be angry that he wasn't left lying – weren't they supposed to venerate him as a hero?

Shimmer didn't intend to give me time to think. She asked:

"So your story shows once again that Bertie is – was – superhuman, just as before it was believed that Rasputin was superhuman."

I laughed incredulously. "Bertie, 'superhuman'?"

"The poison, the bullets, the beating, and still he survived some time in the frozen river, since the autopsy showed he had finally drowned by drowning."

"There wasn't an official autopsy, that's merely what was said by those who found him. The broken-hearted Alexandra wouldn't allow it. And don't forget that the body finally fished out of the river really was Rasputin's, not Bertie's. The Teepees were probably in such a hurry that they didn't wait for him to die before tossing him in the river. Bertie himself was certainly quite dead."

If nothing else, I thought, the proximity of so much clean water would have finished him off.

"But it was Bertie who survived the poison."

"Oh, that's easily explained. Junk food."

They looked at me, uncomprehending.

"Junk food," I repeated. "Lazavert swore he'd put enough potassium cyanide in the cakes to kill a dozen men. Maybe he had.

But a dozen men of Rasputin's time! A hundred years ago. Men whose stomachs hadn't become inured through eating burgers, mercury-flavoured fish and strontium-enhanced chips, crisps, synthetic whipped cream, cola… After what Bertie's stomach had endured, Lazavert's cyanide was nothing."

"The bullets?" she insisted.

"I told you, we were wearing Travelling Suits. We knew Petrograd in the middle of winter was going to be cold. Bertie kept on his underwear, made of ultra-modern super-tenacity fibres and reinforced Kevlar, underneath the fashionable clothes Rasputin gave him. Such material is stronger than chain mail. Remember, Yusupov shot him in the back (as my film showed, though the little coward later claimed it was in the chest), so the bullet wouldn't have penetrated much, but the force knocked Bertie down. Of the shots outside, two missed, one was again in the back, and only one in the skull. And that's the one that did him in."

"The skull! You say so yourself. Yet he still survived the trip to the Neva, and being thrown in the icy water."

"It was Rasputin's body that showed signs of drowning, not Bertie's," I repeated, annoyed. I really was getting fed up with their determination to regard Bertie as some sort of superhero. I'd shared every single one of his Travels, and yet everyone seemed interested only in him, as if I hardly counted.

"He must have – have had – some weakness," she went on, as if I hadn't spoken, "some chink in his armour."

Chink? Big enough for Jabba the Hutt to squelch through even after eating!

"Some Achilles' toe-nail," added Shade, her right hand twisting convulsively, as if it were tightening a noose round someone's neck.

Some chance! I doubted if his mother had ever dipped him in *any* water, let alone the Styx. Mind you, I could just about imagine him bathing in dragon's blood, like Siegfried, but no one mentioned linden leaves.

"Some fatal flaw, like Coriolanus, or Boromir, or Mr Toad," Shimmer added.

Not for the first time, I reflected that things had got a bit confused in the future. Still, in a way it gave me confidence – people who believed Mr Toad was a historical character must have weaknesses of their own.

But why would they be interested in weaknesses in a dead 'superhero'?

Since I didn't answer, Shimmer said: "Well, anyway, you've admitted yourself his worth had by now been recognised and that he had been made Captain. Did you have any inkling then of how glorious his future was to be?"

"No."

Shimmer blinked then changed the subject.

"You mentioned two men again. Were they the same pair as before?"

"No. Well, maybe yes. Their clothes and speech were different, but maybe their faces were similar. The reason they reminded me of the others was that they kept on about waiting for someone."

Shade and Shimmer exchanged a glance, while Shalom simply sat unmoving. But did I detect just a flicker of interest?

Shimmer was about to say something, changed her mind and said instead:

"So would you say that the second time machine – the one you called Baby – was the breakthrough?"

I looked at her, puzzled.

Shade hissed and began to rise to her feet again, but Shimmer made a warning sign with her hand, and she subsided, like a discouraged Yorkshire pudding.

"I mean," Shimmer went on, as if the little pantomime hadn't happened, "you solved that particular problem by going forward in real time in order to then Time Travel Back."

"Well, yes," I said, still not seeing what she was getting at, "there was really no other way to do it."

"And so you began to consider how polarities could be permanently reversed. Having already realised, as only a true genius could, that a time machine inhabits a quantum world, and 'rides' on the echo of particles in the past, was it the Petersburg experience that inspired you to begin your calculations to enter a yet more improbable universe, and 'follow' a 'road' that had never existed?"

I had no idea what she was on about, so I asked: "Would you like a cup of tea?"

For a second, Shimmer's eyes had such a hard look, I imagined even uncut diamonds would tremble in their presence. But once again she forced a smile.

"No thank you," she said. "I understand your reticence to talk about what, in your time, could be dangerous information, but which, of course, in our time is common knowledge. But that doesn't detract from the brilliance of the original conception."

I nodded, as if already aware of that fact.

"That's always been the problem with scientific breakthroughs," she went on. "After a time, they are just taken for granted, and people forget the brilliance, or sometimes the years, even centuries, of hard work that led up to them. How often do we think of the miracle of electricity when we switch on a light? Or recall the years of research that led to cloning, which is now so commonplace? Or the oneirotab which allows us to pre-programme our dreams?"

"Cloning is commonplace in your time?" I asked, mainly to distract her from the increasingly determined questioning about my Time Machine.

"How else do you think…?"

This time it was Shade who hissed and held up a warning finger.

"… do you think we could provide enough livestock to feed twenty-one planets?" finished Shimmer. But I knew that hadn't been her original sentence. Still, maybe it wasn't such a big mystery. I thought it more than likely that Shalom at least – and maybe even the other two – was a genetically-enhanced clone. Or an android. What else could explain her impossible speed and reflexes?

I was keen to learn more (and allow time for Captain Anderson to arrive) but Shimmer was obviously finding it harder and harder to play the nice gal. But I'll give her this: she was still trying.

"Tell us about your next adventure. Something about the Mormons, wasn't it? That's one of the episodes about which we have so much conflicting information."

"Very well," I said, "but I need to go to the bathroom."

"But you went half an hour ago!"

"Erm, I've drunk an awful lot of coffee today."

"It can wait till after. Read!"

It was clearly not open to negotiation. I squeezed my legs together and picked up my notebook.

And at the back of my mind, that question still pricking – just what had Maria meant when she said she might not be coming back tonight?

8: MR SMITH TAKES HIS TABLETS

Convenient to the village of Manchester, Ontario County, New York, stands a hill of considerable size… On the west side of this hill, not far from the top, under a stone of considerable size, lay the plates, deposited in a stone box… I looked in, and there indeed did I behold the plates, the Urim and Thummim, and the breastplate, as stated by the messenger… I made an attempt to take them out, but was forbidden by the messenger, and was again informed that the time for bringing them forth had not yet arrived, neither would it, until four years from that time…

At length the time arrived. On the twenty-second day of September, one thousand eight hundred and twenty-seven, the same heavenly messenger delivered them up to me…

No sooner was it known that I had them, than the most strenuous exertions were used to get them from me. Every stratagem that could be invented was resorted to for that purpose.

(Joseph Smith, Jr, *The Pearl of Great Price*)

Bertie was still looking a bit waterlogged when his father informed us that we were to go Back to find out if the Founder of the Church of Jesus Christ of Latter-day Saints had been telling the truth.

I was both annoyed (would I never get to swim naked in the Nile with Cleopatra?) and puzzled by this. I knew the Mormons, like many another sect, had taken heart from the disgrace of the Evolutionists, and that a delegation from Salt Lake City had offered a very significant amount of money to finance a Trip. But how did this fit in with Bertie Senior's 'Blood and Guts' theory?

It didn't.

Bertie's dad had, it seemed, been considering a divorce, or at least a separation, before his son was assassinated, but had then called it off: it would be unseemly to leave the mother while the son was in the Regeneration Chamber. Besides, he reminded himself, she had sterling qualities: her cooking was superb, she never forgot to warm his slippers, she never objected to his snoring, and she never ever answered back. The same passive attitude, however, she also carried to bed. Bertie once told me that as an adolescent he had gone to his parents to ask about the birds and the bees. His mother had informed him with some surprise that birds flew and bees buzzed, and his father, with a dismal sigh, referred him to Rachel Carson's *Silent Spring*, and also muttered something about the dodo.

Bertie Senior thus found certain attractions in the Mormons, quite apart from their offer of finance, which made him consider actually joining them. Partly for spiritual guidance (he hadn't failed to note that sinners fared much better in their version of the Afterlife than in the traditional Christian one), but, more importantly, for their practice of polygamy (recently legalised again after a huge financial contribution to the new American President's election campaign following the assassination of the previous one by the Society of Orators). He could easily afford to take on more wives, he would still be able to enjoy his first wife's excellent food and slipper-warming without having to spend all his time with her, and at night he might expect to find something more positive to do than snore.

"What you told me about Cain's intended wife being somewhat young by our modern-day standards has made me reconsider the Mormons' attitude to the family unit," he declared. We were alone in his office. "The traditional churches' principles on certain matters are obviously later accretions to the original Divine Plan." He deliberately looked me in the eye from such an angle that I couldn't fail to see the opened window and the top of some clouds reflected in his gaze.

Convinced by my shiver of fear that I sympathised with his new liberal outlook, he added:

"Now of course, it may turn out that Joseph Smith really was a charlatan. But if so, I don't want it made too public, OK? Positive discrimination in his favour. Don't film too many things that might reflect badly on this great Church. Oh, and better not let Bertie know we had this little chat."

He nodded almost imperceptibly at that open window two hundred and fifty floors up.

"Can I be Captain again?" I asked.

"If this mission is successful, that's a strong possibility," he answered.

It seemed pretty clear to me that Bertie's mum was already doomed to a rota system for his bed, as he righteously looked forward to having his own collection of underage Stepford Wives.

⊕

I did my homework as usual, and realised at once we had a problem. Joseph Smith was clearly one of the most blatant frauds the world has ever known. An uneducated farm lad, he starts having visions at the age of fifteen, then in 1823 the angel Moroni pops down and shows him where some Golden Plates or Tablets are hidden, but, being a bit of a tease, doesn't let him get his grubby hands on them till four years later. He finally humps these Plates home, and proceeds to translate them by hiding his head in a hat! Yes indeed. Read his autobiography. Sharing hat space is a so-called 'seer stone', or 'peep stone', which he'd earlier used to try to locate buried Spanish treasure; and also what he later claims are the biblical Urim and Thummim, some kind of dice used to draw lots. In another room, or behind a curtain, various scribes write down what he dictates (the words appearing on the seer stone in the darkness inside the hat). His first scribe is his wife, Emma, who later testifies: "I frequently wrote day after day, he sitting with his face buried in his hat, with the stone in it, and dictating hour after hour…"

What he dictates, of course, is *The Book of Mormon*, translated from the 'Reformed Egyptian' text on the plates. This is the record of two tribes of Israel who in 600 BC got so pissed off with being pissed on by their neighbours that they grabbed a handful of travel brochures and took off for America. There they created a magnificent thousand-year civilisation (of which not a trace has ever been found), got a bit bored, played war games, and wiped each other out to the last man, whose name was Moroni (now resurrected as an angel).

No one else is ever allowed to see these Golden Plates in two whole years, not even his wife. When his father-in-law Isaac Hale demands to see them, he is refused on the grounds that it would mean instant death for anyone but Joseph himself to set eyes on them. Then, in 1829, the 'translation' complete, Moroni gets all possessive as angels are wont to do and demands them back, which really is an awful shame because now no one will ever be able to see them. A year later, *The Book of Mormon* is published.

And people believe it! A thousand members in the first year! By 1844, when Joe is killed (his good friends God, Jesus, Moroni, and a whole bunch of apostles and Old Testament heroes not lifting a heavenly finger to save him), the Mormons are already a force to be reckoned with. (They are reinforced in their faith by other goodies from Joe's hand, such as his translation of the *Lost Book of Abraham*, which informs us that 'our' God came from the planet Kolob where there are lots of other gods, and where all good Mormons will go when they die. They will be very tiny Saints, since Kolob, we are told, is one thousand times bigger than Earth, which would imply a gravitational force so strong that no creature there could be more than beetle-height.) Well, let me tell you, I admired this chap immensely. He came up with the most preposterous story imaginable, and then convinced thousands of people it was true (and those thousands are now many millions: though half of those, it is only fair to say, are Americans, who are afflicted with a potent credulity gene). No pussy-footing for Joe, no mere interpreting of the scriptures: he wrote his own!

While the competition was raging and frothing at the mouth promising everyone hellfire, Joe held out the prospect of eternal bliss, even for sinners. Much more enticing. And how could I not admire a chap who managed to notch up, according to one estimate, thirty-seven wives ('celestial marriages' or not), a third of them already the wives of other men? With the husbands sometimes having to act as witnesses to their wives' new marriages! Even so, he still had time left to help his first wife produce nine kids! And he didn't go gentle into that not-so-good night either, but with pistols a-blazing when the mob came to lynch him in that gaol in Carthage, Illinois!

Yep, one hell of a guy.

But I had to remember Bertie's dad's open window.

As usual, we had the problem of just when to arrive. My Time Machine still suffered from its initial limitations: a three-day stay was the maximum, less if we made any great use of the Spatial Mobility Module. The technical branch was forever putting pressure on me to modify the design.

"You're the only one who really understands it," they said, "we simply followed your specifications, without grasping the underlying principle at all. We confess we still don't really understand why the egg-timer shape is so fundamental. Surely, with your genius, you could help us make alterations to tone up the thing, at least enough to allow us to keep it a longer time in the past?"

At other times, they would badger me to tell them how I came up with the idea in the first place, would ask to see my earlier designs, my experiments, my early failures.

I refused, naturally. "You will understand – and no offence meant," I said, "that if I reveal the train of my amazingly brilliant abstract reasoning, and one of you should accidentally let slip the theoretical underpinnings of my approach, then within a very short time rival companies could well be producing Time Machines as well. But as it is, even if they got hold of this one, they'd have no way to replicate it. Your jobs may well depend on my discretion."

They would argue a bit and then let it be, but once I overheard one of them mutter as he moved away: "If I hadn't seen it with my own eyes, I'd say this guy wasn't capable of designing a sundial, let alone a time machine!"

Insolent swine! He wouldn't even have had a job if it weren't for me.

Anyway, the problem still remained.

Bertie was all for arriving in 1844 so that we could film the storming of the jail in Carthage and the shooting of Joseph and his brother Hyrum. I myself would have liked to film Emma's reaction when Joe informed her that he was planning on taking more wives! Bertie's dad agreed that both these would make gripping TV and might even knock *Big Baby* temporarily off the top slot, but they were peripheral to the main question. In the end, it was obvious that everything pivoted on the reality or not of the Golden Tablets.

So he settled on 22 September, 1827, the date given by Joe for receiving the Plates. If Joe had told the truth – but naturally I believed he hadn't – Bertie Senior hoped we might be able to film some of the astonishing translation process as well.

Winnie hadn't accompanied us to Russia, she said, because of the extreme cold and the potential danger. I thought she might want to join us this time, and indeed she seemed quite interested until, telling her the history of Joseph Smith, I mentioned the name of Moroni. Perhaps the meeting with one semi-mythical being, Cain, had been enough for her, because for a moment or two I thought I saw fear in her eyes.

I didn't mind. Bertie would probably find some way to get himself killed again, and I would comfort her as before.

The regenerated Bertie, happily, smelt a couple of skunks less than his cellular predecessor, and was clean-shaven (to avoid further confusion with hirsute holy men) but apart from that, things went wrong almost from the very beginning.

It was a lovely autumn late afternoon and we left the TM in what seemed to be an old volcanic crater, and took the SMM to Cumorah Hill near Palmyra, western New York State. We landed right on top, and then settled ourselves to wait behind some rocks, using the zoom lenses on our miniature digital cameras as telescopes. Within a short time, a tall, muscular, very handsome young man appeared, glancing round furtively all the time. We were much too far away for him to see us. He was carrying a spade and a sack. He went through some trees into a clearing, where from our vantage point we could see him clearly. He began to dig, and after a very short time, unearthed a stone box, about the size of a large TV set. The box existed! But I immediately told myself that he must have planted it earlier, on the off-chance that he might be followed, in order to give his story more credibility. He had clearly thought his scam through well – I was even more impressed.

And then a shining angel appeared, in a pillar of light, just as Smith claimed he had in the First Vision!

So perhaps he had been telling the truth after all. I don't think I've ever been so disappointed in anyone in all my life. I had believed Smith to be the most outrageous fraudster that history had ever produced – and it turned out he was nothing more than a prophet who communed directly with angels!

What a let-down.

The angel, his face invisible behind the glow, began doing his spiel, the usual stuff about how God was seriously browned off with things on Earth and would Joseph kindly put things right please, and translate these rather flashy Golden Plates pronto. Then he suddenly tensed, swung round, and looked directly at us.

"He's spotted us!" Bertie muttered.

Some people might think that I have treated Bertie badly in these memoirs, trying to belittle his role in our adventures, despite having publicly praised him on so many occasions. I think this is most unfair. Whenever I spot one of his good points, I immediately mention it, like bird spotters mention a rare sighting of the Black-breasted Puffleg.

 So I am glad to report that at this point Bertie had an Idea.

Having an Idea, of course, created a bit of havoc inside his cerebrum, like the dropping of an effervescent tablet in water or the first huge drop of rain on a pile of dust. It took a few splutters before he was able to formulate his Idea in words that I could understand. But when he did finally manage this feat, the Idea came forth with admirable succinctness.

"Let's bugger off!"

I knew he was right. The brilliant glow that hid the angel's features was angled straight at us, and I sensed he could see the SMM as well, despite the rocks that hid it. Damned angel eyes!

I pushed the emergency 'Make-a-run-for-it!' button (we'd labelled all the controls for Bertie) and we zoomed away as bursts of bright light punctured the air where we had been.

Angels you do not want to mess with, believe me.

We put a good twenty miles behind us, and landed in some barren wasteland. I sat there pondering what to do while Bertie tried to build a sand castle out of the dust that swirled at our feet.

We might have had a close encounter with an angry angel, but at least we had got some astonishing film. Or so I thought. On checking the playback it turned out to be fuzzy and unclear. There was an aura around the angel that caused ripples, distortions in the air, so that not even the figure of Joseph Smith was distinct. A close encounter yes, but of the blurred kind. Any amateur film enthusiast could have produced a similar effect with a couple of plastic bags and a table lamp. And Bertie's film was just the same.

So all we had was ten minutes of unconvincing film to back up our amazing testimony.

We would have to return to Palmyra, and try again. Looking on the optimistic side, the Universe was a biggish place, and any hard-working messenger of God worth his wings surely wouldn't hang around after doing an errand, but fly off and do a few chores elsewhere, in some neighbouring galaxy, for instance.

We waited a couple of hours and then flew to the Smith family house on the outskirts of Palmyra. I anticipated that Joe, having been forced to wait four years, would want to start translating as soon as he got home, and I hoped to be able to film his unique system of doing this, and also get some close-ups of the Tablets, the text, and the peculiar translating tools.

We landed again and hid the SMM in some woods near the town. Darkness was already drawing in. I remembered reading that the family house was a couple of miles out of town. But in what direction?

I had already decided not to waste time asking directions if we came across two odd-looking men hanging around. So I was pleased when I spotted a solitary man standing under a cherry oak. I approached him.

"Excuse me, do you know where the Smith family lives?" I asked politely.

Just then another man stepped from behind the tree, doing up his trouser buttons, and hitching the braces over his shoulders.

"Now that's not an easy question," drawled the fly button man, "seein' as how half the people hereabouts are called Smith."

"But they ain't all families," interposed the other. "Quite a few orphans an' widders. So that's less than half the folks."

I didn't want all this nonsense again, so I began to move away.

"Was it John Smith you were wanting," one of them called after me, "or Joseph?"

I turned back. What luck!

"Joseph," I said, "Joseph Smith."

"A pity."

"Sorry?"

"We don't exactly know any Joseph Smith."

"Or a John," added his companion, shaking his head sadly.

"So why did you ask if I wanted John or Joseph?"

" 'Cause half the Smiths we've ever come across are called John or Joseph. It was a fair gamble. Ah, if only life had such even odds!" He shook his head despondently.

"Wait a minute!" said the other. "We aren't waiting for Smith, by any chance?"

"No, his name definitely wasn't Smith."

"So what was it then?"

"Don't tell me you don't remember!"

I was well and truly fed up with these two; whether they were the same as the previous pairs or not. It was time to deal with them.

"I saw a man waiting for you," I announced.

"What!" For the first time they seemed to come truly alive.

"A man. Tall. Air of authority. Waiting for you. He said he couldn't wait much longer."

They threw their arms round each other, and did a little jig.

"At last, at last! I told you we'd been waiting in the wrong place! Or the wrong time!" one of them said.

"Oh no, you didn't. You're the one who wanted to come here."

"That was yesterday."

"Oh no, it wasn't. Yesterday, we were… where were we?"

"It doesn't matter. Tell us, good sir, where did you see this man? Was he really waiting for us?"

"Oh yes, he distinctly said he was waiting for you. You two especially."

"Where, where?"

I furrowed my brow, then wrinkled it, then scratched it, then smoothed it back to how it was at first.

"Oh dear, would you believe it, I can't remember!" I said. "And come to think of it, I believe it was yesterday I saw him. Or was it the day before? Oh well, in any case, he'll be gone by now."

And I sauntered off, whistling, as they both burst into tears.

Well, they'd asked for it!

We soon came across another man, who told us the Smiths were leasing a house on a farm belonging to a Quaker, and gave us directions to get there.

We walked. We squelched through marshland, crossed streams, stumbled through fields, got chased by a bull and even some cows who must have sensed that we were effete men of the future, and finally, worn out, reached the whitewashed wooden frame house. It stood alone in acres of farmland, though it didn't have the porch and gable it now has. There were trees all around it, and this, together with the semi-darkness, meant it was easy to approach one of the four windows facing the front.

Through the first one we saw seven or eight people, probably Joe's parents and some of his brothers and sisters. They were finishing supper, it seemed. We filmed them for a few minutes, then tried another window.

And there he was, sitting on a hard wooden chair, light auburn hair puffed up in a style that reminded me a bit of Elvis Presley when he was young. And leaning over him, a woman with abundant black hair and hazel eyes, not particularly pretty, but tall and slim: Emma Hale, the woman he'd eloped with and married in January of this same year.

And on a table in front of him was the stone box that he'd unearthed on the hillside! He was about to open it. At last we would see the famous Golden Tablets!

But not quite yet. His hand on the box, he paused, and then remarked, with a surprisingly deep and vibrant voice: "The appointed task will be long and hard. I will need more inspiration, my darling!"

So she inspired him.

Throughout these chronicles I have at all times endeavoured to be circumspect and delicate. I do not wish to leave behind me a work that will cause unnecessary distress or unease. It is meant to celebrate the exploits of one who is, alas, no longer with us, not to pander to base tastes.

Therefore, I do not describe exactly how Emma Hale inspired Joseph Smith, preferring to throw a discreet veil over this touching scene between two young healthy newlyweds. Let those who seek lurid descriptions satisfy their sordid desires elsewhere!

Afterwards, as he was gasping and cramming his still throbbing cock away, she wiped the frothy cum off her face and tits with a corner of the tablecloth, removed a pubic hair caught in the corner of her mouth, and said: "My darling husband, that is the third time I've inspired you today. Please let me see the Golden Plates."

"My sweetheart" Joe replied, rubbing perspiration from his thick blond eyebrows with the back of a prophetic hand, "if only you could! If you only knew how I long to share the glory of God – you've got a bit on your nose, good woman, no, no, not that side, yes, that's it, just there – but the angel warned me that it would mean instant death for anyone but me to see them. I dare not disobey.

Remember Lot and his wife; I would find a salty vagina unappealing."

She pouted, but nodded acquiescence.

"So now, my love, please go and sit in the corner, at that writing table, as we agreed, and we will begin the great work."

She did as he requested, and then drew across the old blanket that was hanging on a rope strung across the room, so that she was hidden behind it.

"No peeping!" said Joe, and opened the box!

There could be no doubt about it. Even in the poor candlelight, those Plates glimmered and glittered and glistened even more than Joe's deep blue eyes had during the process of inspiration. Strange hieroglyphs that really did look Egyptian-ish caught the dim light and hurled it back brighter.

Joe reached for his hat. And a most unusual chocolate-coloured egg-shaped stone, which was presumably the famous 'seer stone'. I say 'unusual' because there seemed to be a tiny screen inset into it. Well, that was logical. I'd always wondered how he could have claimed to read from a stone. Now it made a bit more sense. It also explained why Joe needed his hat to keep extraneous light out.

Joe proceeded to translate just as he later described in his autobiography.

"Wherefore, it is a... a cheapskate account... no, a... an *abridgement*, yes, that's it, of the record of the Nephi folk, no, change that, folk of Nephi, no, people, *peoples* of Nephi, and also of the Laman lot, no no, better, *Lamanites*, sounds more biblical, written to the Lamanites, who are a leftover, I mean, remnant, of the Shack – that sounds odd, building?, no, ah – *House* of Israel; and also to Jew and godless bastard – can that be right, try '*Gentile*' – written by way of commandment, and also by the spirit of prophecy and revelation..."

We filmed frantically, using two cameras in case anything should go wrong.

We'd been filming for a quarter of an hour or so, and were starting to yawn, when I sensed movement behind me. I swung round, and dimly made out shapes among the trees. Maybe half a dozen or more people converging on the Smith house in the darkness.

Of course, now I remembered. Joe had boasted to so many people of his visions and of his having been promised the Golden

Plates four years before, that gangs from the nearby towns had been waiting for him from the very first day, intending to steal the gold. It was a particularly credulous period, and Joe did after all have local fame as a treasure hunter.

"You go in through that window," one of the men whispered to Bertie, in the dark mistaking us for members of the group.

"OK," said Bertie, who's an obliging sort of chap, and grasped the windowsill.

But not all the family were eating, translating, transcribing, or reproducing. Someone yelled from an upstairs window. At once, Joe threw aside the hat, slammed the stone box shut, reached for a rifle and snuffed out the candles. All in a matter of seconds. The rest of the house was plunged into darkness. I heard rather than saw rifle muzzles being poked through windows.

Then the firing started.

That's America for you!

I had already hurled myself to the ground, but Bertie had one leg over the windowsill, and his body became the unwilling mediator in the quarrel between the bullets of the attackers and those of the defenders.

He crashed back on to me, splashing me with blood.

I don't mind admitting it, I was tempted to make a run for it. But if I returned to the present again without at least his body to be Regenerated, I knew just how many floors I'd be flashing past.

But who would comfort Winnie if we both died?

I was still hesitating when above us a whirlwind and a whirlpool came to blows, and we got caught in the middle of the struggle. I've never been sucked up into a tornado. But I'm sure the experience would have been like that.

For a few minutes I felt like a lost sock in a tumble dryer. But when the dryer stopped, I almost wished it hadn't. I found myself on what seemed at first to be the edge of a cloud, but turned out to be a kind of aerial catamaran, the two hulls each having an elongated egg-timer shape. Egg-timer? Around both hulls was a three-foot-wide flange, and I was sprawled on one of these.

As was Bertie!

So the shots hadn't killed him! But he was covered in blood and groaning.

"What the hell was that?" he gasped, wincing with pain.

"*That* was me," answered a voice. "So what do you two think you're up to?"

It was the angel Moroni, standing on the flat bridge deck, only now that we could see him up close, he didn't look much like an angel at all. Straggly moustache and beard, for a start, suffocating a tiny mouth, and with frighteningly large oval eyes. And hardly any taller than Bertie.

He now peered closely at my companion, and then gasped:

"Bloody hell! Can it be… it's Bertie, isn't it? Well, well, well! And you," (turning to me) "must be N, the treacherous Narrator. Well, well, well!"

Before I could protest at the gratuitous epithet 'treacherous' being applied to me, he went on: "So what's the game, eh?"

"It's all Bertie's dad's idea, and it may be OK to visit the sins of the fathers on the sons, but not on their sons' unwilling travelling companions, so can I at least go now, please?" I blubbered.

When I got back some members of the support team criticised my reaction. I am one hundred per cent sure those people have never been balanced on the edge of a catamaran miles up in the sky and faced by an irate angel who could nudge you into eternity with a flick of his wing tip.

"You were taking pictures of me earlier on," Moroni went on, "that's why I've been looking for you. I don't want any pictures!"

I could understand that. His appearance, as I said, was decidedly odd, not at all what you'd expect of an angel. "His whole person was glorious beyond description," Joe had written. Just shows what a dab of effulgence can do!

Apparently, though, it wasn't a question of vanity.

"At the moment," he continued, "they only *suspect* what I've been up to, but with *proof*…"

They?

"But we need those pictures to take back to Dad," said Bertie, whom mere mortal wounds could not deflect from his sense of duty.

"Look," said Moroni, as reasonable as cheese on toast, "it boils down to a choice between your needs and mine, which in principle, I admit, have equal merit: so you can keep your film, and be dropped half a mile, or not keep it, and not be dropped half a mile. I can't be fairer than that. Well, lads, what do you say?"

Lying sod! It was at least two miles to the land beneath! Bertie began to scratch his head prior to pondering this extremely difficult dilemma while I promptly fished in my pocket and handed over the cassette I'd used earlier on Cumorah Hill. Moroni slipped it inside his robes.

"Thank you. A souvenir. Besides the danger to me," he went on chattily, "it would ruin the sport."

"What sport?" I asked.

"You haven't cottoned on yet? You must have seen that the Golden Plates are real. Where, or should I say *when*, I come from, we have plenty of gold and not much use for it any more. I recorded *The Book of Mormon* on those Plates myself. Little story I cooked up in my spare time."

Mark Twain had once described that 'little story' as 'chloroform in print'. I didn't mention this. Certain things are best kept to yourself when you're two miles up on a double-barrelled egg-timer.

"My aim is to start a new religion, not only with no proof (nothing new in that) but with such a ridiculous cover story that it will prove my whole point and win a little bet I have on. You'll notice I've deliberately chosen, as my prophet, a not-very-bright chap already found guilty, last year, of 'disorderly conduct' and being an 'Impostor'. A fellow who claimed to be able to find buried treasure, and after they'd been digging a few days in Susquehanna Valley, and nothing was found, said that the treasure had sunk lower due to an enchantment! In other words, a known charlatan, fraud, and confidence trickster.

"Then, having chosen a thoroughly disreputable 'prophet', I'm doing everything possible to make his story completely unbelievable. All the common-or-garden prophets have visions, too easy, so I'm throwing in the Golden Plates as a bonus, but will make sure that no one except Smith ever actually sees them. When the book's transcribed, I'll take the Plates back so that Smith can never show them to anybody, and people will have to take his word alone – the word of a known liar – that they ever existed! I've also written the thing in a language I made up myself."

"'Reformed Egyptian'?" I asked.

"I haven't given it a name yet, but, yes, I suppose that will do nicely. Sounds silly enough! Thank you! As you've just seen, to give an even greater element of farce, I told Smith to put a couple of stones inside a hat, cover his face with it, and then dictate to someone behind a curtain or in another room entirely the words that appear in the viewer. Can't get much more ridiculous than that!"

I noticed as he was speaking some of the same strange hieroglyphics on the flange of the hull.

"As for *The Book of Mormon*, to make the story as suspect as possible, I've stuck in a bagful of anachronisms: a steel sword for Laban, for example, and a nautical compass for Nephi, many centuries before either would be invented; I've used the word 'Jesus Christ' 600 years before he was born; and I've spoken of a mighty Jewish civilisation in both the Americas lasting for a thousand years, and haven't provided a single artefact.

"To make it even more of a challenge, I'm planning to get most of Smith's early disciples to recant later, and openly accuse him of fraud. And, of course, I'll dress up and claim to be God and Jesus, and Peter, James, John, Moses, Elijah… you name them, I'll be them! And using this same false beard every single time!

"And in spite of all this, I bet you we'll still get a thousand converts in one year."

"And what about polygamy?" I asked. That was really why we were here.

" 'Polygamy'? What are you talking about?"

"You know, your idea of 'sealing', of 'celestial plural marriage', whereby Mormon men can have as many wives as they like."

Moroni stared at me, those enormous eyes became even wider, then the slit of a mouth, which had until now been downturned, flipped over into a smile.

"Actually, I hadn't thought of that, but… what a fantastic idea! Whatever made you think of that? That'll win a few converts! Thank you, I'll give Smith a few 'revelations' about that! He'll take to that idea like an obese teenager to a hamburger, or a donut to coffee! Despite that rather nice young wife of his. 'Polygamy', was that the word? Commanded by God! Ha, ha! Perhaps God will even 'command' him to marry the wives of his friends! Oh, can you just imagine the fun!"

Well, let me tell you, I felt a bit bad about that. But how was I to know that Moroni was simply making things up as he went along?

And I swear it wasn't me who suggested that these 'wives' could be as young as fourteen.

At this point, Bertie butted in again. He seemed to be taking about as much notice of his wounds as a dying Shakespearean hero with a bad memory and a complicated final speech to make.

"Even if you don't let us have the film, we can still tell people what we know."

That's Bertie all over for you: balanced on the edge of what I was now convinced was either a Heavenly Chariot or an advanced Flying Time Machine (the egg-timer shape again, only doubled!), miles in the air, giving a tetchy angel a very good reason to loop the loop. I was half tempted to shove him over the edge myself at that point.

But Moroni just chuckled.

"I can tell you're Bertie all right! But go ahead, repeat every word. The more you prove the whole thing is a fix-up, the more people will believe it isn't. That's the whole essence of religion! Look what happened when the geologists produced rock strata older than Bishop Ussher's four thousand years BC date – half the believers said that God had put that older rock there to *test* their faith, and the other half that the Devil had put it there to *destroy* their faith!"

"Anyway, I've got to be going. Lucky for you you're who you are! So long!" He stared one last time at Bertie. "Well, well, well! Would you believe it?"

I got as far as saying, "What...?" before the tornado started again. A few maelstroms later, heads reeling, stomachs rolling, we found ourselves on land again.

At least Moroni had the decency to dump us next to the SMM. Which was lucky for both of us: lucky for Bertie because, despite the casual way he treated his wounds, they didn't treat him back in the same casual way, and it wouldn't have been very long before he bled to death; and lucky for me because if I returned yet again with a dead Bertie, his own fault or not, I would be quite unable to defend myself from yet more slanderous attacks on my character, since my broken body would be attracting opportunistic flies and horrified bystanders two hundred and fifty storeys below the office of the Chronotech CEO.

⊕

To the relief of the medical staff, this time Bertie needed little more than a dozen or so emergency blood transfusions, major surgery, and a few weeks in the ICU. His father was therefore freed from having to worry about him, and was able to give all his attention to a great ethical dilemma.

You see, Moroni had slipped up.

Bertie and I had both been filming the translating of *The Book of Mormon*, but when Moroni had whisked us up to his time craft (if that's what it was), he'd only seen my camera, since Bertie had carelessly dropped his when he was being shot.

With Bertie safe (if in extreme agony) in the SMM, it had only been a matter of minutes to fly back to Smith's house and pick up his camera, before heading back to the TM and home.

So we did in fact have some film, fuzzy though it might have been, showing an angel giving Joseph Smith both the Golden Plates and a few choice revelations. Moroni needn't have worried: his features were completely lost behind his effulgence, which presumably had been beamed down from his Catamaran.

Bertie Senior paced up and down his office wrestling with his conscience. It never had shown much promise as a fighter, and was rapidly reduced to squirming submission. He stopped pacing, sat down behind his desk, and gave his decision.

"The whole Mormon thing then, you say, was a fake from beginning to end, a joke or some kind of wager by this Moroni character, who you think maybe comes from the far distant future, or even another planet. I think it better not to make this public. In fact, we will show the film that you do have. Sceptics can still say the floating Moroni was a stage trick, or that the Plates weren't really gold. It probably won't convert anybody one way or another. Therefore, we are not really leading anyone astray. But it will give believers a bit more reason for their belief. It will no longer be quite so embarrassing to declare oneself a Mormon."

He paused, gauging my reaction. I rigidly controlled every muscle of my face. "And," I said, "it would be cruel to take away the basis of faith of twelve million people, most of them hard-working and sincere and honest tax-payers. Let us leave these innocent if misguided people with their hopes and beliefs."

He smiled at me gratefully.

"Quite so," he said, "quite so. And quite irrespective of all this, you'll be pleased to know I had already decided to make you co-Captain with Bertie."

The next day, after the showing of the two film segments, he declared in an interview that those scenes seemed pretty conclusive to him, that the Prophet's authority was obvious, and that he was going to convert to the Church of Latter-day Saints forthwith, although he understood that others might still have their doubts and fully respected their viewpoint.

His married his second wife a day later. By the time Bertie came out of the ICU, he had two more stepmothers, both younger than him.

9: ABOMINATRIX!

After I finished the tale, Shimmer and Shade muttered excitedly together. I couldn't catch most of what they said, but I did hear – or thought I heard – Shimmer ask, "You don't think that Moroni was working for *her*, do you?", and I saw the other shake her head. "But he recognised Bertie," Shimmer insisted. I couldn't hear the answer to this.

But I could have sworn that Shalom smiled quietly – just for a second – before her expression became as impassive as ever.

The atmosphere in the room had now definitely changed. Up to now, Shimmer had been more or less relaxed, as much as gunpowder can relax, clearly in command of the situation. I couldn't imagine Shade ever relaxing – I had finally realised that her constant hand movements represented the imaginary and quite unconscious manipulation of various weapons – but she too had been one hundred per cent confident. If they had known about the 200 guards outside, it hadn't seemed to bother them.

Now I sensed nervousness, or if not that exactly, a sudden wariness. Whoever or whatever Moroni really was, these women knew of him, and clearly respected his powers.

They didn't seem to like the idea of the two strange tramps, or whatever they were, who kept turning up, either.

And who was the 'her' Shade had referred to? From the tone of voice in which the word had been uttered – like a pious Moslem finding a suckling pig, marinating in vodka, on his dinner table – she was no friend of my Visitors.

Something was wrong in their future. It was becoming clear that these three weren't here just to make sure the Andromedans received accurate reports about the superhero Bertie! I doubted that the Andromedans even existed.

So what did they really want from me?

I suddenly wondered whether Bertie had been (or was going to be) a hero of theirs after all. They were apparently facing some kind of problem from someone, and they considered it possible that Moroni was on her side. And since Bertie and this woman had at least one thing in common – Moroni – could it not be that Bertie had somehow been associated with the former? It certainly seemed more likely for Bertie to be mixed up with some troublemakers than to have ended up an acclaimed superhero on twenty-one planets.

The Omega Cow-pat Syndrome.

For the moment, another matter was more pressing.

"Please," I said, as deferentially as I could, 'now can I go to the bathroom?"

Shimmer swung round on me.

"Repeat again exactly what Moroni said. At the end."

I sighed and glanced at my notes.

"Erm... here it is: 'Well, well, well, would you believe it!' I can't promise they are the exact words – remember I wrote up these stories some time after the events, and I was balanced two miles up in space at the time. Distracting. Not much air up there, either."

"'Well, well, well, would you believe it!'" Shimmer repeated slowly. "So Moroni didn't expect to find Bertie there - that means he can't see the past!"

"Of course he can't" snarled Shade. "I've told you a dozen times Moroni can't be a bloody Guardian. He's just some aberration that Time threw up. Like the Abominatrix herself!"

Abominatrix! I was taking all this in like a hungry Black Hole, but at this point Shimmer turned to me again.

"You said Moroni's craft had a double Egg-Timer shape? Like two figure eights?"

"Yes, more or less."

"So even he was only using your own basic Backward design, then?"

"Yes, I suppose so." It seemed the safest answer, although I wasn't certain what she meant by 'Backward design'.

"We know all this," Shade interrupted violently. "Why don't we just extract the information we need the usual way, and go?"

That didn't sound very nice.

"You know why," Shimmer answered sharply. She turned back to me.

"My colleague is a bit impatient, since they're only waiting for our report to complete the details for the Andromedan Time Capsule that will spread Bertie's glory beyond our tiny galaxy. But what difference does an hour or two make now?"

Although unintended, this gave me the chance to once again avoid answering her insistent questions about my Time Machine.

"Of course," said I, "I fully understand. I'll read you our next adventure at once, it almost certainly contains the information you want. But first, I really must go to the bathroom."

Shimmer looked annoyed, but nodded reluctantly.

Once again, a nod to Shalom.

I left the room, but this time I turned left, towards the stairs, thinking I would go to the second bathroom upstairs, which had bigger windows and might offer a possibility of escape. The way Shalom had stopped me answering Maria's phone call, and Shade's comment about the 'usual way' of obtaining information, had convinced me that I wasn't really very safe with these ladies. And they must have done something to the servants: the whole house was too ominously quiet.

Then I remembered my guest. The passage leading to the bathroom also led to the further small flight of stairs that went to the attic. Too close. And in any case the drop from the bathroom into the garden was almost certainly too high. It's one of those things people constantly forget to check when buying a house. I turned round and headed back the way I had come.

"Forgot," I said, "problem with the cistern."

Shalom said nothing, simply followed me as before. We reached the bathroom. As she stepped back to allow me to enter, she spoke for the first time, her voice a barely audible hiss.

"Remember, you know nothing at all about the Forward Machine. Nothing at all. Your life depends on it."

She pushed me rapidly into the bathroom, and closed the door behind me.

Well!

She could have waited till after! As Macbeth said in a different context, 'There would have been a time for such a word'. I stood over the toilet pan, Shalom's words echoing round my skull like homeless bullets, while my member hung idly like a lonely pink sock on a clothes-line on a damp Liverpool day. The shock of her warning had once again turned the stopcock off.

The fact that I knew nothing at all about the thing I was supposed to know nothing at all about should have helped, but didn't.

Forward Machine?

I must have stood there shaking (transitive and intransitive) for a full two minutes, before a gentle warning knock came on the door, splintering it. Despite the indignant expostulations of my bladder, the release valve remained obdurate. I had no doubt that if I didn't emerge soon, the door would be broken down. Once again, I muttered obscenities at my former friend, pulled up my zip, washed the sweat off my face, and stepped out, my bladder as full as ever.

"What do you mean...?" I began, but Shalom gestured me to silence, and pushed me back towards the sitting room. Had she hissed that warning because she happened to be a human-serpent hybrid, or because she knew my other visitors had hearing acute enough to catch sounds even from this far away?

What had she meant? That if I said anything about a 'Forward Machine', Shimmer and Shade would kill me? Or that she, Shalom, would kill me? Was she secretly working against the other two? Or was the whole thing a ruse to make me confide in her, and thus reveal things they all wanted to know?

We entered the room again, where it was at once evident that Shimmer and Shade had been arguing. I wondered whether the argument had concerned the 'extraction' of information 'in the usual way'. Perhaps they'd be kind enough to extract my urine while they were about it!

"Please continue with your account," said Shimmer, before I could even sit down.

At least, she was still playing the Good Cop. But I sensed it wouldn't be long now before she relinquished that role.

"It was at Roswell," I said quickly, "where we came across Moroni again."

Shade, who had clearly been about to protest, subsided.

Well, I had two more tales to tell. If they didn't find whatever answers they were looking for in them, I would know soon enough.

But with luck, Captain Anderson should arrive before then.

I cleared my throat preparatory to reading the next adventure. *Forward Machine?*

10: ANATOMY OF LOVE

"There were two gurneys, with unzipped body bags on each one. The doctors were at one gurney. There was a small, mangled body in it. The nurse said the doctors complained that the smell was the most gruesome they'd ever come across in their life… She said a hand was severed from one of the mangled bodies, and they turned it over on a long forceps…"
(Glenn Dennis, radio interview, 1995)

For the time being, Bertie Senior's extra wives soothed his troubled soul, and I had great hopes that now we could skip religion and assassination and concentrate on really important things, like did they really have orgies at the Court of Cleopatra. But no, my dream was not to be. Instead of Alexandria in 0047 BC, we were sent to Roswell in 1947 AD.

Still, I had to admit, this could well turn out to be our most significant Trip yet. We might be the ones to finally discover whether there had been a cover-up and whether we were really Alone Out Here.

Sixty years had passed since those events, and each year had only added to the vast array of conflicting 'evidence'. There was only one undisputed fact: something landed, or fell, near Roswell in New Mexico somewhere around June-July 1947.

'RAAF Captures Flying Saucer On Ranch In Roswell Region', screamed the *Roswell Daily Record* on 8 July, 1947. The next day it whispered that the 'flying saucer' was only pieces of a weather balloon.

And for around thirty years, that was that – wild speculation abounded, but no new information came to light. But then witnesses began scrambling out of the woodwork (perhaps the cramped woodlice had finally rebelled), and within a short time we had one flying saucer, then two, then nine; one alien, two aliens, then a whole gang of the little buggers; an immense cover-up run by a shadowy Government organisation called Majestic-12; and finally films of autopsies of the third kind.

The testimony of most of these 'witnesses' was always dubious and inconsistent, even as regards the date of the supposed crash, which varied between 14 June and 8 July, 1947, or its site, which again varied between Corona, 75 miles northwest of Roswell, and the Plains of San Austin, 150 miles west of that.

One witness, however, seemed to have greater credibility than most. Glenn Dennis was a young mortician who claimed he had received inquiries from the nearby Army Air Force Base about the availability of child-size coffins, and procedures for embalming bodies that had been exposed to the weather for days. He also declared that he had encountered a hysterical Army nurse on the base, Maria Naomi Selff, who later told him she had aided doctors performing autopsies on small non-human bodies. He had never seen her again, though later, he said, he heard that she had been killed in a plane crash.

There was a big hole in his story of course, the same size and shape as the mysteriously disappearing nurse.

The rolls of 16 mm cine film, however, supposedly taken in 1947, and shown worldwide in 1995, convinced many people. One purported to show the detailed autopsy of an alien; another much shorter bit of blurred 'tent footage' showed a body on a table and two 'doctors' removing parts from it; and a third (the 'debris' footage) showed control panels designed for six-fingered creatures, and an 'I-beam' with strange hieroglyphic-type markings.

The eighteen-minute alien autopsy attracted most attention. The creature was about five feet tall, with smooth hairless skin, a large head, big round eyes, tiny down-turned mouth. The genitalia (if there were any) resembled those of a human female, but there were no breasts or nipples. Most noticeable of all was the bulbous body. The feet appeared to have six toes, and the eyes were covered by dark membranes. During the autopsy, various organs were removed, including the brain, but there was never any really clear view of these – the cameraman seemed to have a severe case of St Vitus's dance.

As in the case of the Army nurse, the big problem here was precisely the twitchy cameraman who filmed all this – another person who took forty years to lose his shyness, and who even so still kept his identity unknown. Not only that, he had supposedly managed to smuggle the footage out of Roswell and keep it hidden all of that time.

For the determined believers, the aliens in question ranged from the Nephilim (the offshoot of those bad angels who, Genesis tells us, mated with the female progeny of our old friend Cain and that wife of mine who so cruelly deserted me), through galactic researchers checking on their big experiment (Earth), to an everyday intergalactic reconnaissance force preparing for an invasion of our planet.

The US Air Force itself said the debris found was simply part of a balloon carrying low-frequency acoustic microphones, part of the classified Project Mogul to monitor possible Russian nuclear testing. All that was really found was a bit of tinfoil, paper, tape, and sticks – all part of a radar target.

Now, a few months before, I would have been one hundred per cent certain that the whole thing was as ridicuious as… well, as Joseph Smith, for example, with his head in a hat translating Golden Plates delivered by an angel.

So now I was slightly more cautious in my disbelief.

Yet, of all the conflicting evidence, something that bothered me was that they couldn't even agree on the date. And that the appearance of the 'autopsy film' alien didn't tally with the descriptions of the aliens supposedly seen at Roswell by, for example, the Army nurse.

Could there have been two crashes, with two different kinds of aliens? Were they playing Star Wars up there in the sky?

And that tortured face in the alien autopsy film kept tugging at the sleeve of my unconscious. Until…

"Moroni!" I cried.

We were in the Time Machine, nearing our destination.

"What?" said Bertie, my Co-Captain. He was again completely recovered, but a bit subdued. Possibly the result of a sudden overdose of new nubile stepmothers. It might also have had something to do with the eleven bullets they had fished out of him. The only ones that had done no damage were the four that had entered his brain.

"Moroni. That's who that autopsy alien was – ok, he's lost his smile, got himself a bit of a paunch, but those eyes, that mouth! It was Moroni!"

"Don't be silly, it was nothing like Moroni." Dying and half-dying so frequently, and being Co-Captain, was tending to make Bertie annoyingly self-assertive.

"How would you know? You couldn't have seen clearly through all that blood! And he said himself he often appeared in disguise in

Joe's 'visions'. And that his beard was false. He's probably able to change his appearance completely."

"In that case, you wouldn't recognise him at all, would you?"

You can't imagine how painful it is to be caught out in a logical blunder by Bertie. Like Fermat would have felt if he'd been taking a stroll in Toulouse and a seagull had suddenly screamed out the solution to his Last Theorem.

Then I remembered something else.

"The 'hieroglyphics' on the retrieved I-piece in the alien debris film were the same 'Reformed Egyptian' that we saw on Joseph Smith's golden tablets!"

Well, that put him in his place! But then I had another thought.

If the body shown in the longer autopsy was Moroni's, who were the two creatures in the other bit of film and those seen by the 'hysterical nurse' encountered by Glenn Dennis? In other words, if Moroni had died as the result of a mid-air crash, who, or what, had he crashed into? By its very nature, a time machine *while travelling* did not exist in the outside physical world (it was, as everyone knows, on the other side of the Event Horizon) and therefore could not hit a physical object in our world. The only possible thing it could 'hit' therefore would be…

Another time machine!

I hurled myself at the controls.

"What are you doing?" yelled Bertie, pushing me back.

"Out of my way, you fool! We must abort!" I managed to knock him backwards, get my fingers to within inches of the main button.

"We abort, Dad will skin me alive!" And the dogged little bastard grabbed my testicles as he fell, squeezing so hard that I momentarily lost vision and balance, and hit the wrong button as I fell too.

A glass of orange juice appeared from the dispenser.

I hurled him off me, reckless of whether my favoured parts remained in his hand, or returned to their cosy pre-ordained place, and lunged at the control panel again.

Too late!

Considering that space, and therefore time, is infinite, the chances of one time machine being in the same spatial-temporal point as another are also infinite to one. However, as I had learned before, the mere presence of Bertie could considerably reduce any otherwise impossible odds. Indeed, I have sometimes wondered whether his odours might not be a manifestation of some fifth fundamental force, perhaps even that elusive force that unifies gravity, electromagnetism, and the two nuclear forces. I even wrote to a respected Liechtensteinian professor on this subject of olfaction. He wrote back, beginning: 'Dear N, I too have been wondering about this. Bear in mind, to put it in crude layman's terms, that receptor binding leads to a number of possible events including G-protein activation and IP3 induced Ca++ release. Action potentials set up in receptors which are direct extensions of axons that pass through cribiform plate and synapse in glomeruli to second order cells that pass in the olfactory tract directly to inferior frontal lobe of cortex and pass on to other areas including the limbic system…' I stopped reading, and took this as unqualified support for my theory. Add to that a wild card like Moroni, and the impossible becomes possible.

With a whole planet to fall on to, we had to go and fall near 509th Bomb Group at Roswell Army Air Field, whose motto must have been *Disembowel First, Interrogate Afterwards*: a side effect of being at the start of a Cold War? The Truman Doctrine had been expounded only three months before.

The first thing I became aware of as I came to was that I was in a partially unzipped body bag, and being assailed by a most fetid smell. I almost cried out.

Lucky I didn't. Because if I had, I wouldn't be recounting the tale.

I realised at once, of course, that only one thing was capable of thus torturing all my forty million nasal receptors at once.

I managed to open one eye and sure enough there he was.

Bertie's luck had always been bad. But everyone's luck has to turn sometime. And Bertie's had: it had turned worse.

He was laid out on a dissection table. With an Army nurse and two doctors standing over him.

Wait a minute, you say, are you claiming that you and Bertie were the aliens that Glenn Dennis spoke of? Have you forgotten that the nurse swore they were less than four feet tall?

You have to remember that we only travel through time by

STEVE REDWOOD

travelling faster than the speed of light. During the actual 'journey' therefore, we get foreshortened, compressed along the axis in which we are moving, reach zero, and then begin to lengthen again. In this case, our journey got violently interrupted, and we were thrown into 'normal' space before we'd had time to stretch back to our original height. And need I tell you that such sudden deceleration plays havoc with the bowels. Hence the unusually – even for Bertie – pungent smell of which the Army doctors complained.

There were other unfortunate side effects I was shortly to become aware of.

I said that Bertie's body was on the dissection table. I should have said *most* of his body. Even as I watched, one of the doctors yanked out a kidney and handed it to the nurse.

Whose name really was Maria.

Imagine a young Natalie Wood with traces of Liv Tyler thrown in, and you're nearly there. They don't make nurses like that any more, that's for sure.

My heart, I confess, was smitten immediately. There was something about the way she received the kidney, the way her slim fingers curled round it, the pure sensuality with which she then wiped the blood off on her primordial hips.

Oh, don't think I had forgotten the delectable Winnie or my dear sweet Mabel. That would never happen. But Winnie was the wife of another man, and *cicisbeos* were frowned on in our killjoy society. Besides, our friendship had unaccountably cooled of late: at times, she showed a certain… well, almost indifference. As for Mabel, she had made her decision and chosen to help Cain populate the planet. A worthy aim, for which I easily found it in my heart to forgive her; but she could never come back, and would she not wish me to be happy, just as I had wished her happiness when I had taken off and selflessly left her in Cain's loving arms?

But the circumstances were not propitious for romance. I was in a body bag, with my shrunken body so mangled I found the only digit near enough to surreptitiously scratch an itch on my nose was my big toe. I was unable to ascertain which of the two had changed position.

If I gave any sign of life, I realised, I was likely to become a painful medical experiment: I've seen *The X-Files*. On the other hand, by playing possum, I would shortly be privileged with seeing my own

118

innards for the first time. I tried to convince myself that it would be exciting to have Maria's hands removing my spleen, but of course I would be dead. Necrophilia's fine, but only for the living.

I was momentarily distracted from my gloomy ruminations by the plopping sound Bertie's kidney made as Maria dropped it into a large jar.

The doctors continued to rummage, as I pieced together what must have happened. The discrepancy in the dates and locations witnesses reported for the finding of the New Mexico 'aliens' was now explicable: we had obviously 'hit' Moroni's craft, but since TMs travel in time (and only incidentally in space) the nano-seconds between the break up of our Machine and his had translated into three weeks and a hundred miles on the ground. Moroni and his debris were found by the 'cameraman' who filmed the autopsy, and we were the other Roswell 'aliens' that Glenn Dennis had stumbled upon.

Yes, back in Palmyra, New York, Moroni had been a bit different (as Bertie had dared to point out) from the hairless pot-bellied creature of the autopsy film (though his eyes and mouth were the same), but, like us, the accident had thrown his atoms together somewhat haphazardly. I hadn't noticed his six fingers, but then I hadn't exactly been intent on counting them. Probably a case of Lamarckian evolution – he'd developed extra fingers over time from trying to keep them in so many pies.

The doctors fished out Bertie's heart, handed it to Maria, then began to remove the stomach. Reckless creatures! Their surgical masks were no match for Bertie's pugnacious aromas, and they both suddenly retched and dashed out, presumably to seek fresh air, a sick bag, or extreme unction. The nurse, however, stayed in the room, seemingly impervious to the stink. I found out later there was a word for this: anosmia, lack of a sense of smell.

Maria's anosmia saved our lives.

"Pssstt!" I whispered. Short and to the point, that's how I like to be.

She turned towards my body bag, startled.

"Don't be afraid!" said I.

I agree with hindsight that a very mangled and presumably alien corpse saying 'Don't be afraid' wasn't really going to reassure anyone. I was also uncomfortably aware that my head had been rearranged, and that the tongue emitting those soothing words was in fact poking out, and backwards, from the left ear lobe. No wonder they'd decided to autopsy Bertie first.

Maria screamed.

Well, thought I, ever optimistic, at least contact has been made.

How nobody heard the scream I don't know. Perhaps they did, but no one wanted to enter that mephitic room before they had to.

"It's all right," I said, "I'm not really what I seem. I am, in fact, quite tall, rather strikingly handsome, with a modulated cragginess that many have remarked upon, with sensuously wavy hair and just a hint of a dimple in my right cheek, and I wondered whether you'd like to marry me."

Being proposed to by a bag of body parts can only have two effects: make you scream, or make you laugh hysterically. Maria did both.

"You may not think it to look at me now," I went on, unsure whether or not to be encouraged by her response, "but I frequently rub shoulders with world leaders, I am sought out by the major TV channels, and my erections are dependably heliotropic and steadfast. It's true that my dear sweet Mabel – who is," (I added hurriedly) "no longer my wife – well, she is, legally, but she must have died a few million years ago, and I therefore do not think my marriage vows should now be taken too seriously, or allowed to stand between you and me – it's true that she never had a high opinion of my erections, but the reason for that, I assure you, wasn't any deficiency on my part, but her dampening effect upon me, which might, to use medical jargon, be described as 'Cold Bucket Trauma'. I am also quite willing to do the washing up now and then, share the cooking, even do the odd bit of ironing, and should you want children – though it may be a bit early to start thinking about that – I've been told I would make a good father."

This latter statement wasn't true but no one won fair hand by being too honest.

Maria, clearly still in a state of extreme shock, answered dreamily, as though hoping that by playing a conscious role in her sudden nightmare she might bring it to a conclusion and wake up. She still clutched Bertie's heart in one hand.

"I don't doubt your claims. But where would we keep your erection? In the pen holder? Or are you unaware that your erector is separated from the rest of your pieces? As for being a good father, how would you dandle our children on your knees since you do not seem to have any, how would you take them swimming, or teach them to play baseball, or how to beat up the neighbours' kids, or bungee-jumping, or all the other things a good father does? Frankly, I don't see how you could even feed them, unless they happened to be cannibalistic."

Well, she was at least considering my proposal – in a commendably rational and considered way, too. Shock-induced it might have been, but this level-headedness only made her all the more appealing to me..

Encouraged, I answered: "Ah, but we are time travellers, and our bodies are only in this unfortunate state because we have been literally torn between past and present. It's simple quantum mechanics. My tongue at the moment, as you may have perceived, is issuing from my left ear. Had we crashed a nano-second later or earlier, my ear might well have issued from my tongue. Pure chance. But in your future, I am – as I have already modestly hinted – a not unattractive man of whom any future children might be proud, and who would even join in with them in the beating up of the neighbours' kids provided those kids weren't too big."

"I'm sure that everything you say is true," Maria answered cautiously, clearly wondering when she was going to wake up, "but this is not the future, but the present, and when I wake up I'm afraid I'm going to have to help dissect you."

That's what I loved about Maria from the beginning. An honest woman, a straight-talking woman. No simpering coyness with her. My uncrushed eye gazed at her with admiration.

"I'm not the kind of man who would seek to interfere in his wife's professional advancement, but allow me to say that your dissecting me would seriously jeopardize our future together. My friend, as you see, is already dead. I am only alive because I happened to land on top of him, and by chance he cushioned the force of the impact."

I recalled how fiercely the selfish Bertie had struggled to avoid having to cushion the force of the impact for me.

"But if I don't dissect you, I won't get paid, and as at the moment your wage-earning capacities are limited…"

"But if you help us to escape from here, and reach our TM – Time Machine – we can return to the future, and we will have our normal forms."

"Even him?" She nodded towards the eviscerated Bertie.

"Yes, even him, though in his case there would be a slight delay. And his normal form isn't that much of an improvement."

"But what would there be in it for me? There you'll be, safe in the future, and here I'll be, facing a court-martial."

"But I'll take you with me! We'll get married, and…"

"I don't want to hurt your feelings, but I'm quite happy here. This is a good job – when we don't receive things like you." The hysteria was near the surface again.

"But if you help us, you'll be an international heroine in the future. There must be something that you want that you can't have here."

"Nothing, nothing at all."

"Nothing at all? I can't believe that. Think of the wonders of the future – colour television, pre-cooked meals, package holidays, computerised toilet paper, the sexual revolution…"

That one got her.

"The sexual revolution?"

"Yes. You can take a pill and not worry about pregnancy, you can go to male striptease shows, if your boss so much as brushes your shoulder you can sue him for sexual harassment and win millions, you can *be* the boss, you can have breast implants and plastic surgery and face-lifting and liposuction to hide your age…"

"But I don't want to hide my age…"

She stopped, and a peculiar light came into her eyes.

"Tell me, if I come into your future, will I still be twenty-three?"

"Twenty-three?" quoth I, with squishy gallantry. "I wouldn't have put you past twenty! But, yes, you'd be the same age."

"But everybody else here would continue to get older?"

"Of course."

"Including my sister?"

"Oh, if you're worried about a beloved sister, we can take her with us too."

"So in twenty years' time, for example, I'd still be twenty-three, and my sister would be thirty-eight?"

"Well, if she's eighteen now…"

"And in another twenty years' time, I'd still be twenty-three, and my sister would be fifty-eight?"

"I told you, we can take her with…"

"…And then fifty-nine, and then sixty and then sixty-one…"

"We can take…"

"And I'd still be twenty-three!"

At which point, Maria threw her arms up in the air (dropping Bertie's heart) and danced around the room, laughing hideously. I began to wonder whether I had not perhaps given my own heart too freely.

Abruptly, she stopped laughing. "Which year do you come from?" she demanded.

"2007."

"1947… 2007… that's fifty, no, sixty… plus eighteen equals seventy-eight, she'll be an old hag, yes, but she might also be dead!"

She stamped her foot in rage, her heel catching the edge of Bertie's heart, and sending it skittering across the floor.

By now I was beginning to get the idea.

"Erm, don't you get on with your sister?"

This induced a five-minute tirade, the gist of which was the following:

Rosanna was her younger sister. Now if Maria looked a bit like Natalie Wood, Rosanna was very similar, but with an added *je ne sais quoi* imparted by a soupçon of Brigitte Bardot. Armed with this unfair advantage, a dark-as-midnight New Mexican brunette who somehow exuded Gallic blondeness, she had already, at the age of eighteen, won the heart, mind, and, worse, body, of the young pilot that Maria had loved since succumbing to puberty. Maria was understanding about this, and had reacted in a sisterly way – she hated her.

And what better revenge than to reappear in a future where the pilotnapping younger sister would be an old hag, and she could flaunt her youthful beauty in front of her! But…

"She might die before then, and I wouldn't be able to savour my victory. Not worth the risk."

"OK, then, we can drop you off on the way. Say, thirty years from now. Or forty. Whatever. Imagine, you'll still be as young and beautiful as you are now, and your sister will be as old as you want her to be."

There was in fact no way we could just stop mid-journey to drop her off. If that had been possible, we would probably have been able to avoid most of our unpleasant adventures. But when you are in a body bag in an army base and about to be dissected, ethics take on a certain elasticity.

She eventually agreed. I think she had decided that if this was a dream, it had now taken such a delicious turn she would stay in it as long as possible.

"So where is your Time Machine?" she asked.

"Ah, I was rather hoping that you knew"

"Why should I?"

I tried hard to remember what Glenn Dennis had said.

"Are we still near Roswell?"

"We're in the base infirmary, in a supply room."

I would have heaved a sigh of relief if my lungs had still been anywhere near my throat. I'd read that the 'alien autopsy' had been filmed at Fort Worth Air Force Base in Dallas. But that would have been Moroni, of course. If we were still anywhere near our TM, I could summon the SMM as I had in Florence to escape Máchiavelli and his men. The TM might still be all right, since it had been brought down by the shock waves of the temporal collision, and had not 'hit' anything in the usual sense of the word. Except the ground, I reminded myself.

But to use the SMM I needed the remote control.

I fumbled around inside the body bag but as one of my hands was now attached to my coccyx, and the other had developed ingrowing fingers, I wasn't able to make a very thorough search.

"Um, excuse me," I said, "but would you mind emptying me out on the table a minute, and seeing if you can spot a small oblong contraption, black and silver, a few inches long? I need it to summon the Time Machine."

Maria nodded as if this were the most natural request in the world.

She unzipped the body bag, swept Bertie to one end of the operating table with her forearm, poured me out at the other end, and then prodded and poked around in places where only doctors, nurses, and lovers don't fear to tread. She certainly knew how to ingratiate herself into my good nooks. She quickly gave a cry of maniacal triumph.

"Is this it?" she cried, clutching the remote, which had escaped the attention of whoever had bagged us because it had wedged itself into… well, that's not too important.

"Excellent!"

I prepared to summon the SMM without more ado. But because of my ingrowing fingers, I found it difficult to feed in the signal.

"You'll have to help me!" I gasped.

She leaned over me – oh, that starched blouse, that sensuous antiseptic smell! – and was just depressing the final key when the door opened, and the two doctors returned.

"What's this? Fraternisation with mangled alien corpses?" one of them shouted at Maria. "We'll have you court martialled for this!"

"I'm not an alien and I'm not a corpse!" I protested.

"But you *are* mangled, though."

"Yes, and you're supposed to be doctors. How about helping to *un*mangle me?"

"Our orders are to dissect you. How dare you interfere!"

"What about your Hippocratic Oath?"

"You must be joking, this is the army!"

"You can't just murder me!"

The second doctor interposed angrily. "This is an American military base. We've just won the war. We murder who we want. And innards will not address complete human beings, especially their superior officers, unless ordered to."

I had to play for time till the SMM arrived.

"Despicable earthlings," I cried, "even now our huge Mother Ship is hovering over this continent, and my colleagues will use your bodies to hatch their larvae in if you dare harm us!"

"You're talking through the back of your head!"

This, of course, was true.

"I, pathetic terran, am an admiral of the fleet. Inferiors are not allowed to look upon our faces. Therefore we address them through the backs of our heads."

That made them pause.

"Ah ha, so you *are* an alien!" said the first doctor. "And as such you must be executed at once."

The other doctor looked doubtful.

"Aren't they supposed to be viciously interrogated and brutally tortured first?"

"Not if they're Commies"

"But if he isn't a Commie?"

"All enemies of the American people are Commies."

"But what if he isn't an enemy…"

"He's just threatened to hatch his larvae in our bodies! Undermining us from within. Close infiltration through the fifth column. If that isn't Commie, what is?"

He picked up his scalpel with patriotic fervour.

"Stop!" said I. "I warn you, if you cut me, I smell much worse than my companion."

He laid down the scalpel: patriotism overcome by postulated pustulation.

Still playing for time, I pursued my advantage.

"Take me," I commanded with mangled majesty, "to your Leader."

They looked at each other in indecision.

Before they could make up their minds, the wall crashed down, and the SMM occupied the spot where they had been, wobbling precariously on their shattered heads. Well, they'd been a disgrace to their profession, anyway.

"Quick," I cried to Maria, as I scooped up as much of Bertie as I could, "before anyone comes, help me into the machine – and don't forget to pick up Bertie's heart!"

I draw attention to this thoughtfulness on my part to silence those who unfairly criticised me for what happened after.

Maria was magnificent. She yanked me to my feet – wherever they were – and hurled me into the SMM. Bits of Bertie came flying in after me. She had just managed to throw herself in, and the hatch was closing, when the first bullet thudded into it. Within minutes, the SMM was flying low towards the homing beacon in the TM. I already began to feel safe.

Which was a bit premature, as when we got there, our beautiful streamlined egg-timer Machine, lying at an angle in a deep depression, now looked more like two poached eggs stuck together, and was, moreover, being guarded by an army platoon!

But I had no choice but to act. If we lost the element of surprise, we would never escape.

I sent the SMM hurtling straight at the TM, where it docked with an excruciating clang that set my teeth on edge against my hip bone.

Were there soldiers inside the TM? Most likely. They must have found a way inside in order to have been able earlier to drag us out. Extreme measures were called for.

"Maria," I said, hiding my desperation under the icy exterior called for in such situations, "get Bertie's large intestine, and as I open the airlock, slit it open, and hurl it through the gap. Wait ten seconds – by which time the soldiers should have left, or been asphyxiated – then run into the Machine, and press the green button to the left of the main door, which should close it. Then come back for me, help me to the control panel, and let's hope the thing is working."

In certain quarters, I have suffered severe moral obloquy because of that decision, as has my darling Maria. We are painted as some kind of monsters, gratuitously ripping open the highly private organs of the man who later – some opined – helped saved the world.

It is these very people who claim to speak on behalf of Bertie who do not understand the true nobility of my friend. I understood it. I knew that had Bertie been alive, he would have been the first to ask us to sacrifice his organs in order to serve the common good.

Maria's army training again stood her in good stead. No sooner did I open the airlock into the TM than six feet of feculent intestine went flying through like an anaconda stung by a jelly fish. Gagging sounds came from the other side, and the sound of scrambling boots. Maria took a quick glance, then dashed through the lock. A few seconds later, I heard the main TM doors sliding shut, and then she was back, helping me stagger through.

What a woman!

But when I approached the control panel, holding my breath and nose, I saw that everything had been in vain. Part of it was smashed, and though the buttons controlling dematerialisation were still intact, nothing happened when I lowered my bottom over them and punched them. I ripped off the twisted protective plating, and saw that many of the wires inside had fused. It would probably have been beyond my skill to repair them even if I'd had the necessary tools. At least, the ventilation system was working, which saved me from the worst effects of Bertie's bowels.

"We're trapped!" I groaned. "The only thing we can do is go back into the SMM and escape to some primitive part of Africa, where they treat aliens like gods instead of dissecting them."

Maria loomed over me, her black eyes flashing with the searing light of sibling rivalry.

"The only place we're going is the future – you promised! You think I've gone through all this just to watch my sister stay younger than me?"

"But, my darling, the controls are wrecked. At least, if we escape from here, they may send another Chronoporter to rescue us."

This was most unlikely. Especially if they went through my papers, and found the original plans for the Time Machine.

Through the view port, I saw some soldiers preparing to attach explosive devices to the TM. Did I dare to ask Maria for one first, and final, kiss? It would be a very innocent one, since my tongue was no longer in my mouth. I feared she might be disappointed.

Ah, *lacrimae rerum*!

Just then there came a strange squelching sound from above, as though a Giant Freshwater Squid were kissing the Machine, and then we were whisked up and away at a terrific speed.

Impelled by my natural nobility, I put my arm round Maria to protect her, but forgot it was growing out of my backside. It therefore went round *her* backside. I had to admire her. Despite the terrifying situation she was in, she had the presence of mind to give me an almighty slap. My head throbbed with agony and adoration.

After a few minutes, we jerked to a halt. I looked through the view port, and saw that we were in even more barren desert than before. Above, the squid noisily broke the kiss, we wobbled perilously before coming to a standstill, and two massive Egg Timers forming the twin hulls of a flying catamaran glided down beside us.

Moroni's Flying Machine!

The tiny cabin between the hulls opened, and out stepped Moroni himself, or his double, signalling us to do the same.

As if I hadn't already had enough problems, it seemed I would now have to explain to the spirit of a dead spirit why we had accidentally killed him again! The situation called for quick thinking and appropriate action.

So I stayed inside the TM and cowered.

Moroni smiled, and raised something that looked like nothing I had ever seen before, but which very definitely made the statement, 'I am a really nasty super-advanced weapon'. His gestures plainly indicated that either I come out or he would blow a hole in the TM. Obeying this cogent argument, I, or most of me, squelched out, whispering to Maria to stay inside.

I breathed in deeply, grateful to be able to savour the tang of the natural world in my last moments.

But instead of percolating me, Moroni holstered the weapon, held out his hand, and said, beaming:

"Put it there, boy!"

After at least ten seconds' disbelief, I put it there, using the respectable arm growing from my shoulder. Moroni had amazingly solid hands for a doubly dead angel.

"Where's Bertie?" he asked. "He didn't get himself killed again, did he?"

I confessed that this was indeed the case.

"That lad does get into some scrapes! Who else is with you?"

I turned round. Maria wasn't in sight.

"What do you mean? There's only me and Bertie," I said with my most innocent expression. Heroes protect their women: everyone knows that.

"Oh, come on! Think I was born tomorrow? Anyway, let me see if I can remember... Roswell, middle twentieth century, Bertie once more sacrifices himself to save his patently unworthy Travelling companion, can't quite remember how... they're about to be boiled down for glue when they're helped by a mortician... no, no, that's not right, a doctor? Something like that... Ah, I remember, a nurse! Called Narnia, Nuria... Come on, help me here, I didn't get a very high grade in Pre-Atrocity History."

"Maria," I said unwillingly. *Pre-Atrocity?*

"Yes, yes, that's it, Maria! Who later... yes, well, I'd better not tell you about that right now. Besides, that depends on... Anyway, you chaps certainly saved my bacon." His eye membranes nictitated merrily. "Somehow, they'd got on to me, and sent their top hit men, Nergnug and Smugnot. Pitiless bastards if ever there were any! But you splattered them good and proper! So intent on tracking me, they never saw you coming at all. Wham! They're the only ones who could have recognised me, and now you've well and truly finished them off, the frumious swine!"

So the 'Alien Autopsy' film didn't show Moroni after all, but a similar being who was apparently some kind of gangster (or cop?) from his own time!

"But we saw remains of your Machine in an old film," I stammered. "It clearly showed those sigils or hieroglyphics you have here on the hull."

He followed the direction of my glance.

"Oh that, that's just the name of the company who constructed the Machine. The boss claims Egyptian ancestry, so they use an ornate Egyptian-type logo. I think it says 'Horus Brown and Sons, Time Unlimited'. It's on all our Machines, since Brown has a monopoly."

"But why are you here? You won't find many Mormons around here."

"Oh, I didn't come for them. They're ticking along just nicely. I wanted something a bit more exciting. I'd just popped back to 1925 to get one of my drones to inseminate a certain Grantham shopkeeper's wife with a little cyborg who'll be called Margaret and will destroy England, and on the way Forward nipped into Los Alamos to make sure the Bomb was coming on OK. I was just hightailing it Uptime again when I sensed a temporal dislocation, and stopped to investigate."

God, this angel was a devil!

But so what? So long as he was on our side...

"Anyway," he went on, "enough of me and my hobbies. Introduce me to Maria."

I called her, and she stepped out, brandishing her scalpel aggressively. What a woman!

"You can put that down," said Moroni, smiling. "I'm a friend. Sort of. I noticed that your Machine doesn't seem to be working, and I can probably fix it for you. But first I must ask you to let me touch your forehead. It won't take a moment."

Maria backed away a little.

"It's all right. It won't hurt you. And it's entirely up to you. But if you refuse, I will not let you return to the Machine."

Maria stepped up to him, her face grim.

Moroni touched her forehead with fingers outstretched – all six of them, I finally noticed – then smiled again, and moved back.

"Thank you. I had to be sure you weren't one of them. Now I'm in a bit of a hurry, but one good turn deserves another, so if I can just take a quick look at your controls…"

And he stepped past us into the Chronoporter, only to stagger out again immediately, his face green.

"Bertie?" he asked.

I nodded.

"So it was all true!"

So saying, he took an almighty breath, and dashed inside again. All I could see for the next few minute was a flurry of hands and fingers. He dashed out every now and then to gulp in fresh air.

Finally, he staggered out, and stayed out.

"Done," he said. "The electronics are very elementary, though the brilliant concept behind it is the one we still use. And you'd better get back home quickly. Bertie is starting to decompose, and is near the point where it might be impossible to Regenerate him. And if that happened…"

He made a gesture with his hand as if slitting his throat, and then added, seeing my puzzled expression:

"Ah, N, my dear chap, not only is Bertie going to change the future, he is the future! Provided nothing goes wrong. Well, I have to be off, but if there's any time you need help, just shout! I won't hear it, but I assure you it's the recommended course of action."

He waved a cheery goodbye, entered his cabin, and suddenly the catamaran wasn't there any more.

I could hardly believe our luck. We'd managed to escape from Roswell, and earned the gratitude of a powerful being from the far future into the bargain.

Or was it more than just gratitude? He'd implied that his own existence depended on Bertie's. But how was that possible?

I got back into the TM, and set the controls to take us home.

At least, I thought to myself, our crash at Roswell had saved us from having to meet those two irritating tramps again!

Just before we dematerialised, I spotted a weather balloon descending to earth.

⊕

Well, I got a lot of flak from Bertie Senior about the condition of his son's body, but I was in such an unfortunate state myself that even he didn't have the heart for too many recriminations. The Centre's medical staff sighed, demanded another rise, rolled up their sleeves, consulted anatomy charts, wiped the sweat off their foreheads in time-honoured fashion, and set about unjumbling my body. Bertie was already in the Regeneration Chamber, which they now simply called 'Bertie's Room'.

Maria came to see me in the recovery room a few days later. She'd checked the records, and found out that her sister had indeed finally married the pilot. She'd flown over to see her. It turned out that she had soon lost her uncanny beauty, the pilot had been unfaithful from the start, he'd then divorced her and married some English girl, and poor Rosanna had led a thoroughly miserable life. Three attempted suicides. She was now a shrivelled seventy-eight with nine cats and a paranoid goldfish. Maria had literally danced round her. Seems sisters sometimes get like that.

Maria gave a new meaning to my life.

I was, of course, missing my dear sweet Mabel terribly, which was why I needed something, or someone, to help fill that aching void. I had thought the special friendship of Winnie would be enough, but lately she always seemed to be suffering from an inordinate number of headaches. Bertie had once told me, his face creased with unhappiness and frustration, that the headaches had in fact begun soon after they had got married. It must have been the result of the time transference. No way could he blame her. He still worshipped her. But it was… disappointing.

I could understand him. I had also found she was limiting me more and more in the varieties of comfort I could offer her whenever he died.

Strangely enough, the presence of Maria changed all that. Now Winnie visited me every day, and tried so hard to please me that twice the medics had to replace the stitches on parts of my anatomy.

If only she had been that keen before! I still had great affection for her, her smile still thrilled me – though since she'd had the teeth brace removed, it had lost some of its mysterious allure. But Maria and I had shared moments more intimate than any in human history. She knew me inside out. My heart was completely lost to her.

Besides, despite her new ardour, Winnie still gave me the odd impression that she didn't really like men at all.

There was one clear exception. Leonardo da Vinci. Her eyes would mist over whenever she mentioned him (which was often), and time and time again, Bertie told me, he would find her poring over reproductions of his pictures. Indeed, he said, more than once he'd found her weeping quietly as she looked at the Mona Lisa in their bedroom.

So why had she come to the future and married Bertie? For money? That was what she'd said in Florence. That had to be it.

But now she could easily have become extremely rich by herself. A ten-minute interview with the Mona Lisa could fetch a hundred thousand pounds. A nude centrefold in *Playboy* alone netted half a million. But she rarely took advantage of these opportunities.

So if she wasn't really bothered about money, back to the same question: why had she married Bertie?

And why did she now seem to treat Maria as a personal enemy?

And something else was worrying me.

We had believed we could go into the past, and solve great mysteries without affecting the present. And indeed I still hoped we were not affecting the present.

But the past was a different matter. Someone or something was hiding changes we had made, but not always doing the job too well. Maria and Glenn Dennis, for example.

Dennis claimed he had spoken to Maria after the 'alien' autopsies. Only then had she disappeared. But that was impossible: she had come with us before the autopsies were finished. It was as if there were a jagged edge, a suture, an overlap, where the changes we had brought about had insufficiently replaced the original past, and debris from the old Past was still hanging around. Like Dennis' memories.

But more significant was something I had guessed at before. In the very act of solving the mysteries, we were also, at least in part, causing them.

What had just happened here? We had crashed into Moroni's enemies, and our bodies and theirs had provided all the bodies seen by the various Roswell witnesses and on the three bits of film.

But before we made that trip, whose bodies had the Roswell witnesses been seeing?

Perhaps we *had* changed the past, after all. Perhaps in a different timeline, Moroni's enemies had crashed, not into us, but into Moroni himself. Or, perhaps, no one had crashed, but Moroni had landed to play one of his little tricks, his enemies had landed to pursue him, and they had killed each other. Or perhaps, again, either Moroni or his enemies had got into a fight with the US military. Perhaps aliens really had landed. Perhaps there'd been a plague of dwarves or hobbits. All these options produced bodies. Very neat.

If that were the case, the crash we had just caused might be simply one version of the Roswell events. In another version, maybe Moroni really had died. But that would imply parallel timelines. Glenn Dennis' memories, however, were in our timeline, when they should have been in a different one, the one where Maria never came with us.

Besides, I never had liked the idea of parallel dimensions. Too glib.

There was another possibility, unlikely though it seemed. What if we, Bertie and I, were not so much changing the past as filling it in? These things had already happened, but somehow they had *un*happened, and we had to fulfil our function? As if someone had been stealing bits of the past, leaving dangerous holes that we had to fill in. In other words, those Roswell bodies really had been ours all the time. Even before we went there. It brought us back to the all-time-is-eternally-present idea. We had crashed at Roswell, and gone back to solve the mystery of who had crashed at Roswell, simultaneously.

I went through our other adventures. Bertie's proposal of marriage, and the wealth she imagined would come with it, had given Mona Lisa – so I believed – her smile. Leonardo carried the picture around with him all his life because we had taken the real person away from him. Cain had no way of finding a wife (short of incest) until we went back, and I selflessly sacrificed my own happiness and provided him with my own spouse. In the case of Rasputin, it is most unlikely that he would have survived the poisoning as Bertie had done: Bertie's impregnable stomach had given rise to the very legend we were solving. And now, with Roswell, we (with Moroni) turned out to be the very aliens we had gone to investigate, and it was we who had taken away the one reliable witness to our own presence – Maria the Army nurse.

But that left Joseph Smith. And there this theory seemed to break down. Our presence had, on the surface at least, made very little difference to the course of events. We had only played a minor role. Indeed, the only relevant thing I could think of was my inadvertent suggestion about polygamy, which possibly had won many more adherents for Mormonism.

Wait a minute!

One of them was Bertie's father.

Who had provided the funds to build the Chronoporter in the first place! And who sent us to film Joseph Smith!

This seemed to suggest that the only reason for our presence in Palmyra was for us to meet a self-styled angel who would adopt my suggestion about polygamy which would eventually lead to my being sent back by a man who fancied extra nookie.

So was Moroni then the key?

But Moroni himself had implied that his survival depended on Bertie. And why had he insisted on touching Maria's head? What had he been looking for?

And – the memory suddenly returned – why had Winnie seemed uneasy when she'd heard Moroni's name?

And why did Bertie have to die, or nearly die, every time we went Back?

I gave up, took a pile of aspirins, and fell into a doze dreaming of Maria, now lying in a barge like a burnished throne burning on the waters of the Nile. Truly, age had not withered her, and nor, I sincerely hoped, would custom stale.

11: A TOUCHING MOMENT

This time, when I stopped reading, my Three Graces' reactions were even more muted. They seemed to be trying to take in the implications of what they'd heard.

I wondered whether I dared ask a couple of questions that had been bothering me ever since that adventure: why had Moroni touched Maria's head and decided that she wasn't 'one of them'? And what had he meant when he'd referred to 'Pre-Atrocity History'?

But I decided not to ask. I was afraid of the answers.

"So what we thought was a daring pre-emptive strike by Bertie on Moroni's enemies was simply bad driving? Was that just more of Boadicea's propaganda? Can we have been overestimating him all this time?" I may have been imagining it, but Shade almost seemed to have a hurt look on her face. As if she'd been betrayed.

"If we're overestimating him, how come the Revolution's spread so qui...?" Shimmer stopped herself, realising I was listening, then went on more quietly: "Anyway, accident or planned, it disposed of the only people powerful enough to stop Moroni. On the other hand..." She turned to me.

"Can you just read that bit again, Moroni's last words about Bertie?"

Again? But I nodded. Anything to gain time.

" 'Ah, N, my dear chap, not only is Bertie going to change the future, he is the future! Provided nothing goes wrong.' "

"'Provided nothing goes wrong.' So he really doesn't know the future – or the past – for sure!"

"Of course he doesn't!" snapped Shade. "How many times do we have to go through that? But what was all that nonsense about Wild... Winnie and that Italian painter? Did you say she was crying over a picture? Crying?"

Her voice had the same intonation as that of someone who has just discovered that her neighbour eats live slugs for breakfast. Unwashed. With their fingers.

"Enough of that!" Shimmer's voice sliced across the room like an electrical discharge.

There was a most uncomfortable silence, during which I

marvelled yet again at the unnatural beauty of my visitors. Shimmer's eyes were sapphire coated with silver, her hair now still, each hair shining with the brilliance of stalactites caught in an impossible ray of sunshine, her face a combination of symmetries that man has only been able to dream of. Her beauty was so acute I felt it piercing me like the icicles her hair reminded me of. And Shade was almost a negative image of her, no less perfect. The black leopard to match Shimmer's pure white tiger. They were both too beautiful, too perfect.

Inhumanly beautiful. Inhumanly perfect.

I glanced at my watch. Just gone nine. Anderson had to be here soon.

My bladder passed on an apoplectic-verging-on-the-apocalyptic message.

"Look, I need to go to the bathroom agai–"

"No!" Shimmer.

"But…"

"No more wasting time!" Shade, after a final glower at her colleague. Then, to my surprise: "And don't you have anything to drink? A real drink? Like whisky?"

"Indeed yes, of course." And I nodded towards the drinks cupboard. I got up – slowly, so as not to upset either them or my bladder – and fetched a bottle of Laphroaig – the dire situation called for dire sacrifice – and three glasses (I could have done with more than a dram myself, but alcohol was a bloody diuretic, wasn't it?), which I placed on the coffee table in front of them.

Since none of them made any attempt to move, I then poured a heartbreakingly generous measure into each of the glasses, and made to pass the first glass to Shade, who was nearest to me.

Our fingers accidentally touched.

Might that not have been a magical moment, that explosive second of contact where two people who have believed themselves to be adversaries suddenly look full into each other's eyes, and understand that they have always been meant to be together?

Shade, however, recoiled like a cobra from a mongoose, a spasm of disgust passing over her perfect face.

No, I didn't hear wedding bells there!

Shimmer reached over for her drink, followed, a few moments

later, by Shalom. The latter had the same unreadable expression she'd had since the beginning.

Perhaps as compensation for Shade's brusque action, Shimmer, though now not wasting time on false smiles, said:

"Might I suggest that you have been overly modest, titling your account *Bertie's Finest Hours*? You seem to have been as much a protagonist as Bertie. While not implying that his innards didn't behave on the operating table with the heroism to be expected of the innards of such a man, it still remains true that it was your quick thinking in enlisting the services of the nurse that finally saved the day."

I looked at her gratefully.

"I'm glad someone appreciates that! Indeed, to tell you the truth, at first I was going to call my account *Time to the Power of N*, but everything changed, of course, with our last adventure, of which you must have heard. Bertie's fate then fully caught the public imagination, and a sort of retrospective glory was spread over all his previous exploits."

"Yes. Maybe we have been somewhat misled by our sources, many of which rely, of course, on those same contemporary accounts. It is becoming clear that Bertie owed much more to you than we thought."

I nodded, pleased. Obviously, I'd misjudged her.

"And, of course, none of his glory could have been achieved without the Time Machine. *Your* invention."

I nodded again, more doubtfully this time.

"We've all seen the schematics, of course, of your Time Machines, and yet even after so many thousands of years of having time travel, no one can fail to be utterly astonished at the sheer brilliance of the design, a conceptual leap that science had never seen the like of. Though you did say something rather strange," her voice was deceptively casual, "something about the original plans for the Time Machine: that if Chronotech had found them, they might have refused to try to rescue you."

I knew I'd been stupid to read out that particular sentence as soon as I was in the middle of it. But I just hadn't seen it coming. With three pairs of eyes examining me with more attention than Scrooge checking that Bob Cratchit hadn't been at the coal-box, I'd been too nervous to be able to glance ahead before reading.

"I only meant that I felt I couldn't trust the Company, so I'd kept back some of the theoretical information needed to construct the Machine. And some of the more vital components I constructed myself with the help of people I could trust outside the Company. If Chronotech had the whole design, I would no longer be indispensable to them."

This explanation was about as convincing as a scream in a vacuum, but Shimmer seemed to accept it.

"A wise decision, given the then revolutionary nature of your discovery. And yet, to me, the fact you then went on to design a Machine that went Forward instead of Back – a Machine that seemingly broke even the Laws that you yourself discovered – is an even greater achievement. We now use such Machines almost on a daily basis, of course, but I – and I know I speak for all my colleagues at the Records Department – even now cannot comprehend how you were able to make that further, impossible, conceptual leap."

Remember, you know nothing at all about the Forward Machine.

"If the first Backward Machine was an invention of genius," Shimmer went on, "how much more so was the Forward Machine! Whatever made you hit on such an incredible (for the time) idea?"

Squelch! I was right in it. The only consolation was that once again my bladder grew terrified and temporarily stopped nudging me.

Shalom was observing everything, but not with her usual impassivity. I noticed she had put her whisky down, and had moved to the edge of the sofa, poised like an arrow with the bow drawn back.

I had to say something.

" 'Forward Machine'? Are you saying that's how Bertie arrived in the future?"

For once, Shimmer was taken aback. "How else could he have got there?"

"Well, I thought maybe someone came Back from the future and took him there, Like we brought the Mona Lisa back to our time."

"But… it *must* have been you – Bertie said it was you."

Now I was surprised. Why ever would he have said that?

I needed time to think.

"Look," I said, "why don't I just read you our final adventure together – since after all it's Bertie you've come to learn about – and you may well find some of the answers there."

I knew damn well they wouldn't, and was even beginning to suspect they weren't particularly interested in our adventures! What they really wanted to know was something about the Time Machines, though I couldn't see why.

Shimmer and Shade exchanged glances, and after a few seconds Shimmer nodded, but with an expression on her face that indicated plainly that my time was running out.

As I opened the folder again, I wondered once again where the hell Anderson had got to.

And just who was that 'someone' that Maria had met? Was it possible she'd fallen into a trap? I didn't like to think of other possibilities.

Still, I reflected, if Anderson didn't arrive in time, and if things got really bad – as I was feeling more and more certain they would – well, I could probably save myself by sacrificing my prisoner in the attic.

I wondered what they would make of our old friend Leonardo da Vinci!

12: THE CRUCIFIXION CONSPIRACY

And there were also two other, malefactors, led with him to be put to death.

And when they were come to the place, which is called Calvary, there they crucified him, and the malefactors, one on the right hand, and the other on the left.

(St Luke)

Bertie Senior's new-found happiness didn't last very long. It wasn't his son's latest grisly death, which he took in his stride; it was something far closer to the bone. One night he discovered three of his new wives wantonly disporting themselves with dildos in one hand and copies of his bank balance in the other, and came to three reluctant conclusions: first, that he wasn't perhaps as great a lover as he had believed; second, that dildos were an international conspiracy against the male sex; and third, that the young women had only married him for his money. Luckily, they hadn't been Temple marriages (which are for eternity), so he soon got shot of them. Quite literally, according to some evil tongues.

This unfortunate experience naturally led him to question the validity of the Mormon faith. He had, he decided, been a bit hasty in converting so quickly. Not only had the standard of Bertie's mother's cooking gone down in vengeful proportion to the number of wives he took on, he had also recently felt a couple of sharp pains in his chest. They might have been the result of his renewed marital activity, but they might also, he feared, be a Sign, a warning swish of the Reaper's scythe. It was time to search again for a dromedary-friendly needle.

I had a horrible fear that he might send us to check up on the origins of other religions. I didn't fancy that one bit. Sweltering in the Arabian desert with Mohammed? Starving with Siddhartha Gautama? Discussing the prophetic secrets of pyramids with Charles Taze Russell (before the end of the world in 1915, obviously)? No, thank you!

But we were saved from that. He decided to stick with the religion he knew.

"We still don't know if there are aliens or not," he mused one afternoon, as we looked out over the city he virtually owned, "but

141

perhaps this isn't so important after all. There's an even greater question. Despite Moroni's trickery, we know there is a Creator, because Cain actually met him, and you said you might even have spotted him yourselves chasing Adam. But what about the story of Jesus? In particular, the Crucifixion and the Resurrection?"

I knew what he really meant: had Jesus truly sacrificed himself for *all* men, including filthy rich magnates like himself whose life had been as pure as snow driven through a chimney?

And I also guessed what this was leading to. I had a very bad feeling about it.

If, as I suspected, we were at least partly responsible for the very mysteries we were solving, might we not also somehow become responsible for the murder of the Son of God if we went to investigate it?

And if we did, there was Someone who might take it rather badly. The same Someone who, as far as I could see, had spent most of the Old Testament taking things rather badly. The Middle East still isn't very densely populated.

I put forward a host of irrefutable reasons why we shouldn't go to that particular place at that particular time. Bertie Senior listened with his usual attentiveness.

⊕

He didn't want to be accused of sending us back to film the Crucifixion just for the sake of sensationalism. The whole Programme, after all, was predicated on the idea of solving old mysteries. So, apart from finding out whether the Crucifixion ever really happened at all, we were told to try to solve the mystery of the two thieves.

St Luke says that one of the thieves crucified with Jesus believed in him, saying 'Lord, remember me when thou comest into thy kingdom.' And that Jesus answered: 'Today shalt thou be with me in Paradise.' Very heart-warming, and the kind of uplifting conversation that ought to grace all good crucifixions. But then both Mark and Matthew tell us that 'they that were crucified with him reviled him'. Not so nice at all: quite down putting, in fact.

So our first job was to see which of these two versions, if either, was correct.

Rather significant, I thought, that Bertie Senior should be so concerned over the fate of sinners.

Our second job, though, was the important one. Crucifixions were the in thing in those days, a way for the Romans to display their advanced civilisation to the surrounding barbarians. Six thousand followers of Spartacus had died in that manner along the Appian Way seventy years before as proof of Imperial enlightenment. So being crucified was nothing to write home about, even if your hands had been free to do so. Rising from the dead, though, was, even then, considered a pretty clever thing to do. If we could show that Jesus really did manage to pull off that little trick, then that would go a long way to proving that he was who he said he was. And as our technicians swore that they had now improved the TM enough for it to stay for up to five days in the past, we were confident we could come back with an answer.

"Oh, and if you can also film the Turin Shroud and the Oviedo Sudarium you might be in line for a bonus," added Bertie Senior, as he waved goodbye to us. I had no idea what the Oviedo Sudarium was, but it didn't sound very nice, so I mentally decided to forget that small task.

It was only as the Machine was about to take off that I had a disquieting thought: if Moroni was behind the Mormon religion, could he also have been behind other religions as well? Islam really didn't seem his style, not enough razzmatazz But the Jesus story itself? When I thought about it, I realised it could easily have come from Moroni's twisted imagination: spirits impregnating virgins; water being transformed into a popular alcoholic beverage; evil spirits hitching suicidal rides in pigs; a saviour getting bumped off by the very people he's come to save; a prophet who acts as if his willy is no more than an irrelevant accident. Yes, this absurd story certainly bore all Moroni's hallmarks.

No, it couldn't be. I shrugged off the thought. I was getting obsessed.

What we were NOT expected to do was solve the mystery of the Nazca Lines in Peru.

⊕

"So you think you're the first? Haven't you ever asked yourselves," said Jesus, "just why there was no room at the inn when I was born?"

He was in the courtyard of the Roman fort, and, far from being shackled, was wandering around among the soldiers.

We hadn't. "Filled with paparazzi trying to get an exclusive on the Three Kings?" Bertie suggested. "Brits chasing the winter sun?"

If this strikes you as a not wholly appropriate manner to address the Son of God, bear in mind we'd just had our Time Machine confiscated the second we materialised, and not only that, but when they'd seen it, the Time Police drafted in for the event had laughed their helmeted heads off, treating my great invention as a prehistoric relic!

"Dr Flintstone, I presume!" one of them had quipped.

Sassy bastards! OK, so they had foldaway models they could slip into their shirt pockets, but where would they have been without my prototype? "You're just pygmies standing on the shoulders of a giant!" I yelled (Jesus frowned), but they didn't understand: ah well, culture was already well on the way out when we left: *Hello Magazine* had become required tertiary education reading.

Perhaps it was a good thing they didn't understand. I recalled what their colleagues had said about being able to get round Temporal Paradoxes, and held my newly re-implanted tongue.

As for Bertie, after his recent experiences there was very little that could faze him.

Jesus almost came up to my left armpit, bearing an uncanny resemblance to Engelbrecht the Surrealist Sportsman immortalised by Richardson and Hughes. You can see why we were initially a bit doubtful about his claims. I personally believe that his small stature may well explain the mystery of Why the Stone was Moved, but we'll get back to that.

Jesus didn't seem to notice Bertie's tone, anyway. "Time Travellers, that's why! Hundreds of 'em! Supposed to have come to honour me, and then hog all the accommodation, leaving me and the Womb in a stinking manger!"

It struck me as a bit odd that he should refer to his mother as 'the Womb', but I suppose he might have picked up that way of thinking from the Holy Ghost. Some wasps, so I've read, have a similar habit of laying eggs in other creatures. And no one says how wonderful that is, or starts a cult to the Virgin Hymenoptera!

You think you got a big audience for your birth? I thought to myself. Just wait and see the full house when you snuff it! OK, as it happened, that's exactly what he was doing, but I wasn't to know that then.

I must admit that I felt no more friendly towards the other Travellers than he did. Until now, I'd assumed that we were the world's only Time Travellers – apart from the Time Police, and, perhaps, Moroni – and when we get here, the place is packed out with them! All from our own future, of course. The ungrateful bastards could at least have stopped off en route, and shown their gratitude by leaving me a few bottles of far-future whisky.

Unlike Moroni, none of them seemed to pay any particular attention to Bertie. A few of them had vaguely heard of us – all right, of him! – but that was all. I began to wonder whether I'd been wrong in assuming Moroni to be from our future.

At that moment, a Roman soldier passed by, and for no reason at all, gave Jesus an almighty shove. Incensed, Bertie sprang forward, and knocked him to the ground. I expected him to be beaten to death by the other soldiers lounging by, but they just laughed, and one of them even offered him a cigarette.

A cigarette?

"You're coming on well," said Jesus, as he got up and dusted off some dried sheep dung and nodded approvingly at the man who'd just pushed him, "but you forgot to sneer and spit in my face." He turned to us. "A few have got into the spirit of the thing, as you see, but some of them are such poor actors, it'll look more like a medieval miracle play than a crucifixion! And there still aren't anywhere near enough soldiers. I don't suppose you'd mind slipping on skirts and helmets, and looking pitiless and aquiline for a bit?"

"You mean, these soldiers aren't real? I mean, real soldiers?"

"Good Lord no, all the original soldiers got murdered by a Christian fundamentalist Traveller who came into the past to Save me. Before I could explain that I didn't want Saving, she'd zapped the lot with some sort of Death Ray. Typical female emotional overreaction! Nearly ruined everything. The Time Police frisk the lot the second they arrive now, of course."

As we knew to our embarrassment. When we'd stepped out of the TM in the early Friday dawn, two Teepees, dressed just like the ones who had brought us back from St Petersburg, in black uniforms (why

145

do these types never wear pink or turquoise?), had stopped us.

"Spoilsport or Pervert?" they asked.

"I don't understand," I said with as much dignity as is possible when one is being lifted, turned upside down, shaken, and frisked. They confiscated my pork scratchings.

"Most people who Travel here either want to stop the Crucifixion – without much success, as you must already know – or indulge in a bit of the old *schadenfreude*."

The frisking suddenly became extremely – one could say *too* – thorough. "What's this?" one of them sniffed suspiciously. "Why's it hidden there?"

"It isn't hidden," I said, squirming, "it's… it's for my haemorrhoids."

That wasn't exactly true, but I didn't feel like explaining that the surgeons had misplaced a couple of minor items when they were trying to put us back together after Roswell.

I thrust away the bowel-wrenching memory. Jesus went on:

"Trouble is, word's got round that I spell trouble, and even the locals are keeping low-key now. Haven't seen a Scribe or Pharisee for days! Pilate's also been giving me a bit of a headache, tried to resign twice yesterday. Worried about his reputation. I've had to promise him a place on God's right hand side in Heaven (luckily, he never thought to ask me just how far from his right hand side). Why, even the unclean spirits have made themselves scarce!"

I was beginning to think that this chap wanted to get himself crucified.

"I'm beginning to think you want to get yourself crucified," I said. I usually like to say what I think, though I frequently have to make an exception with Bertie's father, of course. And, these days, sometimes, with Winnie, too.

"What else do you suggest? I have to do something. Father's obviously never going to shuffle off his immortal coil. Still fit as a bloody fiddle. A million press-ups – at his age! – and he doesn't even break sweat! I'm heir to a throne I can never inherit. Unless I seize it by force."

This I could understand. The same thing had recently happened in England, when Prince Charles, just before his fifty-eighth birthday, had finally lost patience and, after confiscating all her dogs and hats, had the Queen locked up in the Tower. Her presence there greatly increased the revenues from tourism.

However, I couldn't see how being crucified would help Jesus, unless he intended to take the nails with him and hammer them through God's unsuspecting head.

"My crucifixion will be a great PR job. Future ages will worship me, not Father."

I'm a real softie, as you know. Look how I'd forgiven Mabel for abandoning me in the Land of Nod! I didn't want him crucifying himself for nothing, so I pointed out that God, in fact, was still worshipped – in my time at least – despite nagging doubts as to why he'd had to use the Holy Ghost instead of pleasuring Mary himself.

Jesus smiled. "Ah, but that's just the first couple of millennia. People will finally come to realise that sending me down to be crucified to save the world, instead of having the guts to do it himself, was morally reprehensible. Only slightly less savage than Saturn eating his children, really. Hardly paternal. There'll be a hate campaign on something called the Internet. By the third millennium, so the Time Police have told me, Christians will worship me alone, with Father seen as a servant of the Devil."

I was a bit suspicious about what the Teepees might have told Jesus about the future state of Christianity. They must have realised that, just in order for them to exist, the Crucifixion, and everything that followed from the spread of Christianity, had to go ahead. In such a situation, they would not hesitate to tell little white lies to make sure the Crucifixion did go ahead. Indeed, I was later to find out that their pressure went beyond this. As for what they had done to the woman who had killed the original Roman soldiers, I dreaded to think.

And look what the bastards tried to do to us afterwards!

"But how will this help you get the throne?" I asked.

"When the angels find out that Father has just let me die, without lifting a blessed Finger to save me, I'm pretty sure they'll back me in a coup."

"Will you win?"

"I'm not a fortune-teller! But yes, I think I will. You see, God is only as powerful as the number of people who believe in him and worship him. And whatever happens, I'll be treated with a bit more respect, that's for sure!"

At this point he was felled by another ersatz Roman soldier hoping to make a good impression on him. This one remembered to spit. Wiping the spittle from his face, Jesus looked up, thanked him, and said with a rather cocky expression: "Oh, by the way, I intend to rise from the dead, wander around a bit before Ascending. Might take a stroll to Emmaus, always wanted to go there. Don't you think that's a rather super idea?"

I forbore to answer. I was pretty sure the Teepees had given him that idea, too.

(Judas later told us that Jesus was already dying from some horrible disease, picked up from all that laying on of hands and raising dead bodies without washing the divine digits after, and so he was simply trying to make the best of a bad job: better to go out with the glory of a Crucifixion than an ignoble wasting away. Maybe so. But Judas didn't strike me as a particularly honest fellow. Come on, thirty pieces of silver just for pointing out the shortest chap in Jerusalem! Daylight robbery!)

I still wonder which came first in this ridiculous loop. Jesus had decided to get himself crucified because the Teepees (and other Time Travellers, no doubt) had told him that in the future he would be worshipped because of this act. But presumably they (like me) only got the story from the Gospels because it had already happened. But it only happened because Jesus had been told it was going to happen. Unless, of course, the Gospel writers had made the whole thing up, which meant that Jesus was about to do something which had never happened in the first place. In which case, he would be altering history, after all. But then the Teepees wouldn't have allowed that to happen. But then they themselves would be the product of an alternate history.

Another of those endless circles. At least, all that had nothing to do with us. My earlier fears dissipated.

I scratched my head and dragged Bertie off for an early breakfast. Nothing but bloody unleavened bread: I'd forgotten it was still the Passover period.

I knew Jesus wasn't due to be crucified until the third hour, which for some reason I never understood actually meant nine in the morning, so we struck up a conversation with another Traveller from the twenty-second century who was also being roped in as a substitute

Roman, and who had arrived a few weeks before us. An ornithologist, apparently, who'd spent his whole life studying hummingbirds. He revealed that the Gospel writers had indeed been a bit creative with the truth. The five loaves and two fishes, for example: in actual fact, that's what had been left *after* the Sermon. It also transpired that the unclean spirits who drowned with the Gadarene swine were really a largish group of smallish Ayon pygmies, Travellers from Papua New Guinea, who had roused Jesus' ire by a spirited defence of animism and an equally gutsy apologia for cannibalism. He chased them through the streets. A moneylender, still smarting from an earlier outburst of the prophetic wrath, told them how Ulysses had escaped the Cyclops Polythemus by clinging to the underside of the giant's sheep, and persuaded the Papuan pygmies to do the same with the crazed pigs. No one, however, had mentioned the cliffs. It also seemed that Lazarus, although he *had* been raised from the dead, had tottered around in circles for a few seconds, groaned, said "Christ, I feel like death warmed up!", picked his nose, and then keeled over again, as dead as a Monty Python parrot. Elisha had done a much better job.

Now, of course, all this wasn't to say that Jesus wasn't really the Son of God, simply that things weren't as cut and dried as some would have us believe.

Anyway, we agreed to go along with his plans, and got our Roman uniforms. Bertie looked rather sweet; his Regenerated legs were surprisingly shapely. There were about a hundred of us in on the act. The other Travellers knew nothing – their function was to return to their own times, and confirm the historical reality of the Crucifixion. I must admit we felt a bit superior with our nice uniforms and our little secret. If only we'd known!

Well, I guess you all know the story, so I won't repeat it, just clear up a couple of errors.

Judas, for example. We'd grown kind of fond of Jeez, eccentric or not, so we strung Judas up, made it look like a suicide, and used the pieces of silver to pay for snacks during the Crucifixion. That was the technicality the Teepees later used against us. (Yes, I know all about that story in Acts that, 'falling headlong, he burst asunder in the midst, and all his bowels gushed out', but that was just a bit of exaggeration by Peter, hoping to distract people from the three cock crows.)

The thunder and earthquake, of course, was just future technology, as was the Star of Bethlehem, which I was told normally crowned the Dome of the future World Stock Exchange.

But I do want to tell you about Bertie. I owe it to him. I know I may sometimes have spoken of him with a certain asperity, but when it really mattered, he came up trumps. British pluck at its best.

It will also help to clear up some apparent contradictions in the Gospels.

First, though, I have to refute those who accuse Jesus of being a cry-baby for shouting out on the Cross, "My God, my God, why hast Thou forsaken me?". Let me tell you that he displayed amazing fortitude throughout the whole proceedings, and that when he uttered those words, he winked at Bertie and whispered, "That'll turn 'em against him!" He was a credit to all people of unostentatious stature.

Ah, you say, and how come Bertie was so close, how come no one else saw the wink? Yes, well, those contradictions I mentioned…

You see, one of the thieves, cottoning on to the fact that the Roman soldiers weren't soldiers at all, and feeling insulted at the prospect of being crucified by blackleg civilians, did a bunk half an hour before the Crucifixion was scheduled! No sense of history, of occasion.

"I've got to have two thieves!" yelled Jesus, who by this time was, not unnaturally – he'd been up all night – showing signs of tension. "Symmetry!"

Symmetry my foot! It was those Teepees putting pressure on him again. Well, they stepped in, made us draw lots, and poor Bertie drew the short straw. I'd like to think that this was an entirely aleatory event, even if the same unfortunate appearance that had secured us instant access to Leonardo's studio probably influenced the distribution of the straws. And yet I now suspect there was something almost pre-ordained about his choice. As if all his other trials had been somehow leading up to this final apotheosis.

I could, I suppose, have tried to summon the SMM to get us out of there fast, but I realised that if I succeeded (unlikely, with the Teepees guarding the TM), I would in fact be changing the past. Jesus had died with thieves on either side of him. The Travelling zapper had created another hole in the past, and Bertie's destiny was to fill it in.

Bertie himself seemed a bit doubtful about the honour.

"Fuckit, fuckit, fuckit!" said he.

For a moment, I thought he was conjugating a long-forgotten Latin verb, but then realised it was a heartfelt, if rather selfish, complaint against his destiny.

But Jesus whispered, "Don't worry, I'll see you're all right!" After that, I didn't feel so bad about it, and indeed was rather hurt by the mute reproach in Bertie's eye.

We bade tearful goodbyes, and up went Bertie with a martyred expression.

"Lord, remember me when thou comest into thy kingdom," he said, remembering to keep to their funny way of speaking, and Jesus swore he would, and that they'd share a bottle or two that very night in Paradise. But then he realised they could be heard, and he whispered to Bertie, "You're better start reviling me, quick, or they'll get suspicious", so Bertie dutifully weighed in with some really vile insults, to which the other thief added heartfelt refrains.

But I noticed one Jew, who gave me the impression of being a doctor, scratching his head in surprise. He'd been even nearer than me to the cross, and must have heard the earlier part of the conversation. I guess the other gospel writers later dismissed his astonishing testimony, but St Luke chose to believe a fellow physician, and included a (doctored) version in his gospel.

Jesus got a bit more than he bargained for, poor chap. He was all hyped up to take his Crucifixion like a Man, and even used his knowledge of carpentry to coolly criticise the shoddy construction of his cross and the poor quality of the nails, but he hadn't counted on the three crosses being so near to each other. That, I'm sure, is why he, supposedly a god – or, at this stage, a demigod – died before the other two, who were mere mortals. If you were on a cross next to Bertie, and if you happened to be so short that your head was not far above Bertie's lower regions, wouldn't you too yield up the ghost as soon as possible? And divine nostrils are well known to be particularly delicate.

It also explained why the group of mourning women were keeping their distance and 'beholding afar off', as the Gospels so tactfully put it. I asked someone which one was Mary Magdalene, wondering whether she'd be up for a quick drink afterwards.

Still, despite Bertie, Jesus managed to hang on for six hours up there, including three hours in almost complete darkness (something arranged by the Teepees for effect), and it wasn't till the middle of the afternoon that he finally died.

At this point, I noticed two rather badly-dressed Sadducees get up and walk away, chuckling and eating bananas. I overheard one of them say: "So much for empty threats! Didn't have to wait long, did we?" It was impossible, of course, but I thought I recognised them.

The Teepees were ready, and the veil of the temple was rent in twain, the earth did quake, the rocks rent, and the ersatz soldiers went off to their nearby encampment for a celebratory drink, and, as they believed, to receive their Crucifixion Medals, before returning to their own epochs. My humming bird enthusiast invited me to join them. I gratefully accepted the offer, and had started to follow them when he said:

"I meant, well, of course you'll want to stay with your friend till… well, you know. We'll keep some drink back for you."

"Thank you," I said, my thirsty leg caught embarrassingly mid-air, "of course I couldn't leave while… See you later."

To pass the time – why did Bertie always have to do everything so *slowly*? – I secretly filmed Jesus being taken from the cross. Mary Magdalene had now approached, but not the other women. Was this a sign of interest in me? I do have a rather imposing figure, a noticeable air of rugged nobility, I can't deny it.

"Hssstt!" said Bertie, trying to catch my attention.

I moved closer, carving 'Maria loves N madly and rightly so' on the True Cross in order to disguise my real intention. "What?" I whispered.

"Jesus is dead now, isn't he? Can't you get me down now? This is bloody painful!"

I thought rather resentfully that it hadn't been that comfortable for me either, six hours on my feet like that! But before I could do anything, Mary Magdalene stopped her silent weeping, looked across at me and hissed:

"Oh no, you don't! You two have caused enough trouble. We're not having any more hitches. Shove off!"

As she spoke, her hood slipped back for a moment. I was only able to see her head for a second, but that was enough – Mary Magdalene was a Teepee!

I mouthed "Sorry" to Bertie, and went off to think about things.

Cross or no Cross, you don't cross someone as cross as her!

After pondering deeply, I decided I would, after all, join the other 'soldiers'.

Now there has been a lot of misunderstanding and quite unnecessary ill-feeling about this. I've been accused, not only of allowing Bertie to be crucified, but also of going for a booze-up while he was still hanging on the cross.

That has to be seen in the context of the following problem:

Our original brief had been to stay and film the Moving of the Stone as well, but Bertie's crucifixion had put that idea in jeopardy. It was impossible for me to save him, and I couldn't keep his corpse here for three days, because it might begin to decompose, and make it impossible to Regenerate him this time. The medics had been tetchy enough after the last Trip.

On the other hand, if we Travelled back now, it would leave the job half done. Jesus' dying was no proof that he was really a god. A lot of quite ordinary people have chosen that way to leave the world throughout history. The locals Jews, in fact, perversely took it as an obvious proof that he wasn't a god. The real test would be whether he would rise in three days or not.

Though the Teepees had assured him that this would indeed be the case, even Jesus himself wasn't a hundred per cent sure that he could manage that nifty little number. Towards the end, it had finally clicked as to why the Teepees were so desperate to help him. "If my body doesn't rise from the dead, history will be changed, and you lot are well and verily buggered," he said bluntly, "so you'd better make sure that if I don't manage it by myself, my body isn't there when they move the Stone."

I don't wish to sound unchristian, but perhaps Jesus was so insistent on this point because he didn't want future ages to find his bones, and learn how short he really was. People have certain minimum requirements of their gods. Religious discrimination of the lowest sort, but there you are.

In short, if I didn't leave Jerusalem quickly with Bertie (or Bertie's body) it might rot beyond Regeneration; but if I did leave, I would have no way of knowing whether Jesus really did rise from the dead or whether the Teepees moved his body for him. In other words, our mission would have failed completely.

But then I had an idea!!

It was such a good idea that I make no apology for having given it a paragraph by itself and two exclamation marks.

It concerned the little get-together that the hummingbird enthusiast had invited me to.

Those 'soldiers' all came from well into the future. So they would almost certainly have advanced medicines as well as advanced machines. Because, however advanced those Machines, there must always exist the risk of an accident, of being trapped in the past. Therefore, wouldn't it be logical for them to have anti-decomposition tablets, sachets of formaldehyde or something, to preserve them until they could be rescued? And if so, and if I could procure some, then I might be able to keep Bertie in good condition, and so be able to stay here the planned three days, and complete the mission.

I was almost feeling optimistic as I strolled towards the camp.

Because of the whistling, I didn't become aware of the unusual silence until I arrived there. The trestle tables, plastic mugs, and empty crisp packets were still there. The Travellers weren't. The encampment was deserted.

But not completely. There was one person still there.

A Teepee!

"Ah, I was waiting for you!" he said.

Funny how a far-future weapon looks so similar to our own. Though the one now pointing at me was probably capable of sprinkling bits of me in the asteroid belt.

"Can't leave witnesses," he said.

My first thought was that this sounded ominous; my second, that it sounded really ominous. I was beginning to piece things together. Jesus had said that some well-intentioned Time Traveller had massacred all the original Roman soldiers. So the Teepees had 'bussed' in a hundred new 'soldiers' so that he could go ahead with his highly eccentric plan to seize ultimate power. They clearly hadn't been expecting Bertie and myself, but a couple more soldiers made no difference.

But a hundred people who knew what had really happened couldn't be allowed to return to their own time to reveal that knowledge. Because then Christianity, at least in its traditional form, would be recognised as a put-up job, and that too would inevitably alter history.

I reacted to this slight contretemps in my usual way: I fell to my knees, and pleaded for mercy. My detractors have chosen to regard this as an act of cowardice. Nonsense: history teaches us that if you fall to your knees and plead for mercy, you sometimes *receive* mercy, which may give you a chance later on to skewer the balls of the bastard who made you plead for mercy in the first place.

OK, the blubbering might have been a bit over the top, but, come on, we all have our little idiosyncrasies!

"Oh stop that idiosyncratic blubbering, I'm not here to kill you," said the Teepee, his voice hinting a contempt which showed clearly that the obtuse fool was unaware of the deep cunning of my strategy.

"So why are you pointing that thing at me?"

"Because it makes people blubber, and that's one of the perks that make up for my low salary and this ridiculously tight and cod-sinister-looking uniform."

"Oh, I see." I stopped blubbering. "So what did you mean about 'can't leave witnesses'?"

"Actually, I phrased it rather badly. In fact, that's exactly what they are going to do: leave the witnesses. Here, in the past, in order not to have witnesses anytime else. Well, not exactly here, of course, but somewhere else, where they'll never be found."

"Why do you say 'they'? You're a Teep... from the Time Police, aren't you?"

"Well, in a manner of speaking. By 'Time Police', I suppose you mean the people who confiscated your Time Machine this morning?"

"Of course."

"Yes, they are Time Police. But what makes you think there are Time Police from only one era?"

I had to think a few seconds.

"Of course! Each generation, there'll be new Teepees! They'll evolve, just as our police did from the Bow Street Runners!"

I began to feel a great relief.

"So you come from a different time from the Teepees who frisked us?"

"That's right."

"But your uniform..."

"...is exactly the same. Just because I'm wearing it doesn't mean it's necessarily mine. Couldn't it have belonged to someone else?"

I glanced at his weapon. "You mean…?"

"I do, indeed."

"So why are you here?" I asked.

"I've been sent to help you."

"Sent?" My mind immediately leapt to Moroni. "Who sent you?"

"That doesn't matter. The important thing is that you and Bertie return to your own time with your Time Machine!"

Of course! My TM was the prototype. If it got stuck here in first-century Palestine, the later more advanced Time Machines might never get built.

But the Teepees – the other ones – must also have known this. I said as much to my new ally.

"Of course they know that! They fully intend to return your *Time Machine* to when it belongs. But without you and Bertie. They believe other machines will be constructed anyway, whether you are there or not, because the engineers will still have your plans."

I didn't point out that I had never let them see the original plans,

"But they still risk changing their own past! What have they got against us? Why, they even rescued us in St Petersburg after the Rasputin affair!"

"Maybe so. All I know is that this time they were ordered by someone from their future to stop you and Bertie returning, and that I was ordered by someone else even further in the future to stop them from stopping you and Bertie returning. For all I know, there may be other Time Police from still further in the future being told right now to stop me from stopping them from stopping you! So I suggest we get a move on!"

Just then, a strange tube-like object materialised beside us. Three Teepees – at least, I assumed they were Teepees – leapt out, with weapons already trained on us. Before anyone could fire, however, a net snaked down from above, enveloped the three, and swept them wriggling up into the sky, where they promptly disappeared.

"You see?" said my Teepee, lowering his weapon. "They'd been sent to stop me, and someone else was sent to stop them. You can't imagine the stress in this job! We get a special bonus called the Philip K Dick Paranoia Dividend. There could be a thousand different factions playing leapfrog along the time waves, each one trying to stop the other from making illegal changes. Most unauthorised changes do get Rectified sooner or later, because the further you go along the Line, the more potent the Time Custodians are, until you reach the Ultimate ones, but sometimes there are annoying delays. Once someone buggered around so much with the past – my past, your future – I found I was a women's hairdresser with a lisp – a hairdresser, the indignity! – for three months until things were put right again. Another time I woke up in the morning and found my wife had three-foot-long pubic hair! It's OK for everyone else: things change overnight, but since they change too, they are quite unaware of this. So if a woman suddenly sports three-foot-long pubic hair, they believe it has always been this way. But we have trans-temporal chips implanted which enable us to remember how things really were. We wouldn't be very efficient otherwise."

He shook his head sadly.

"And just when I'd got used to the Tuft of Venus, in fact found that I couldn't really get turned on without it, some officious Custodian Rectified it!"

I wasn't interested in these follicular follies.

"So what do I do now? Bertie's still hanging around on the cross."

"I know. They're just waiting for you to take his body back to your Time Machine, where they'll capture you, put you with the others, and take you where no one will ever find you."

"But how did you know I'd leave Bertie on the cross and come here?"

"It was a fair guess. We do study the people we get involved with, whether it's to save them or to kill them. We call it Profiling."

I decided this wasn't a good time to be offended.

"So what do I do now?" I repeated.

"Can you control your Time Machine from a distance?"

"Not the Machine itself. Only the Spatial Mobility Module."

"That will do. Bring it here. They won't try to stop that. They'll be waiting in or around the Time Machine for you to arrive there with Bertie's body."

"And then what?"

"I come with you, and fry all the guards." He looked lovingly at his weapon.

"Do you enjoy your work?"

"This aspect of it, yes."

I wasn't happy at the thought of all this cop killing. After all, they

157

had saved us in St Petersburg. He understood my expression.

"They'll only be dead for a time, of course. They'll be Snatched back into their own time, Resurrected, and given a day's extra holiday as compensation for their death. Or maybe a month's hard labour for cocking up!"

"There are Teepees at the Cross too," I informed him.

"Hmm, they *are* being careful! This Bertie appears to be more important than I thought."

I flushed.

"They're after me too," I said rather haughtily.

"Yes, it seems that you play some small part too."

"Some small part!"

"Teepees at the Cross, too, eh? Let me guess... one'll be Mary Magdalene, I bet, that's their style, another... yes, another, I wouldn't mind betting, could be the other thief, as backup..."

I hadn't thought of that!

"But how do...?"

"The police mindset, the mindset. Well, no matter. We'll have the element of surprise. Summon the Mobility Module now, time's running out."

I did so, and then cowered down behind a rock

"There may be Teepees in it. I don't want to get in your way, under your feet," I explained.

But the Module arrived safely, and empty.

"Come on, get in!" ordered my protector. "We have to move quickly now."

I allowed myself to be thrust into the SMM.

"Golgotha ho!" he yelled.

We arrived in almost no time, and he blasted Mary Magdalene before she had time to even lift her hood or utter a 'hail Mary'. He'd been wrong about the other thief, who was hanging there quite dead (unless there'd been a double-cross on the cross), but he blasted him too, just to be sure.

"Bloody hell!" said Bertie.

He wasn't dead yet! Stubborn little bugger!

"Get him down! We've got about five minutes before the Teepees realise something is wrong."

Just when you need a claw hammer you can't find one! I yanked and tugged, but couldn't get Bertie's nails to move a micron. I really didn't see why Jesus had complained about their quality. I recalled Longfellow's poem about the crossbill which had also tried to pull the nails from the Cross with its bill, getting it rather twisted in the process. And, yes, you guessed it, it also failed.

"Come on," yelled my protector, "if we take too long, they'll send a force to investigate!" I had no choice. The cross itself was too big to fit into the SMM. It was a Mohammed-Mountain situation: if I couldn't pull the nails out of Bertie, I'd have to pull Bertie out of the nails.

Have you ever tried to remove upholstering from an Edwardian chair? Where bits of fabric are always left like untidy halos round the tacks? Well, the same thing happened with Bertie, though the left hand did come off quite easily for some reason.

Bertie screamed and swore at me something rotten. I forgave him, he'd had a rough day.

I got most of him off the cross, and into the SMM, then off we went at the same breakneck speed towards the Teepee control point where we'd been searched earlier. I spotted my Time Machine in a compound. Surrounded, as my new ally had surmised, by half a dozen unprepared guards.

I docked and, at a signal from him, opened the airlock into the TM. He plunged through, mowed down two Teepees who were in the way, then burst through the main hatchway into the compound, blasting away joyfully.

But one of the Teepees inside the TM wasn't dead, and I spotted him raising a weapon in my direction. Acutely conscious that it was of paramount importance that I survive in order to get Bertie safely back to our own time, I put aside my natural warrior's instinct, and selflessly used his body to shield myself. I congratulated myself on the wisdom of my decision as I felt at least three bullets thud into him. I knew he would thank me when he realised why I had done it.

"Right then, that's it, mission completed!" said our ally, appearing at the entrance again. He noticed the surviving Teepee. "Tut tut!" He finished him off, sheathed his weapon, leapt in, and dragged the two bodies outside where he piled them on top of the others.

"It's been an honour to serve Bertie – and yourself, of course. And I get a bonus! Have a safe journey."

He slipped his hand inside his uniform – and disappeared. Another miniaturised Time Machine, I supposed.

I looked briefly at the carnage outside– however could Bertie be so important? – and set course for home.

Bertie didn't speak: the bullets had finally killed him.

⊕

Well, I was faced with the usual incomprehension and ingratitude when we got back. Bertie once again got all the credit, although all he'd done was dangle indecorously from a cross for a few hours, and receive a few bullet wounds, while I'd had to make all the difficult decisions.

After again showing his displeasure, which necessitated my immediate hospitalisation, Bertie's dad made me alter a few details. In the public version, for instance, Bertie insisted on sharing a cross with Jesus, and also told him a few jokes towards the end to cheer him up. Almost at once a cult sprang into existence hailing him as the new Messiah, with myself cast in the role of Judas.

Compared to his treatment at Roswell, Calgary had been a doddle for Bertie, although he himself didn't see it that way. Broken legs, bit of internal stretching and a few holes – our medical team, now with great experience and always prepared for the worst, had him up and moving in no time.

I spent a long time wondering what happened to the other 'soldiers'. And the thief who'd done a bunk. Had the Teepees murdered them? And then, one day, I was sitting with Maria watching a programme on Nazca in Peru, and marvelling at the long parallel lines and the enormous drawings created there in the red desert rock around two thousand years ago. In total, they cover an area of two hundred square miles, and the designs are so big that they can only be appreciated from the air.

Including an enormous hummingbird!

So that's where they took them! Those Teepees made damn sure they couldn't return to their own times to reveal what really happened in Jerusalem. No doubt they destroyed everything the Travellers tried to build, any messages they tried to leave. But they had forgotten the obvious. The mindset, the mindset…

Their landing strips still stretch into the distance, a constant reminder – to me at least – of how close these chronicles came to never being written.

As for Jesus, I guess I'll never know for sure what really happened. Maybe he really did do it by himself (after all, he only just failed with Lazarus) or maybe the Teepees shifted the body, to leave the tomb empty.

But last night I had a dream in which he appeared and said, "This is an oneiric circular. Thanks a million, you lot. It did the trick." Behind him, an enormous caged and fettered figure with a very loud voice – I'd say a voice of thunder if I didn't think you'd accuse me of exaggerating – was threatening all kinds of things, from plagues and boils to floods and meteor impacts.

I woke up, feeling rather pleased that Jesus really was the Son of God and not just one of thousands of madmen who have claimed to be divine throughout history.

Then I remembered Joseph Smith's visions, and once again was filled with doubt. Could Moroni be playing with me as he had played with the Mormon Prophet? Neither Bertie nor I ever heard or saw anything that actually proved that Jesus was a god.

And with beings like Moroni and, it appeared, even more menacing characters hanging around in the far future, and way too interested in Bertie and myself, it no longer made any sense to accept Pascal's famous wager.

13: THE LADIES SHOW THEIR HANDS

I closed the folder and waited for their reaction, trying to ignore the insistent accordion movements of my bladder.

If my voice had begun to tremble a bit by the time I finished, it was not so much my memory of Bertie's gallant sacrifice as the fact that, to my nervous imagination, Shade had taken on even more the appearance of a shark, one, moreover, about to indulge in a feeding frenzy. I found I had been unconsciously squirming back in my chair and that my shoulder blades had already cut through the fabric to graze the wall behind.

"And that's it? Nothing else?" Shimmer sounded incredulous.

"That's it, that was our last adventure."

"I told you the Mary Magdalene idea was too obvious," Shade hissed.

"We didn't expect it to work," retorted Shimmer, "and it served to remind us just how powerful are enemies are!"

She turned back to me, and gave a long blonde sigh, as if pretending that I wouldn't have heard those comments.

"So the story we heard – that Bertie first tried to bribe Judas to point him out to the authorities as Jesus, and when this didn't work, due apparently to a noticeable difference in height, he insisted on keeping Jesus company on the Cross to give him moral strength, and to tell him some Jewish jokes so that he could at least die laughing – that story wasn't quite true then."

"Um, no."

"Well, this has all been very enlightening, and we must remember to alter the records accordingly. But you haven't told us how or why Bertie then came to the future. Or why you didn't accompany him."

"No," I said, "I didn't write anything about that because obviously until you came, I had no idea Bertie had gone to the future. He simply disappeared."

I saw a streak of black lightning, and simultaneously felt myself being hauled into the air and being shaken upside down. I heard the swishing of liquids inside my body as my bladder tried to turn the tables on my kidneys. Surely the coffee I'd taken after my Bristol speech should have evaporated in my fearful sweating by now. The room looked quite different from that angle. I noticed dust on top of the doorframe: so difficult to get reliable servants.

The other two Visitors hurled themselves at Shade, and managed to break her grip on me. I landed in the old-fashioned fireplace.

By the time I had picked myself up, the three were sitting quietly on the sofa again. Shimmer was tenderly stroking Shade's hair and calming her down.

"You shouldn't have lied," she said. "My colleague can't stand lies."

"I didn't lie!" I lied.

"So you say Bertie just disappeared? And you had no idea where?"

"That's right."

(Convulsive movement from Shade.)

"Um, you won't believe this, but I must go to the bathroom again," I added.

(Convulsive movement from Shade.)

"I don't know how long we can restrain our sensitive colleague if you go on like this. You are trying to tell us that you didn't notice that the Forward Machine was gone?"

I made one last feeble attempt.

"What Forward Machine? What are you talking about?"

(Convulsive movement from Shade.)

"I'm going to count to two and then allow my simmering colleague to boil over," said Shimmer, with a charming smile that was hovering around the minus 273.15 degrees Celsius mark.

Only to two? Well, perhaps the pace of life was a bit faster in the future.

"All right, all right! Bertie disappeared in the Forward Machine or whatever it is you bloody well call it!"

The sigh that came from Shimmer and Shade must have been very similar to that emitted from the judges of the Inquisition when the accused finally confessed to heresy, and they could now cease the unpleasant duty of ripping out their entrails and reward them with a good cathartic roasting in the auto-da-fé. But, to my consternation, whereas Shimmer and Shade noticeably relaxed, Shalom became more tense, and I had the sudden certainty that the most immediate threat to my continued existence came from her more than from the other two.

STEVE REDWOOD

Women! No way to please them!

"Thank you, N," said Shimmer. "We already assumed this, of course, but, as historians, we prefer to go to primary sources. Now all we need from you are the plans for that Machine, and then I think we can leave you to enjoy a tall tea and Coronation Farm. We are greatly indebted to you for the information, some of it quite startling, that you have given us."

I looked at them, and they looked at me. Despite the exaggerated politeness of the words, there was now no mistaking the menace in her voice. But neither was there any mistaking the menace in Shalom's poise: she was like a bullet in a rifle just after the trigger has been pulled.

"But why do you need the plans?" I asked. "You said earlier you've got plenty of Forward Machines now."

"The plans! Now!"

Oh shit!

"I haven't got them."

"Fetch them!"

"I mean, I haven't got the plans. At all. I never did have them."

The imaginary bullet that was Shalom seemed to pause mid-air.

Shimmer shook her head sadly. She seemed genuinely distressed, like someone taking a pet to the vet's to be put down.

"N, the game is finished. We tried, very hard, to do this the nice way. We gave you every chance to give us the information voluntarily. So let me make our position clear. In our time we are facing a revolution which we could easily have crushed except for one thing: the enemy has the advantage of the Forward Machine, the one that we have long suspected Bertie arrived in. In other words, *your* Forward Machine. They can go into the future, bring back super-advanced weapons to use against us, 'anticipate' many of our moves, and, of course, lay traps for us wherever they like. Because of you, many of our best people have died. Yet we are tolerant people. My colleague Shade Gentleheart, for instance, would not normally crush a fly if she could avoid it. We understand that it wasn't your intention to cause us so much trouble. So we will not kill you if you give us the information to enable us to construct another Forward Machine, so that we can crush our enemies."

"We'll do more than just crush that Bertie!" snarled Shade.

164

Shimmer threw her a warning glance, then shrugged.

"I suppose you've already guessed, anyway. That's probably why you omitted details about the Time Machines in your account, and why you now deny having the plans. Trying to protect Bertie. A noble sentiment, but… The reason we told you he was dead was precisely to try to avoid unpleasantness and misplaced loyalty on your part" (her voice oozed hurt regret), "but do you really want to sacrifice yourself for him? From everything you've said, you weren't exactly the best of friends, and you yourself have claimed that the legend of the inseparable time travellers is a lot of nonsense."

Bertie was alive!

Things were beginning to come together. Far from admiring Bertie, these women hated him. Somewhere in the far distant future he had well and truly put his foot in a certain viscous substance that possibly smelt even worse than he did, and earned their enmity. But for some reason also – to do with the Forward Machine, apparently – in that future he was untouchable, and indeed, almost appeared to have become some sort of folk hero, or saviour, of revolutionary forces led by someone Shade had called the Abominatrix.

"Um, has he been causing trouble again?" I asked.

From the looks they gave me I surmised that the gorgons hadn't died childless.

"Look," I said, "if Bertie has been naughty, then of course I want to help you as much as I can. But what has he done?"

"The plans, N, now!"

"But I don't see how a… what do you call it, Forward Machine… is so important to you," I said, trying to gain time. Where the hell was Anderson? And if I didn't get to have a piss soon… "I mean, if you're cross with Bertie – and believe me, I could quite understand that – why, you could come back to an earlier time, and kill his mother, couldn't you? Then he'd never be born. I've seen Terminator, you know. Or, instead of coming here a month after he's gone, why didn't you come a day before he left, and stop him going in the first place?"

It worked. Shimmer couldn't resist a contemptuous reply.

"How can a supposed Time Traveller know so little? We can't change the past, or if we do, the change is Rectified before you can say Quack Robinson! But the Guardians can't cover everything. They can't detect the transfer of *knowledge*, for example. When we return with the knowledge of how to construct a Forward Machine, we can turn the tables on the Abominatrix. We're free to do what we like in our own futures, because we're not creating any Paradox. No law of Causality will have been broken. There was no point arriving before Bertie left, since there was no way we could ultimately stop him going. But we know that you designed his Machine. Do the same for us, we'll be on our way, and you, vermin though you are, will be allowed to live out your useless life."

She'd finally given up on the flattery idea. Bad sign, very bad sign.

At least it was now clear why they'd really come. Yes, they had wanted to find out more about Bertie, especially any weaknesses, but, more important, to discover how he had gone into the future. They had not unnaturally assumed my account of our adventures would include details of how I had come to invent the Forward Machine.

Something else seemed pretty clear, too. If they got hold of a Forward Machine, Bertie (and a whole bunch of other people) was a goner. Because if they could travel into his future, even if only a week, a day perhaps, then they could easily lie in wait for him. If they saw that he was, let's say – to take an extreme example – going to visit a dermatologist two days later, they could either lay a trap for him there, or go Back in time and put poison in the skin cream, or plant explosives in the place, or a hundred other things. I saw now why the rebels had been successful. With such a Machine, attack was possible at any point.

"But you've got Forward Machines! You said you used them regularly in the future."

"No one's ever succeeded in building one except you, though looking at you... Even the great Constructors Trurl and Klapaucius were unable to do it. We need a Forward Machine. We cannot Return without the plans. We *will not* Return without the plans!"

"I can't remember the design."

"Yes, you can."

"No, I can't!"

I waited for another "Yes, you can!", but Shimmer spoiled the pantomime effect by saying:

"We have drugs which increase tenfold the pain felt by a person having a leg pulled off."

Clearly, in terms of ethical philosophy, a few extra millennia hadn't produced notable advances. As far as I was concerned, their idea of a leg break just wasn't cricket. I told myself it was a good sign that they'd only mentioned one limb.

I was already missing the good cop-bad cop routine.

Well, I thought, all I had to do was tell them what I knew. Lead them to the attic. To Leonardo da Vinci.

End of problem.

End of Bertie.

Sad, but if he would get into such scrapes…

Besides, surely he was used to dying…

I remembered how Moroni had first addressed me in our Mormon adventure: "And you must be N, the treacherous Narrator." Was he referring to my little mutual-comfort arrangement with Winnie, or did he mean that I had betrayed Bertie in the end? In that case, why lose a leg, if I was destined to crack later? As Falstaff so succinctly pointed out, honour cannot set-to a leg.

All I had to do then was point these psychotic women in the right direction, and I'd be off the hook.

I opened my mouth.

My Visitors leaned forward. Shalom a bit more than the other two.

I closed my mouth. I'd remembered her warning.

Would I be off the hook?

There was only one reason I was important to these people, only one reason why Shimmer at least had stopped Shade from relieving me of the necessity of ever going to the toilet again.

They needed a Forward Machine to win this war. And they believed I was the only person who knew how to build it.

The moment they found out that I couldn't design a normal egg-timer, let alone one that broke the laws of physics, my life wouldn't be worth a single Turkish lira – and the last time I checked, there were over two and a half million of them to a pound!

Of course, they might let me live, in gratitude for my information.

But I doubted it. I had a feeling they didn't like men much in general, and me in particular. I sensed that they might, on a good day, after a successful assassination for instance, step to one side to avoid crushing a cockroach taking a stroll, but that they wouldn't make such an effort for a man.

No, most probably, the minute I told them what they wanted to know, they would snuff me out like a nun an unclean thought.

At this point, I suddenly felt a sort of belated loyalty to Bertie. Yes, I know there are those who believe I hadn't always treated him as well as I might have. I'd let him die a few times. But those deaths hadn't been final: Bertie had always eventually been Regenerated.

And, now that I looked back, why, when I had generously allowed him to shield me in Jerusalem with his already crucified body, I had even felt something like affection as the bullets thudded into him! What greater proof of friendship could I have shown than to allow him the honour of sacrificing himself for me?

But what my Visitors wanted was to go into his future and kill him – at the very least. An easy death was clearly not on their minds, as Shade had subtly intimated. He had really pissed them off. More than he had me. Only this time it really would be death. No coming back.

Buggered if I was going to let these three homicidal Furies go into the future and kill him for ever! Well, not without a bit of token resistance, anyway....

Besides, I didn't want my memory blotted in future History: "The Narrator, who accompanied the indomitable Bertie on all his many adventures, at the end betrayed him with no compunction." No, no, it wouldn't look good.

I opened my mouth.

My Visitors leaned forward. Shalom a bit more than the other two.

"Never will I betray my friend!" cried I. "You are fools if you think that you can make me reveal anything that might hurt one so dear to me. Do your worst. You can but break my body, my spirit never."

Hopefully they would put those stirring words in their report, and I would go down in history as a man who was willing – at first – to risk all to protect his friend.

Shade whooped with delight, and began to rise, while Shimmer looked at me rather oddly.

"What a funny thing to say! Well, we'll just remove the first leg, and see if that changes anything."

No longer *one* leg, but *the first* leg. Talk about escalation! The problem with these people was that their arguments were so strong they left you without a leg to stand on.

"And don't think," she added, "that these utterly silly heroics will be mentioned in our report!"

Damn!

I realised at once I had been rather selfish.

It was all very well for me to face down these three psychopaths, to give rein to my natural British pluck, to my natural desire to protect a friend with my own life. But unfortunately I just didn't have the right to recklessly put myself in needless danger like that.

I had, after all, promised to take care of Bertie's widow. How could I break a promise to a dying man? And there was Maria to think of, too. How could I drag her sixty years out of her own time, and then just abandon her here? No, no, I had to think of others, and not let my own obstinate valour blind me to their needs.

I opened my mouth.

My Visitors leaned forward – Shalom a bit more than the other two.

I closed my mouth.

I'd just remembered what they'd said about the difficulty of making permanent changes in the past. And how they hadn't been able to kidnap Bertie when he was still here because he was part of the whole history of time travel. Well, so was I! No way could they kill me without those Ultimate Time Guardians or Custodians or whatever noticing. So, they probably wouldn't dare kill me.

There was another consoling thought. Since those mysterious Guardians seemed to have the power of Rectifying changes in the past, there would be little point in these ladies killing me, anyway. Indeed, doing so would only draw attention to their illegal presence in our time. I was safe.

From Shimmer and Shade, that is. But Shalom? I still didn't know whether she had been warning me about what her colleagues would do if I spoke, or what *she* would do.

But then I reflected that I didn't know my own future, and that it was possible that that future was precisely that: being tortured and killed by these 'historians'. Especially if I indulged in silly and pointless heroics. Maybe the Past that the Guardians 'guarded' had included the cruel and hideously painful murder of a certain legless, yet completely sober, narrator! In that case these women would have no worry about their interfering.

Maybe.

I was beginning to realise that the whole paradox of a paradox is that it is a paradox!

I opened my mouth.

My Visitors leaned forward. Shalom a lot more than the others.

I tried once more to play for time (even though I was no longer sure what time was).

"My only wish is to help you, of course. But how can Bertie have caused you so much trouble? He's only been gone a month."

"You really are an exceedingly stupid specimen. You're still thinking as if he only went to another place, not another time. What's important isn't how long he's been gone, but how far in his future we come from."

Of course! He might have been there, in their future, for a year, ten years, longer. He'd only been gone for a month from my point of view because these delightful ladies had decided to visit me at this point in my own time. By now he might be an old man. He might even have finally found a cure for his halitosis.

This impossibly optimistic thought was interrupted by Shade, who had finally lost patience and was now looming in front of me like a condensed and incensed Balrog. A grip of steel was already round my ankle. I should have felt pleased that she was going to remove my leg without the pain-enhancing drug mentioned by Shimmer.

"Enough! Give us the plans now!"

I opened my mouth. From the corner of a terrified eye, I saw Shalom slip a hand into her uniform…

And a sharp silver light suddenly flashed from the metal bracelets round the wrists of the three women, together with a high-pitched whine that even a dentist would have shuddered at.

"The TSM, someone's near our TSM!" hissed Shimmer.

So they hadn't come in the pocket editions used by the Teepees in Jerusalem. That was odd; I had the impression from everything they'd said that they came from further Uptime than the Teepees had. Perhaps the pocket editions were for one passenger only. What did the 'S' mean? 'Space'? That they travelled through time *and* space to get here from one of those twenty-one planets?

Or perhaps 'space' in the sense they needed more of it to take back someone's broken and tortured body (with or without legs) to prevent its being found after their departure!

"I've got 200 men outside," I blustered.

Shade looked relieved.

"We're in luck!" She was already opening the door, her right hand grasping a pistol-shaped weapon.

"Wait!" said Shimmer. "We can't kill them!"

"Why not? He's just let on there's only two hundred."

"You think the Guardians won't notice the sudden destruction of two hundred men? Stun only!"

"But…"

"I said, stun only!" She turned to Shalom, who was also on her feet. "You stay here, keep an eye on our host! Any nonsense, and…"

Shalom nodded. I noticed she hadn't even bothered to draw a weapon. Against how many enemies, I wondered morosely, did they consider it necessary to use more than their bare hands? Fifty people? A hundred?

There was a blur of movement, and suddenly I was alone in the room with Shalom.

In such circumstances there are usually certain tried-and-tested options. Try to bribe her? Promise her a reduced jail sentence? Swear I knew Brad Pitt personally and could introduce them to each other? Appeal to her softer instincts? Try to overpower her?

I almost smiled as I realised the absurdity of all of these ideas, especially the last two. But then she spoke, for the second time.

"I'm sorry, N, but I'm going to have to give you a Mindsweep. Bertie asked me to avoid it if I could, but your knowledge is too dangerous," she said.

You can imagine my feelings. I'd been entertaining this lady in my own home for three hours, given her some of my best whiskey, she never so much as says 'Hello', she peeps in at a private bathroom ritual, and when she does finally break the ice – apart from some ambiguous words intimating my imminent demise – it's only to inform you that she's going to Mindsweep you, and whatever that was, it didn't sound nice!

Before I could point out that this was deplorable social etiquette and ask her whether she might not wish to reconsider, she had clamped her fingers to my temples.

It felt as if a gang of electric eels were practising the butterfly stroke in my head.

I screamed, and somehow managed to jerk my head free.

"Stop! I'll tell you everything!" I blubbered.

"That's the problem."

And once again she held me in a grip of iron. Now I had the impression that my head had been transformed into a large department store, and that the doors had just been opened for the January sales.

And then Winnie, now dressed in the same black outfit as the others, came into the room!

"Winnie," I cried, "help me, she's going to kill me!"

Shalom pushed me away, and hurled herself across the room so fast that I didn't really see her move.

Winnie received a drop-kick that would have burst a rugby ball or a best-selling author's ego, and staggered back. After this, she shouldn't have stood a chance, but she somehow defended herself and proved to be almost as rapid and deadly as her opponent. I guessed you had to learn survival skills backpacking in sixteenth-century Florence! The next few minutes were for me just a blur of black on black. Both women moved so fast I hardly had time to distinguish one from the other. One second, one of them would be framed in the doorway, the next second she wouldn't be there – or a good chunk of the doorway, either! Another second, the knee of one would be turning the solar plexus of the other into a lunar plexus, the next the leg that owned the knee would be twisted at least three hundred and sixty degrees. One of them used my precious grandfather clock as a weapon and brought it crashing down on the other's head, while the victim simultaneously tore out the pendulum and used it as a sword.

The fight seemed to last for hours, but couldn't have been more than a few minutes. And when it was over…

Winnie's body was lying inert in the middle of the room!

"Foul murderess! O black and midnight hag!" I yelled, hurling myself at Shalom, who had collapsed against a wall, getting her breath back.

She still managed to give me a blow that landed me the other side of the room.

"You fool!" she shouted, "That's one of them!"

"No, it's you who's one of them," I replied, struggling to my feet, livid with rage and grief.

"I'm not one of them! I'm one of us, you prehistoric cretin!"

"Liar! It's Winnie, poor sweet Winnie, who was one of us! And I'm the other one. There were only two of us!" I feebly lunged at her.

"There are two of us *now*," said Shalom, knocking me back where I'd come from, "or at least one and a half, but if we don't get out of here fast, there'll soon be none of us!"

"You murdered poor sweet Winnie!"

"'Poor sweet Winnie' my cubic boron-nitride-studded boot! She was sent to spy on you!"

"You're crazy! We met her in Florence. She was the Mona Lisa! A Torquay lass what's more! And you've killed her!"

"She's not the real Mona Lisa. She's a mole. She was sent to keep tabs on Bertie, and on you too, minor pawn though you were."

Before I could recover from that deadly insult, Shimmer appeared in the room. She saw Winnie's body and turned to Shalom, who at once answered her unspoken question by grabbing her streaming hair, swinging her in a circle three times, and slamming her against the wall. Shimmer crashed to the ground in a cascade of masonry. But simultaneously, Shade burst through another wall (bloody British workmanship) and felled Shalom with a blow that sounded like the Titanic hitting the mother of all icebergs. As Shalom dropped to the ground, Shade gave a cry of savage triumph, and hurled herself on top of her, pounding her head against my new red oak floor, which splintered under the blows. Shalom still fought back, but by now Shimmer was back in the fray, jumping up and down on Shalom's stomach like an out-of-control pile driver. Shalom's struggles became weaker, and she finally ceased moving. The other two members of the gentler sex continued to pound her for a few more seconds, emitting shrieks of rage and blood-lust.

Well, that did kind of suggest that Shalom really was not one of them.

Though by this time I was so confused I wondered whether I might not be one of them myself.

Too late, it occurred to me to try to make a run for it. I got as far as where the doorway and half a wall had been, before what seemed like a grappling hook went round my neck, and I was hauled back into the room, and deposited on a small coffee table which somehow still remained the right way up.

Shalom lay crumpled in the middle of the floor, not far from

Winnie. Who, it appeared, wasn't dead. She stirred slightly and groaned. Pausing only to kick Shalom a few more times, Shimmer took a syringe from what looked like a small medical kit in one of her many pockets, bent down, and injected something into Winnie's arm, dropping the syringe on the floor beside her.

It must have been good stuff; the equivalent of the resuscitation pills I'd hoped to find in Jerusalem when Bertie was being crucified. Winnie dispensed with the traditional stirrings, opening of eyes, groaning, and asking "Where am I?", and instead scrambled to her feet and saluted Shimmer. She acted as if she hadn't seen Shade.

"Was it you who set off the TSM alarm?" asked Shimmer.

"You think I'm that careless?"

"Must have been that traitress then. To distract us."

"Who the hell is she?"

"I don't know. She'd passed all the Department security tests. They must have got at her before she joined. And activated her to protect this primitive specimen. Or stop him talking."

Shade rubbed her bruised knuckles across her mouth. She looked at Winnie with a sneer.

"And did a very good job. Didn't seem to have much trouble with the *star* of the Department."

"Ah, it's the ever-jocular tenebrous Tiger shark! You think you could have beaten her – by yourself – if I hadn't weakened her?"

"Yes," said Shade. "No trouble."

She and Winnie glared at each other, like two boxers at the weigh-in.

"Enough!" Shimmer's voice lashed across the room. "You can sort out your personal feuds when you're off-duty. Now we can't waste time. If that's one of Boadicea's people, she'll have been transmitting, and it won't take them too long to notice the transmission's stopped. We have to get the information now, and get out of here."

"I'll help you as much as you want," I said, "but just tell me first who you are."

I looked pleadingly at Winnie, but it was Shimmer who answered.

"Isn't it obvious? Although records from this period are very patchy, we knew that Bertie had a crush on the Mona Lisa, who our Research Centre told us was really a young woman named Wenefride who'd gone back-packing in Italy, and decided to stay. Agent

Wildflower volunteered to replace her, we operated on her, and fattened her up, so that she was almost identical to the original Wenefride. Except that she still had the combat skills of a Black Defender, of course."

My Winnie! I felt a tear start to my eye.

"Her orders were to kill Bertie, if she could – although we already surmised that the Third Law of Temporality would doom her efforts to failure – but, more feasible, she had to keep as close to both you and Bertie as she could, at all times. That way, we hoped she would discover the design of the Forward Machine."

"Winnie, say this isn't true! After everything we had between us… the sonnets I wrote you while Bertie was being poisoned in Yusupov's Palace…"

"You pitiful specimen!" sneered Winnie, "do you think I could have borne to listen to those rhythmical aberrations, or even come near you, if it hadn't been for the Cause? Speaking of poisoning, who do you think really spiked that wine that nearly finished off Bertie on that first Trip?"

"It was Borgia wine! Leo used it through jealousy!"

"That wine was fine! Some of the best I've ever tasted. At first. You forget the Borgias were connoisseurs as well as assassins."

"But Cesare meant to punish Leo for his bridge falling down. It killed half his men!"

"Including a captain whose wife Borgia was after! He was *grateful* to Leonardo for his mistake!"

"But it was Leo who opened the wine. To poison Bertie. To force us to use the Time Machine."

"All that romantic fool intended was to get Bertie drunk, and find out the secret that way. Did Leonardo strike you as a murderer! I added the poison when they weren't looking."

"But why?"

"To 'save' Bertie from Leonardo, and make sure you let me come to the future as his wife. The perfect mole! Bertie may have been as clever as Ulysses – or so we had been led to believe – but not even the cleverest man in the world would ever have suspected the Mona Lisa. Especially the cunning way I insulted Bertie when we first met, knowing this would only encourage him to play his one and only card – take me to the future."

Small doubts which I'd forgotten came back to me. Why had Winnie believed Bertie so easily when he'd told her he could take her to the future? How had she known about hormones a few hundred years before their discovery?

If they could make so many mistakes, I thought, maybe they weren't invincible. Small consolation for me.

"So you really aren't from Torquay!"

"Torquay? *Torquay?* Give me a break, will you! I said I was from there because we knew you were from there, and it would help to soften you up!"

"But at least the girl you replaced…?" It was difficult to restrain the tears.

"The girl I replaced came from Blackpool!"

Oh low blow!

It was a saddening thought. We believed we had solved the mystery of the Mona Lisa smile – a mixture of an early teeth brace and happiness at having been proposed to by Bertie – and it turned out it was really a mixture of an early teeth brace and the barely suppressed gloating of a pitiless secret agent of the whatever damn century they came from at having found a perfect way to spy on Bertie and myself.

"You're not so clever as you think!" I said bitterly. "Just lucky. If my poor darling Mabel hadn't come to the Land of Nod with us…"

"Who do you think put it into her head to go with you?"

I continued to resist the evidence of my foolishness.

"But if the woman intended as Cain's wife hadn't been killed…" I paused. Things clicked. "Oh dear!"

"'Oh dear', indeed, you testosterone troglodyte! *I* arranged for that accident. I then frightened you into believing the future of the human race depended on Mabel being sacrificed. I knew that you would choose me over that frumpy – though extremely long-suffering – wife of yours. That way, with Bertie as husband, and you as lover (if such a word may dignify your abysmal actuations) I could keep tabs on both of you. Either stop you designing a Forward Machine (probably impossible) so that Bertie would never go to the future, or at least find out your design. But Bertie seemed to know nothing about the Machine, because for some reason you never talked about it, not even to him."

"But you changed history by killing Cain's wife! The Guardians or whatever you called them will get you! Mabel was never intended to mother half the human race."

"Maybe she didn't!"

"But…"

"What you (and Cain) thought was his wife was another of our agents. She pretended to fancy me to give me an excuse to leave Mabel behind, so I could keep you as a besotted admirer."

"We saw the body!"

"Only a Back death. She was Retrieved and Resuscitated."

"But Mabel still…"

"A month after out Trip, the angel Gabriel brought Cain's real wife. She probably produced Cain's children. I expect Mabel became her servant or the children's nanny."

My sweet Mabel!

"Don't you want to ask about my blue underwear?"

I now at last became fully aware of 'those subtle and poisonous curves' of the Mona Lisa's lips that Oscar Wilde had referred to.

I didn't answer this cruel taunt. It was now clear she'd flaunted herself in front of Cain knowing that Bertie would leap bravely, but stupidly, to her rescue, and get himself killed.

And after that, of course, she didn't need to accompany us on any more of our trips.

What a fool I'd been! No wonder her portrait, when at Fontainebleau, had been referred to as 'courtesan in a gauze veil'! Those Frenchmen had been more perceptive than me.

And then came another shocking thought.

"Is Maria a mole too?"

"Maria a mole? Not unless she's one of Moroni's. She's the reason I couldn't get at you after Bertie disappeared. The lucky bitch!"

"Well," I said modestly, "I suppose she could have done much worse. I have my good points…"

"Lucky because she escaped two 'accidents' I'd arranged for her. That's why I sent a message to my colleagues to come, and finally put an end to this business."

Shade burst into our little lovers' tiff.

"Let's stop wasting time!" she snarled. "We've listened to all his silly stories, and not got one word about the Forward Machine. Which leg shall I break first?"

"Which one do you usually break first?" asked Shimmer, somewhat distractedly.

"The nearest one."

Shimmer sighed. "Very well, go ahead. He had his chance."

Thinking of Burridan's ass, I faced Shade straight on.

Shade's smile was so sinister I felt my femurs cringing. "Very clever. Both, then."

I'd done my best. If I kept quiet any longer, I'd have two broken legs, and be babbling the truth anyway. I really would have preferred to save Bertie, but two legs was asking... well, two legs too many.

"You're not so bloody clever, you lot!" I said, hoping to disguise my submission beneath a show of defiance. "I know about as much concerning the construction of time machines as Bertie knows about deodorants! Want to know how he got into the future and caused you so much trouble? *You* did it! *You* sent Winnie Back, and the only reason there's a Forward Machine is because Leonardo de Vinci invented one to follow Winnie! Just like he invented the first one. If you hadn't sent Winnie Back, Bertie would never have gone Forward! You brought all your troubles on yourselves!"

14: THE PRISONER IN THE ATTIC

It had happened one afternoon in July, a few weeks after Bertie and I had returned from Jerusalem.

I was sitting in my inner garden contemplating a spider hurtling towards its resentful dinner which was twitching in a web straddling a rose bush, and pondering whether flies had any form of religious belief to help them through such moments. I was also wondering whether I might not at last insist on a visit to ancient Egypt – after all, with the spectacular (if somewhat slow-moving) Crucifixion scenes, our ratings had soared and finally put that bloody *Big Baby* in its place.

Suddenly there came a slight hissing sound, a kind of membrane seemed to stretch over the garden, and pop! something very similar to our own Chronoporter materialised right in front of me, causing me to spill my 1915 Baron de Sigognac Armagnac.

Out stepped Leonardo da Vinci!

He was a few years older than when I'd last seen him, but still looked quite strong and dangerous – the more so as he was brandishing what looked like a particularly sharp-tempered medieval Saracen scimitar. Trust Leonardo not to be content with the Italian short sword of the period! Not enough brio for him.

I understood immediately why he had this unfriendly attitude. We had, after all, taken his Mona Lisa away from him.

And there was another small detail that I'd thought it better not to include in the public account of our adventures.

When he died, Leonardo left something like 13,000 pages of notes. These were taken back to Italy by his friend Francesco Melzi, whose son Orazio inherited them all. Orazio, however, was a person who these days would probably have been a Sun 'reader'. He dumped the lot in an attic, and forgot about them. But word got out, and people descended from all over Europe, either buying, stealing, or simply ripping out pages as souvenirs. The result was that half the papers were lost forever.

Well, almost for ever. Around ten years ago I met an Italian student in Torquay who invited me back on holiday to her place, a rather grand farmhouse in Tuscany – gentlemanly discretion forbids my identifying exactly where. Francesca's father being of the unshakeable belief that his daughter's purity should be sullied only by a wealthy man with exceedingly honest intentions, she had to use the loft to demonstrate her quite natural physical desire for me, and there I came across a complete Leonardo notebook (which I like to call the *Codex N*, worth far more, let me tell you, than the measly thirty million dollars that Bill Gates paid for the *Codex Leicester*). How it got there, I've no idea. A lot of these farmhouses were once part of princely estates.

Of course, at the time I didn't know what it was, as I could hardly read a word of it. But I could see that it was very old, and the multitude of sketches reminded me of Leonardo's notebooks, which had recently featured in a television programme. My first instinct was to ask Francesca, but I quickly reflected that if the manuscript was indeed valuable, as I suspected it was, her father would at once claim it. He was rich enough already. I found a scholar in the nearby town and showed him a couple of pages. He expressed astonishment, said it was definitely Da Vinci, but that he must be misreading something because it seemed to be part of a design for a machine that could travel through time! At this point, luckily, he had a heart attack and died on the spot.

Well, I grabbed that manuscript, and left the shop, and Italy, at once, I knew the Italians would claim it as national heritage. How could I sell it without running into legal difficulties? While I pondered this, I set about trying to learn enough Italian to translate it myself. A study of the other notebooks in a facsimile edition helped me a lot, but the task still took me two years. This was a few years before the discovery of the Universal Language Centre in the appendix, and besides, it was written in Leonardo's left-handed mirror writing, with a few codes and ciphers thrown in. All his life the artist had been terrified (and with reason) of plagiarism.

But it was worth the effort. The antiquarian had been right: the notebook contained nothing less than detailed designs for the construction of a time machine!

Leonardo has been greatly admired for his plans for, among many other inventions, flying machines. Although he had an unfortunate habit of just missing the mark – despite his brilliant anatomical work, he never quite made the leap to understanding the circulation of blood, and, in astronomy, despite acute observations on the planets, he never made that other leap to heliocentricity – he had somehow hit on the unexpected properties of the egg-timer shape, the fundamental principle of any time-reversal process. But he lacked, or the sixteenth century lacked, the materials to actually make one. So he turned his magpie attention, as usual, to something else.

Look at it from my point of view. Leonardo da Vinci had been dead an awfully long time. He had no needs. I, on the other hand, was then 28 years old, with lots and lots and lots of needs. Like a job. Money. Women. Self-respect. I couldn't see how I could sell the notebook without running into big problems. But there was another way.

That's when I got in touch with Bertie's dad. Offered him 'my' design for a time machine in return for a promise to be the first person to travel in it. First, it had been pilots who attracted the women; then the astronauts left the pilots stranded mid-air. What couldn't a time traveller achieve? Of course, if I'd known my constant travelling companion was to be the multi-trillionaire's son, I'd have sold the plans on the black market and settled for a less exciting lifestyle.

I never let Francesca know what I'd found. After all, the notebook hadn't really belonged to her any more than to me. But I did send her a box of chocolates each Christmas. I'm not an ungrateful or heartless man.

Leonardo's present menacing attitude was, therefore, not entirely unreasonable.

"You stole my *bambina* and you stole my papers," he said, his voice like an electric saw with a short, "and I'm going to demonstrate to you that my studies in anatomy, and especially of the nerve centres, have not been wasted."

I didn't like the sound of that. This, after all, was a man who was quite happy secretly dissecting corpses in his room at night, and who designed battle carts with mobile scythes, and cannon, and flame-throwers. And all that when he was in a good mood.

STEVE REDWOOD

I would have made a run for it, but I was trapped in my deckchair, and the blade of the scimitar, which I could swear was grinning evilly at me, was within instant decapitation range. Have you ever tried to get up out of a deckchair in one swift flowing movement? Already I knew he guessed the truth, but I parried weakly:

"A lot of people have been through your papers. You are – and, may I say, most deservedly – a famous man."

It didn't work. He seemed to increase in sound and fury, like a juicy political scandal, or an amorous frog. "You stole my plans for a time machine!"

My laugh was weaker than a mummified mosquito.

"Ha ha," I said, and then optimistically added, "ho ho!"

Yes, it sounded as ridiculous as it looks!

"That," said he, "was my own reaction, albeit more full-blooded and with much more genuine humour, when Winnie let slip, the very day I finished painting her, that Bertrando had threatened to kidnap her and take her to the future. I thought that, apart from being a bit simple, he must also be completely crazy. I had myself already designed a theoretical time machine, as a kind of mental exercise, but I knew it would require impossibly lightweight materials that simply didn't exist. Nonetheless, my suspicions were aroused, and I asked Niccoló to search your room at the inn, and also decided to get Bertrando drunk on Cesare's wine to see what he might reveal. He did indeed start to say strange things, and when he mentioned something about an egg-timer shape, I knew the coincidence was too great to be accidental. But then, as you know, he suddenly got ill. Although I hadn't planned this, and was indeed a bit surprised, I realised it gave me the chance to lay a trap for you.

"When that bigot Michelangelo tried to break into my studio, it was at once obvious to someone of my amazing intelligence that this was the feeble ploy of a vastly inferior mind to distract me, so I headed straight away for your inn. When I saw the machine, I knew! Only *I* am clever enough to have realised the fantastic possibilities of the egg-timer shape for temporal relocations! I managed to break off a bit of your machine to analyse the material it was made of later!"

His story didn't quite fit in with what Winnie had told me, but I didn't have time to worry about that.

Inspired by the scimitar, the blade of which was now whispering to me that it couldn't go much longer without a nice cool drink of blood, I said:

"Of course, you're quite right, and that's precisely why our first trip was to come to see you, to thank you personally. We wanted to let you see for yourself the child of your genius. But we didn't want to distract you just as you were on the point of finishing that wonderful painting. And before I could be alone with you to discuss your invention, Bertie got ill, and my only thought naturally was to get him back here safely for medical treatment."

I figured I could get away with it.

He hesitated, and the scimitar's grin turned to a look of puzzled consternation.

"Then why were you hiding the machine?"

"We weren't hiding it from you, we were hiding it from everyone else." And then, hoping to distract him, I added: "It's wonderful to see you again. But how did you manage to get here, and how did you know where and when to come? No normal human being could have achieved that."

My ploy worked.

"I am not, as you well know, a normal human being. I was almost sure your time machine was based on my plans – extrapolating from notes I had already made, or maybe notes that I would be making in the future. When Winnie was taken from me, I at once destroyed all the relevant notes I'd made until then. My thinking was, as usual, impeccable: if the notes didn't exist, then no one would be able to find them in the future, make a time machine, come back into the past, and steal my Winnie. In theory, Winnie should have reappeared immediately. It didn't happen."

I nodded sympathetically. My life depended on my sympathy and his empathy.

"I was therefore faced with two possibilities. Either your journey to the past had now *become* the past, replacing the original past, and so nothing could undo it. Or, although it was extremely unlikely a mere five hundred years would produce anyone as clever as me, it was not totally impossible. In that case, maybe the machine I saw hadn't been based on my notes at all. Maybe the brilliant concept had been arrived at independently by another being almost as remarkable as me, one having the advantage of centuries of scientific development, and numerous research grants and assistants to aid him. Though having seen you and Bertrando, I doubted this. In either case, Winnie was lost to me. *In 1505!*"

I almost guessed his next words.

"It was then obvious that I would have to go into the future to get her back. Although I had destroyed my notes, I still remembered them. Total recall. One of the many advantages of genius, I suppose. I realised I would have to alter the design of my machine so that it would go forward in time. So that I could rescue Winnie and, of course, kill the people who took her from me."

I nodded sympathetically. The scimitar perked up.

"I secretly worked on this for half a decade. But then I had another fear. If your machine had been based on my notes, and if those notes no longer existed, there would be such a Paradox that perhaps you wouldn't exist either. Time might simply wipe out the anomalies. I was quite happy with the thought of Bertrando not existing…"

I nodded sympathetically.

"… or you…"

I nodded.

"…but perhaps Winnie too would be trapped between two impossible time periods. I had to know exactly when she was, to find her. So I rewrote all the original notes for the Backward Machine, to make sure that they would after all exist again in order for you to find them. But I destroyed all the notes for a Forward Machine once I had constructed it, to make sure you couldn't find them and move away into the future ahead of me and my sanguinary vengeance."

I nodded sympathetically. The crafty bounder! That's why I found nothing to help me build a Forward Machine!

"So now I've just got three things to do, and then I'll be off again. Find Winnie and take her back with me. Kill Bertrando for taking her from me. And kill you for stealing my plans."

I tried, but failed, to nod sympathetically. The blade curved in a radiantly wicked snicker.

"Look, sir," I said, "kill Bertie if you want, he's the one who absconded with your Mona Lisa, but you can't kill me!"

"'Mona Lisa'? Who's that? And yes I can!"

I stared at him in surprise, but then remembered that the name

'Mona Lisa' wasn't given to the picture until long after his death.

"Sorry, I meant Winnie. But I've done nothing wrong. I simply came across your notebook, and honoured your genius by turning your plans into reality, so that others could know of your brilliance!"

"You told people that the plans were mine?"

"Of course! You don't think I would pretend to have designed it myself, ha ha! Any idiot would know that only a universal genius like yourself would be capable of it."

"Yes, that's true. They certainly could never believe that someone like you... Well, if everyone knows it was really my invention... No, I think I'll kill you anyway, now that I'm here."

"There are a dozen guards just outside this inner garden. If you kill me, you'll spend the rest of your second life in prison – while Bertie and Winnie live happily together, and come to visit you twice a year. If he lets her!

That stopped him. The blade fell, thwarted and dejected.

"Indeed, looking at you," I went on, "I really do think you ought to have something to eat before killing anybody. Why not come in, and we can discuss the best way to kill Bertie?"

"I've already decided on that," he said ominously.

He took two diagonal sweeps in the air at about belly height, followed by a short vertical thrust. I sometimes wish I didn't have such a vivid imagination.

However, I seemed for the moment to have deflected his fury against myself. Once inside the house, it would be easy to summon a few guards to overpower him. After that I could consider what to do.

But then Bertie strolled in through the secret gate!

It was true that I had more than a dozen guards patrolling the grounds (we'd had word of an American plot to kidnap me to learn about the time machine), but I might as well have had none. Leonardo had avoided them by simply materialising in my private inner garden, and Bertie, of course, as my fellow time-traveller (together with Maria and Winnie) was always allowed through without question.

His appearance had a revivifying effect on the scimitar. It glowed with joyful anticipation. Maybe it also sang; I don't know, because the sound would have been drowned beneath Leonardo's roar of rage.

Bertie didn't show enough intelligence to head right back out of the gate through which he'd come, but he did show enough to start running, just before the scimitar swung in an arc that confirmed me in my previous analysis of just what Leonardo intended to lop off first.

Well, off set Bertie, careering round the garden like Hector fleeing Achilles round the walls of Troy. He was much younger than Leonardo (thirty years or five hundred years, depending on your point of view), but his constant deaths hadn't been good for his health. And the medics, understandably a bit fed up by now, had been a bit slapdash the last time – they hadn't bothered to regenerate his crucified feet, but simply patched over the holes. It was a race he was doomed to lose.

Bertie had circled the garden three times (selfishly cutting through an island bed the third time, leaving a swathe of crushed and mortally wounded daylilies that Maria herself had planted) when he spotted Leonardo's time machine, which, as I said, looked very similar to our own. For a person distracted by the whooshes of a monomaniacal scimitar, it would have appeared that it was ours.

So Bertie leapt in, and just managed to close the airlock in time. Instead of accepting defeat, Leonardo began taking huge slices at it, reckless of what damage he might be doing to his own machine.

Then it disappeared!

A few seconds later, the guards I'd been able to summon while Leonardo was distracted burst through the hedge, and soon the incensed artist had become a senseless one.

That was a month before I received my lady Visitors.

What, you say you kept the great Leonardo da Vinci locked up for a month! Can such cultural barbarism be? Surely, with Bertie gone and the Mona Lisa now to all intents and purposes a widow, all you had to do was let the artist and his model get back together again.

To which I answer: and what about loyalty to my dear friend Bertie? Winnie was his lawfully wedded wife. What if he came back and found I had casually and callously sacrificed her to a five-hundred-year-old-man? How would I be able to look into his poor trusting bemused eyes then? Was it for me to presumptuously take it upon myself to break the holy sanctity of marriage?

I was also, I confess, slightly influenced by the fact that Leonardo, when he discovered that I had indeed claimed to be the inventor of the Time Machine, refused to give me his word that he wouldn't kill me the moment he was free, for taking away the glory that should rightfully have been his. He also swore to announce to the whole world that I was a fake.

I could see myself suffering the ignominy of having to return all my honorary degrees, of seeing all the statues dedicated to me razed to the ground – probably with myself under the rubble – of women aborting the babies created from my expensive sperm sold in phials twisted into the shape of my signature.

This, naturally, weighed much less with me than did my concern for Bertie's honour, but it might, I realise in retrospect, have had some small influence on my decision.

It was also too risky to allow Winnie to come to the house any more. Leonardo was quite capable of inventing something similar to the bird which had dishonoured the statue of David, and launching it to warn her of his presence. I called her and told her that I'd been expecting Bertie that day, but that he hadn't turned up. The couple of guards who had seen him enter the grounds naturally felt such admiration and loyalty for me that they didn't hesitate to support my story, and opened offshore bank accounts the very next morning.

Even so, Winnie still arrived two days later, and intimated (while stroking my vas deferens, rather suggestively, I thought) that if her beloved husband had indeed had a tragic accident, perhaps the best way to keep his memory alive would be for her to stay beside his best friend recalling his grand exploits.

Before Roswell, I'd have been overjoyed at this opportunity to warmly display our shared admiration for my friend. But Maria had changed all that. I was madly in love, and had been from the moment I first spotted her in her enticing nurse's uniform, even before she poured me out of my body bag and slid her slender fingers through my innards in search of the Spatial Mobility Module remote control. If you've ever had that experience, you'll know there's nothing quite like it! Besides, even before Roswell, I'd had to admit to myself that Winnie had often appeared more interested in talking about the technical aspects of time machine construction than in demonstrations of tenderness. Indeed, I'd almost begun to wonder whether the Americans weren't paying her to secure restricted information.

So that evening I told Maria, who was now living with me, that Winnie had made a pass at me, and thus got her effectively banned from the house. I also told her about Leonardo: it would have been almost impossible to keep his presence hidden from her. I expected reproaches… and I received them! Maria said she'd often wondered how I could ever have invented anything as advanced as a time machine, and confessed that she'd only pretended to believe me to keep me happy. This was a bit of an unpleasant surprise, I must admit. Still, after a time, she seemed to have forgiven me my little deceit, though I felt we weren't quite as close as before.

How could I have known that banning Winnie from the house would drive her to get in contact with her superiors and bring the wrath of the future down upon my head?

Besides, 'locked up', while technically correct, gives quite the wrong impression. It is traditional to lock criminals in cellars but lunatics in attics, so I only kept Leo chained for a couple of days in the cellar, while I had part of the top floor of the manor house converted into a secure holding zone. He had his own bedroom with bathroom en-suite (with flying ducks on the tiles to appeal to the artist in him), a lounge, and another bedroom which was quickly converted into a study cum studio by the addition of books and an easel. I had bars put on all the windows, of course, and instructed my guards to check ceiling, floor, and outer walls each day. The devious artist was not beyond creating a diamond drill out of the graphite in a pencil, or an onager out of the bed frame and springs.

(The scimitar I had turned into a ploughshare: I pitied any field that might decide to offer resistance.)

Despite his fulminations against me and my progenitors and offspring (which I found odd, as the former had disowned me years before, and the latter had never arrived, possibly because my sperm perished in the arctic temperatures that my sweet Mabel emanated when performing her matrimonial duty) both I and Maria treated him very well. Each day we offered him a choice of dishes from nearby Italian restaurants (the first day he hurled a *bistecca alla fiorentina* back at me: I'd forgotten he was vegetarian). His bedding was changed every day. Television, video, music, solitaire, we gave them all to him.

And books. We took him as many biographies of himself as we could find. He must have had an unusually well-developed appendix, and a strong desire to read about himself, because even without the injection of stem cells from addled parrots' eggs, he had more or less mastered English within a few days. His vanity was not without foundation. He lapped up the books, and would sometimes forget to threaten me with a terrible fate for hours at a time. Vasari's *Life* he would read time and time again, and had even torn out and stuck on the wall the opening passage: 'The heavens often rain down the richest gifts on human beings naturally, but sometimes with lavish abundance bestow upon a single individual beauty, grace, and ability, so that whatever he does, every action is so divine that he distances all other men.'

Freud's 'Leonardo da Vinci was like a man who awoke too early in the darkness, while the others were all still asleep' also won wall space, Leonardo muttering, "I don't know who this fellow is, but he'll go far." However, he spent the rest of the morning engrossed in his *A Childhood Memory of Leonardo de Vinci*, laughing his head off at the great man's weird interpretations and mistranslations.

He got very depressed, however, when he found out how his works had decayed with time, especially the *Last Supper* in the monastery Santa Maria delle Grazie: his experimental pigments hadn't lasted fifty years even. Neither could he understand why the *Mona Lisa* in Paris was so protected.

"It's in a box!" he said.

"Yes, it's bulletproof."

"But who would want to shoot a picture?"

"Good question."

We took him books on other artists, too. Some made him roar with laughter.

"Take a look at this! After I died, that fanatic Michelangelo painted himself as the flayed skin of St Bartholomew in the *Last Judgement*!"

But he got really pissed off when he realised that in present-day Florence, Michelangelo was far more of a tourist attraction than he was. A lavishly illustrated book on his great rival narrowly missed decapitating me as I ducked hurriedly out of his rooms. I made my peace with him by informing him that his horse and rider study for

189

The Adoration of the Magi had five years before fetched the highest price ever paid for an Old Master drawing, although I did not inform him that this record was actually shared with Michelangelo's *Study for the Risen Christ*!

To bring him up to date, I also procured brochures from some of the modern art galleries. He was quite incredulous. When he saw the first examples of surrealism, cubism and Dadaism, he began to finger his beard in a perplexed manner; pop art, collage, and post-dogmatism induced quite vigorous tugging; and by the time he reached unmade beds with dirty knickers, bricks haphazardly strewn around the floor, pickled (and skinned) politicians, spin paintings, and so on, he was pulling out whole tufts of hair in disbelief. He was stunned by an article in *The Times* about a visitor to the Tate Gallery, during the judging for the Turner Prize, who had a bad stomach, and vomited into a huge bucket she saw on the floor. It turned out that the bucket was part of the exhibition, and the presence of the vomit swayed the judges, who brought thirty years of experience to their task, into giving it second prize, instead of third, as they had been planning. They felt the vomit made an unusually astringent Conceptual Statement about the quality of modern life.

We also took him science books and video documentaries. The more he read and saw, the more depressed he got.

"There's no longer any room for the great individual genius," he lamented. "There's too much knowledge. Even my remarkable mind cannot take it all in. Advances now can only come from worldwide collaboration between hundreds of laboratories, thousands of specialised scientists, and those computing machines they have."

I visited him whenever I could, although many days it was impossible. Within a couple of days of Bertie's disappearance, the cult which had sprung up around him immediately after his crucifixion began to talk about his 'Ascension', equating his disappearance with the resurrection of Jesus, unperturbed by the fact the angels had delayed a month before collecting him. It was then that I began the lecture tours and television and newspaper interviews, and as my fees increased in proportion to the supposed heroic acts performed by Bertie, I sprinkled my accounts with them more and more. Soon it was out of my control. At some meetings, the faithful would grow dangerously restless if they weren't given new exploits of their hero to gasp at, and I found I was trapped in a widening spiral of hagiolatry, my own safety depending on my satisfying their need for more and more Bertie derring-do.

However, I stayed home when possible, and after going through the ritualised greetings ("Will you promise not to kill me if I let you free?": "On the contrary, I'll tear you from limb to limb", and similar contrapuntal variations on the same theme) Leonardo and I had many interesting discussions. Paradoxically, the more he described, with both an artist's and an anatomist's attention to detail, what he intended to do to me if ever he got free, the fonder I became of him. Although he still blustered, the five years without Winnie had somehow... diminished him. And, deep down, I believe he rather enjoyed being pampered, and also that he'd decided it wouldn't be a bad thing not to see Winnie until some time had passed since the loss of her husband. Nonetheless, I didn't take any chances, and before I entered his 'suite', my guards would first shackle him to the bars covering the windows, a long chain leaving him ample room to move around – but not quite enough to reach me where I sat in an armchair near the door.

"Bertrando can never come back," he said, on one of these intimate occasions. "As you discovered, I realised that the only logical way to displace the sands of time was with a Time Machine in the shape of an hour-glass or egg-timer with an internal spring. Time would first flow in one direction, then the spring would be activated at the end of the journey, which would flip over the egg-timer, thus reversing the flow of time, so that you would end up precisely when you had started.

"At first, I confess to my shame – but as it's only to you, it doesn't matter, because I doubt if you understand what I'm saying in any case, and you'll be dead once I get free – I took a completely erroneous theoretical route. I thought of the river of time, rather than the sands of time, and therefore initially considered it would be more feasible to design a time machine that would go forward (following, as it were, the flow, the current, of the river) than to go back (swimming against the current). But time does not flow, it is a still pool, it is everywhen. Imagine that you are an insect (as indeed, compared to me, you are) on a globe, which represents the whole of time, you can in theory move in any direction you wish. But whichever direction you move in – and that direction will always, in the normal course of events, be experienced as forward – you are, as it were, carving out a new road. When you travel back in time, you are travelling along a road already made. But when you try to go fast-forward, there is no road, it is as if you have to hack your way through virgin jungle with a blunt machete.

"So when I decided to follow you to the future, I had to incorporate into the design infinitely more energy than I would have needed in a backward-going machine. But I had a new advantage. I had a chunk of 'your' machine which allowed me to analyse its materials, and try to teach myself to create similar ones, although the task seemed impossible. But then I wondered to myself whether anyone else had come into the past, and I trained a dog to sniff out anything resembling the constituents of your machine. I searched the area for many months thoroughly. And indeed I found a complete time machine!"

I now know, of course, that what he'd probably found had been Winnie's time machine, but at the time, thinking that Winnie was the real Mona Lisa, I assumed it had belonged to the two strange characters who had seemed to be wandering everywhen.

"Applying Negative Superstring theory (I don't suppose you lot have even discovered it yet!) in an hour-glass context, I managed to convert that machine so that it would go forward in time, following the tachyon track you left. But as I wasn't sure exactly when I would find you, I didn't set any limits to the forward motion. I might need to keep edging forward century after century until I caught up with you. That slave of yours must have accidentally set my Machine in motion (if we may use the word for something that doesn't actually move) but he'll be (or, we can say, will have been) unable to stop it, since it is attuned only to my own brain waves. It will keep going forward until it runs out of energy, and the spring snaps, which, at a rough calculation, will be around..." he paused a moment, "...I'd say around 2.30 pm, 25 July, 9009."

25 July? St Christopher's Day? The patron saint of travellers? Very apt.

"But it cannot come back! Once the spring has snapped, it will be like a broken clock. In theory, I suppose, a new spring (I am speaking figuratively, of course, we are in fact in post-quantum physics here) could be inserted, so that the Machine could, from some future time, be sent forward yet again, and it could return to the point it was at when the new spring was inserted. But it can never return to a point before that time. A time machine can either go back and then return, or forward and then return, but it can never reverse the direction of the initial journey. In other words, you will never see Bertrando again."

To my surprise, I felt a small pang. I suppose Bertie was like a scab that you get used to, and miss when it eventually falls off, leaving surprisingly tender skin underneath.

Of course, all during this period, I was trying to find some way out of my dilemma with Leonardo. By the end of the second week, I believe he had given up all serious intention of killing me but was too proud to say so, while as time passed I no longer needed to consider Bertie's honour so much. If Bertie was never going to come back, there was no point in keeping Leonardo and Winnie separated.

The ideal solution, then, would have been to get rid of him by sending him – and Winnie – back to Florence in the early sixteenth century. But how could I do it? Bertie had gone off in Leonardo's machine, and security wasn't so lax at the Chronotrek Centre that I could sneak two stowaways aboard 'my' time machine. In any case, all trips were still suspended in honour to Bertie's memory.

I could only hope that in the end Leonardo would become more reasonable. I never ceased to remind him that he'd been dead for 500 years when I found the *Codex*. But for me, I pointed out, the time machine would never have been built; it was only because of me that his great project had come to fruition. I promised that, if he in turn promised to reveal nothing about his part in the invention for the time being, I would leave a sealed envelope to be opened upon my death, revealing all, so that future ages would at last realise the real extent of his genius, In the end, I was almost sure, he would agree to my terms, in return for freedom, and the chance to be with Winnie – and both of them, I added, were likely to live much longer, and thus be able to spend much more time together, in our present century than they would have in their own time.

Only then, I'd have a new problem: how would Winnie react?

In the end, the matter was taken out of my hands when three ladies from the future dropped in.

15: STRAINED ALLEGIANCES

I gave my ladies in black a summary of all this, trying not to notice Shalom's body still lying on the floor, and asked them if they wouldn't mind directing their questions at Leonardo in future, though I'd be quite willing to have them provided with tea and scones while they discussed the more technical aspects of time machine construction. If I could find my servants, that is.

Shimmer and Shade first stared with disbelief, then Shimmer nodded and muttered something like "I knew he wasn't capable...," glancing at me with even more contempt than before (women do so tend to see things in black and white), while Shade looked at Winnie with a sneer on her face. As for Winnie, she had gone pale and fixed me with a look as rigid as the smile of a politician who's just lost an election and has to congratulate the winner. The expression of casual superiority was completely gone, to be replaced by one of shock and... could it be fear? I remembered what Bertie had told me about her obsession with the *Mona Lisa*.

"Take us to this creature at once," commanded Shimmer. "No, Agent Wildflower and I had better stay here in case any of Boadicea's people turn up. N, show Agent Gentleheart where he is – and I think you know exactly what will happen if you try any tricks."

That wasn't quite correct. I knew the *kind* of thing that would happen if I gave Shade (Shade Gentleheart, I ask you!) the slightest excuse, but I didn't know the *exact* way she would cause me unspeakable pain – a toss-up, I supposed, between the complete removal, lateral displacement, or unusual compression of each and any of my body parts.

As we passed through the hall, up the main stairway, and along the passage, I saw why the house had been so silent. The bodies of two servants were slumped along the walls. My Visitors, before my arrival, must have given them the afternoon off.

Shade noticed and answered my look of concern (would I have to prepare my own supper?):

"They're not dead. It's not allowed." She sounded aggrieved.

We passed the bathroom and I turned towards Shade. From her expression, I knew it wasn't worth the trouble even asking her. At what pressure, I wondered, does a bladder burst?

The door at the top of the small flight of stairs leading to what I called 'the Florentine Quarter' was, of course, locked, but while I fumbled for the key, Shade toed the unconscious guard aside (no pay rise for him!) and smashed the lock with a kick that would have earned her a multi-million pound contract with Real Madrid (although I suspected that game would be too effeminate for her).

This door opened on to a small hallway which led directly into the makeshift lounge. Shade entered, and I followed, for once without the slightest fear that Leonardo would attack me and escape. He was slumped in his armchair – presumably knocked out by whatever my visitors had used on the other guards and servants within the house. Shade slapped him a few times in vain, sighed, took out a syringe similar to the one Shimmer had used on Winnie, and injected a tiny part of the contents into his arm.

He opened his eyes immediately.

"Are you da Vinci?" demanded Shade, while I tried to signal him to answer politely.

But he wasn't looking at me.

"Why, you're a fine figure of a woman, to be sure, slave stock I'd say, I'd like to do a nude study of you. Please disrobe!"

Most women would have been more than happy to be immortalised by Leonardo, but Shade reacted as I feared she might.

"You dare to imagine me naked, vile beast!" she yelled, and had pulled the poor man to his feet by his beard and slammed him against the wall almost before I had time to wince. At this rate, the decorators would be in all week.

"You need the plans for the Forward Machine!" I shouted.

I'm convinced my quick thinking saved Leo's life. Shade took a deep breath (which accentuated the 'fine figure' Leo had noticed with his artist's eye, but I didn't mention this: some people just aren't that good at taking compliments), shuddered, grabbed Leo, now groggy again, by the collar of the tweed jacket I'd lent him, grabbed my arm with her other hand, and hauled us both out of the room, down the stairs (that hurt), along the passageway, and back into what had a few hours earlier been my elegant salon, but now looked like a set for *Terminator*.

There she released us, and Shimmer stepped forward.

"Mr da Vinci, it's an honour to meet you, and in other circumstances… but we are very short of time. N here tells us that

STEVE REDWOOD

you have the plans for the Forward Machine. Please give them to us."

Leo was certainly tough. Despite Shade's battering, he was able to stand there, although swaying slightly, and look defiantly at the blonde woman.

"What do you mean, 'Forward Machine'?"

"The Time Machine you came here in. We want the plans. Now."

"Plans!" he almost laughed. "There aren't any plans, you silly woman! No one's going to rob me a second time! The plans are in my head, and that's where they're going to stay!"

"In your head?" Winnie, who had been standing back as if not wanting to be seen, spoke with a voice full of fear.

I began to say, "I already told you that...," but at the sound of her voice, Leo jerked round so quickly that he threw even Shade off balance. He gave a gasp of delight when he saw Winnie, and stretched out his arms towards her. She shrank back, a look of pure misery on her face, avoiding both his attempted embrace and his questioning eyes.

Slowly, he dropped his arms, looked at her uniform, identical to that of the woman who had just beaten him for nothing, glanced at me and saw the confirmation in my eyes.

I'd kept him locked up for a month, trying to make him see reason, become more flexible. Completely in vain.

With that one guilty look, that turning away of her eyes, Winnie achieved what I'd been unable to do in all that time.

She broke his spirit.

His strong muscular frame seemed to fall in on itself, and the self-confidence and magnificent egoism fled.

Shimmer waited a few seconds – I believe even she was affected, if only for a brief moment – but Shade, with a cruel smile in Winnie's direction, forcibly swung Leonardo round to face her, and demanded the plans for the Forward Machine on pain of the instant breaking of sundry limbs. Perhaps she thought he had a little panel leading to a secret compartment in his skull. I doubt if any Gordian knot had ever got beyond infancy in her presence.

Leonardo just stared at her, but when she gave him a slap to help his hearing he managed to raise his great head and glower angrily at her. She raised her hand again.

But Shimmer now took over. And she was angry, very angry. She went and stood in front of him.

"So you're saying that all the knowledge on how to construct a Forward Machine is only in your head? That even if we continued Back to your time, we would find nothing on paper, nothing recorded, no equations, calculations, schematics?"

Although tottering on his feet, Leonardo found the energy to mutter, "That's what I said, woman! Are you stupid?"

Whoops!

Shimmer stared at him as a falcon might have stared if the mouse in its claws had stuck out its tongue.

"So we have no choice, then. We have to take you to the future, and extract that knowledge. That will be very painful for you. And after that, I will teach you never to call me stupid again. That will be *extremely* painful for you. And then perhaps we'll throw what's left of you to the squoggle-catchers as an extra titbit". Her voice was nectarine-smooth.

Winnie's voice cut in. Something in the tone I'd never heard before.

"But that's not necessary. We only need the information. After that…"

"It wouldn't be *necessary*, I agree."

Shade now joined in.

"What's the matter, getting soft, Agent Wildflower?"

Winnie ignored her, kept her eyes on Shimmer. I saw the tension throughout her body.

"But we *dare* not take him to the future, for the same reason we dared not simply kidnap N. The Guardians would notice the Temporal Ripple."

"Not so. N is a vital part of the history of time travel. It's clear, even as far back as the adventure with Rasputin, that the Guardians were keeping an eye on him as well as Bertie. That's why we haven't been able to use our usual methods to get information. But they have no reason, no reason at all, to be watching Leonardo."

"Even if that is so, he was a famous artist in his own time, and there have to be Ripples if he doesn't live out his life there."

"But he already has lived out most of his life, and done all the things for which he was famous. Removing his last year or two affects nobody."

Winnie didn't answer, but kept staring into Shimmer's eyes.

"Moreover," Shimmer went on, "by being here, he is out of time! It's as if he doesn't exist. Even if they wanted to, the Guardians couldn't trace him. So he can be taken to the future with total impunity. And will be."

Winnie was now almost trembling. "Leave me alone with him for ten minutes, please, I know I can persuade him to reveal the principle behind the Forward Machine. That's all we need. That's the only reason we came Back."

"Agent Wildflower, do I need to remind you that you not only failed to notice that Leonardo designed the first time machine, you not only failed to discover N's secret all the time you've been in this century, but that in addition to all this, as N so acutely pointed out, the Forward Machine, which is causing us defeat after defeat – and the death of one of my best friends - was invented because of you?"

"But that's just it! He's only here because of me. I don't deny I've failed in my duty, I've shamed the Department. I will accept punishment willingly. But this man – this wrong-headed ingenuous sentimental old fool – is innocent. There's no need to harm him…"

"Innocent!" Shimmer roared. "None of them are innocent! How dare you speak such treason?"

Winnie's eyes flashed with reciprocal fury.

"*Treason?* I suffered months of surgery to take on the pudding appearance of the Mona Lisa! I lost half a year of my life getting to enter Florentine society so as to meet Leonardo. And just when I was finding something like happiness, I gave it all up in the name of duty. I shared a bed with what must be one of the smelliest men in history!" (Ah, so she had noticed!) "I allowed myself to be groped by his so-called friend over there time after time when Bertie was being Regenerated. I have never shirked my duty, however hard and obnoxious it might be."

I put these latter comments down to words spoken in the heat of the moment. I've noticed that women tend to exaggerate at times. Sweet Mabel had been the same. Probably a bit of PMT, as well.

"And this is the three-times Agent of the Year we were all encouraged to emulate?" sneered Shade. "The only thing she manages to do well, it seems, is rut with animals!"

Winnie swung round on her, and Shade went into a fighting stance.

"Never call Leonardo an animal in front of me!" hissed Winnie.

Of course, she meant to say Leonardo and N, but she was clearly under a lot of stress.

"What else is he?" snarled Shade.

Shimmer had recovered her self-control and intervened coldly. Her best friend killed. *Oh shit!* And what was eating Shade?

"While Agent Gentleheart is perfectly right, we can settle our differences back home. Now we must move. We'll take that traitress with us too," nodding at the body of Shalom, "resuscitate her, and punish her. Or perhaps use her as a bargaining chip with Boadicea."

Shade glanced across at me. "And that thing?"

"We have to leave him. And alive too, unfortunately."

"Can't I just break his legs and arms?"

"All right, but make it snappy. No, wait, on second thoughts, better not. That might draw the Guardians' attention. Indeed, the fact that Leonardo is the real inventor, and not this cringing specimen, is to our advantage. They'll be too busy guarding the wrong man. After we have the information, we can do exactly what we like with this Leonardo and no one will notice because according to them he's already dead.!"

She really had it in for him! Yes, he'd called her stupid, but did that explain such antipathy?

But Winnie hadn't finished. Her whole posture oozed rebellion.

She turned to Leo, and said:

"Did you really invent the Forward Machine only to come to find me?"

Leo was still swaying on his feet. Shade's slaps weren't normal ones. He said nothing, just looked at her. The answer filled the space between them.

Winnie turned to Shimmer.

"I ask you again, Captain, I beg you, leave him here, with me. Let me find out the secret of the Forward Machine, I know I can persuade him. If I fail, I will bring him to you myself. Within two days. You have my word."

Shade stared at her with disgust.

"She *likes* him, the great Agent Wildflower, who we're all supposed to admire and look up to, she *cares* about this slobbering creature!"

Winnie ignored her, her eyes fixed only on Shimmer. "If you

accept this, I swear I will learn the secret of the Machine. Even if I have to torture him myself to get it. But I will not allow him to be tortured just for the sake of it."

Shimmer glowed like a nuclear bomb about to explode.

"You will not *allow*?"

Winnie flinched before her fury, but stood her ground.

"Captain, have you forgotten what the Great Uncluttering was all about? It was to stop just this kind of senseless suffering."

"This... beast... called me stupid!"

"Because you are!" growled Leo. He clearly hadn't learned much about realpolitik from his pal Machiavelli. Even Bertie would have had more sense. I felt like kicking him myself.

Shimmer tensed and I thought that was the end of him, but she again showed rigid self-control, and didn't even turn towards him. Her eyes were locked on those of Winnie in a silent battle of wills.

What would have happened? I don't know. From what I learned later, I tend to think Winnie's training and indoctrination would have won out in the end, that she would have accepted that she had done all she could for the artist.

But Leonardo at that moment slithered to the ground, his last bit of energy wasted on those reckless words. Shade looked down at him with disgust, and then kicked him in the stomach. It wasn't, to be honest, a very hard kick, more an experimental one, perhaps to see if he was just feigning weakness.

It was still a bad mistake!

For a second, maybe two, Winnie just stood there, her eyes completely blank, as if replaying in her mind what she had just seen.

Shimmer looked at Shade furiously, and began to step in front of her. Too late. Winnie hurled herself on her fellow agent.

I'd thought the fight between Winnie and Shalom had been violent, but by comparison with what came now, that had been like duels staged by geriatrics in a local village play.

Imagine that Vesuvius and Krakatoa had taken on human form and were having a really bad hair day, and you have just a glimmering of what I saw. Winnie had lost to Shalom before, but I now realised that this must have been because Shalom had taken her completely by surprise. Or perhaps it was her mysterious feud with Shade that gave her added power.

Or perhaps it was something quite different.

This Winnie was now an awesome creature whose every movement was designed to maim or kill. A cat cornered by a dog, a striking cobra, a hawk swooping – she was these and much more. But Shade too was a born fighter, and all the time was emitting a strange screech of joy, a banshee wail, that made my head throb. Once again, their sheer speed prevented me from following all their movements, although this time it was easier to distinguish between the two because of Shade's black features.

I was terrified just watching them, but Shimmer unhurriedly moved to the far side of the room, and sat elegantly on the windowsill and looked on, as if she were judging auditions for the role of Emma Peel or a new Charlie's Angel.

Why didn't she join in? Certainly not because of any fear or dislike of battle, of that I was sure: I'd seen her in action against Shalom. Most likely, she considered her mission so vital that she didn't want to take the slightest chance of failure; why involve herself in a fight between two inferiors? Winnie, though she had protested, had not disobeyed her. And, if she were planning to do so, she would, even if she won, be so weakened by Shade that she could pose no real threat.

And indeed, although it soon did begin to look as if Winnie would win, both combatants were slowing down so much that I was almost able to see the expressions of effort and pain on their faces. Within a few minutes, I felt sure, it would be over.

And then I recalled how Shimmer had revived Winnie after the earlier fight, and also how Shade had brought Leonardo back to instant consciousness!

As all three of my original Visitors seemed to be dressed identically and carrying the same equipment, wasn't it likely that Shalom too had been carrying the same small medical kit? Including a syringe that packed more punch than a psychotic mule on amphetamines? And if it had worked on Winnie, might it not work on Shalom herself?

Or was she really dead?

And in any case, why even think of interfering? Why not allow events to reach their inevitable conclusion? Shimmer would take both Leonardo and Winnie out of my way for ever and solve all my

STEVE REDWOOD

problems. My secret would be utterly safe, and I could expect to live to a prosperous old age with my Maria…

… and never be able to look her fully in the eye; appropriating Leonardo's notebook was one thing, allowing him to be dragged to a horrible fate was another…

… and always know that Leonardo and Winnie (and Shalom, too, for that matter) had probably been converted to squoggle-catcher food without my even trying to stop it…

… and know too that, however much I might consider myself Bertie's better, he wouldn't have hesitated one second before throwing himself into the fight if he had been here...

If Shimmer succeeded in taking Leonardo to the future and extracting his information, he and Winnie and Shalom and Bertie and who knows how many of Boadicea's people would all become squoggle-catcher food.

Now squoggles, whatever they were, might well be thoroughly unpleasant creatures and fully deserve to be caught – I was entirely open-minded on the matter, and therefore I had no particular wish to see their catchers go hungry – but my self-interest, mollycoddled and pampered as it always had been, wavered before the onslaught of so many potential deaths, and, despite a gallant rearguard action, finally toppled before the uneven odds.

Damn it all!

Go stuff yourself, Moroni, I refuse to be remembered to the end of time as the treacherous narrator!

I began to edge my way towards Shalom's body, which lay almost in the centre of the room, just a few feet from Leonardo, who was stirring slightly. Twice I was knocked back by the writhing bodies of the combatants. Shimmer must have seen me, of course, but I guess she thought I was trying to reach and help Leonardo (primitive creatures sticking together), or maybe intending to assist Winnie in the fight, and rightly deeming that my contribution in the latter case would be less noticeable than a divorce lawyer's ethics, didn't think it worth the bother to stop me.

The third time I made it. Pretending to have been hit yet again by the flying bodies, I groaned and fell across Shalom, my hands scrabbling urgently inside her uniform. The first thing I encountered almost made me forget why I was there – the uniform had had, shall

202

we say, a flattening effect – but I forced my delighted hands to relinquish their serendipitous find, and to continue the search. I soon felt different contours, those of a small pouch. Terrified that at any moment I would be hauled to my feet by Shimmer and smashed against any remaining bits of wall, I managed to open it and almost at once located the syringe.

It was then that I became aware of the silence.

I glanced round and up fearfully.

Leonardo was now on his feet again, just about. Shade was twitching feebly on the floor on the other side of the room. Winnie was on one knee over her, her breath coming in desperate gasps. Shimmer had risen to her feet and was standing a couple of feet away, poised and deadly, like an angel of doom painted in gold.

"Now that you've let off steam, Agent Wildflower, decide. Either help me carry all these bodies to the Time Machine, including your artistic friend, and for old times' sake none of this will go in my report; or continue to defy me and suffer the same consequences as that traitress there."

Her voice suddenly changed.

"N, what are you doing! Get up at once!"

It was too late. I knew it was too late. But something of Leonardo's stubbornness must have rubbed off on me over the last month.

Besides, hadn't Shimmer said she couldn't kill me because of the Guardians?

I jabbed the syringe into Shalom's thigh and pressed the plunger, waiting for Shimmer to pound me to dust.

It never happened.

Instead I heard a voice from what was left of the doorway.

"Hold it right there, you!"

Captain Anderson and Maria's escort! At last!

An ex-SAS man, Anderson had instantly sized up the situation with British intuition. Beautiful blonde woman, big hairy man. He advanced a step into the room, pointing his gun at Leonardo's chest.

"Trying to escape, eh?" he growled.

One of the guards with him put his hand comfortingly on Shimmer's shoulder.

"You'll be all right now, ma'am."

Shimmer, who until then hadn't moved, trying to assess the new situation, screamed like Faust when the Devil finally came for him. and the guard flew back through the door.

Shimmer spun round like a whirling dervish, and Anderson had time to move the gun about a millimetre in her direction before a pitiless kick to his crotch lifted him a few feet in the air.

But the distraction had given Winnie enough time to get to her feet and she had already thrown herself, but with nothing like her earlier velocity, on the blonde whirlwind. At the same time I felt Shalom's body jerk, and then she too was rising like a jack-in-the-box.

Surely she and Winnie could now defeat Shimmer?

Shalom zoomed into the fray…

…and knocked Winnie flying! Too late I realised that she'd been unconscious during the time that Winnie had been trying to come to terms with Leonardo's presence.

"You fool!" I shouted, "she's one of us!"

"I've already told you she's one of them!" answered Shalom, as Shimmer lifted her up and pile drove her onto her knees.

"She *was* one of them, but now she's one of us!"

Shalom answered after a few seconds, as she twisted Shimmer's foot so that the toes gouged the back of the knees.

"You primeval idiot, there's only two of us… who's that?"

She was referring to Leonardo, who had just lurched into view.

"That's Leonardo. He's one of us too."

The lovelorn painter, who had just seen Shalom giving Winnie flying lessons, stumbled towards Shalom and aimed a feeble punch at her. She kicked him away with one foot, her hands being busy trying to make Shimmer resemble one of the giraffe neck women of the Karen tribe in Thailand.

"I thought you said he was one of us!" she said.

"He is. But he thought you were one of them."

Our profound conversation was interrupted again as Shimmer broke the neck lock and pushed Shalom's head through the television, which miraculously had survived unbroken till now. I had long been planning to change it, anyway. Shalom, nothing daunted, rose and head-butted the blonde Captain with her television head, while she floored the weakened Winnie with what was left of a standard lamp. I wondered what programmes were on. Repeats of *Buffy* or *Xena*, perhaps? *Robot Wars*?

Whether it was the educational value of British television I can't say, but Shalom, once free of her new headgear, at last cottoned on to the fact that Winnie had been attacking only Shimmer, and she proceeded to do the same, confining her attacks to the blonde woman. Probably she'd decided that it would be better to leave herself with one enemy rather than two.

Even Shimmer was unable to defeat the two of them, though she came very close to it, and finally fell before the combined onslaught.

Shalom and Winnie eyed each other warily, neither sure if she was facing an enemy or a friend. I realised that although all the combatants were armed, nobody had made any attempt to reach for a weapon. Was it some strange code of honour?

"Stop, you're both one of us!" I cried. "Winnie was trying to save Leonardo!"

"Whatever for…?" Shalom began.

"It's a complicated story…"

Just then the phone rang. It was still working? I wasn't going to answer, but then I realised that I might be able to warn someone of my plight. I looked nervously at Shalom before picking it up. Maria's voice came all in a rush.

"Is that you? Look, N, I'm sorry, I swear this wasn't planned, but that person I bumped into… you remember that pilot, the one I was crazy over, the one who left me for my sister, and then left her for that English girl fifty years ago? Well, this extremely dishy guy came up to me in the street, and said, 'Look, I know this sounds like a pick-up, but I swear I've got a photo of someone the spitting image of you, which I found when my granddad died…' Well, to cut a long story short, it was the pilot's grandson from his second English wife! Incredible, eh? Of course, I didn't let on who I was, but… he's so like his grandfather was… those eyes that send shivers… and well, you have to admit you did lie to me about the Time Machine, and you *are* fifteen years older than me, which may be why in bed, well, I won't say you aren't adequate, I suppose, but… well, what I'm trying to tell you is, I do hope we can remain friends, close friends, I really do. Must hang up now, Tom's so impatient, so much for English pudeur, sorry about your supper."

Click.

At that point, the ceiling surrendered and collapsed.

And I finally pissed myself.

16: SHALOM TAKES CHARGE

"Well," said Shalom, "we have a major problem."

It was half an hour or so later. We were all in my study, in the other wing of the house.

Winnie and Shalom had maintained their uneasy truce while they dragged the unconscious servants and guards out into the garden, and Shimmer, Shade, and Leonardo into the study, just in time before the whole of the east wing finally collapsed due to the unladylike demolition of its walls.

When I'd cleaned myself up a bit, and managed to control my weeping sufficiently *(Maria, my Maria! O, fill my bitter cup with nepenthe!)*, I told Shalom everything that had happened while she was unconscious, and how Leonardo was the real inventor of both the Time Machines. After staring in disbelief, she threw her head back and laughed:

"So that's why there was never a clue about the Forward Machine! We thought it was because you were unbelievably astute and cautious, and it turns out you had about as much knowledge as a stick insect!"

She'd had a certain charm when she was mute.

Leonardo was lying on a divan near the window: a piece of falling masonry had finally knocked him right out, but his breathing was steady. Winnie was standing over him, throwing nervous glances at him, once or twice furtively soothing his brow. I was sitting at the table a few feet away from them, head in hands. Shalom was, like Winnie, standing. Although they sported bruises and cuts, and winced with certain movements, they both looked as if they'd just had nothing more than a particularly strenuous game of hockey.

A major problem. I looked across at the furious faces of Shade and Shimmer. Their bodies, propped up against a wall, were hidden behind a mass of chains that even Jacob Marley's ghost would have found excessive, so their faces were about all that was visible, and even these were half-hidden by fang- and venom-proof leather gags.

"I don't mean just them," said Shalom, intercepting my glance. "I mean you and Winnie and Leonardo – in fact everyone here. Maria and any guards or servants who knew about Leonardo's presence, too. The easiest and most direct solution would be if you were all dead. That's simply a professional opinion. Nothing personal."

Well, it sounded personal to me.

"I thought you were one of us!" I said, offended.

"What she means," said Winnie calmly, "is that the problem of the Forward Machine remains to be solved. She has little choice but to kill *me*, of course, but I don't really see how she can avoid killing you either."

"Me? Why me? It was me who saved her!"

"Irrelevant. You know who invented it."

"But…"

"The Federation suspects that Bertie came to the future in a Forward Machine invented by you, and if Shimmer Mellowdrop and Shade Gentleheart don't return, they will send more agents to interrogate you. And if they fail, they will send still others. It's inevitable that in the end you will talk. Therefore, the logical thing is to kill you to prevent this. Best Benthamite principles."

She didn't seem particularly bothered by this.

"But Leonardo invented the damn thing, not me!"

"No one knows that except you. And Maria, of course. Shalom will have to kill her too." (This time I definitely detected satisfaction in her voice.) "But as for Leonardo, no one would ever think of going to sixteenth-century Florence to look for a time machine! So there's no need to kill him. Indeed, just the opposite: he has to be put back in his timeline before deadly Paradoxes are created."

"Oh," I said, "so she only needs to kill the rest of us."

My voice was filled with fine irony, but Winnie nodded.

"Perhaps we should let Shalom speak," I said.

"She's right," said Shalom.

I was outraged. "I just saved your life!" Hadn't I said that before?

"And you may feel justifiably proud of yourself. And not only my life, but you probably saved the Revolution too. Your name will live forever in future history."

"Bugger future history! I want my body to live in present history!"

There was an uncomfortable silence after this. The heroism count in the atmosphere was way too high for comfort.

"And Maria's too," I added. My heart was broken, but in sensitive souls like mine you can't snuff out love just like that. *The bloody pilot's bloody grandson!*

Shalom looked reflectively at Winnie.

"Of course, Leonardo has to go back, that's obvious. But I don't want to kill you," she said.

Oh, how nice!

"Yet you're quite happy to kill me...!" I began, but no one took the slightest notice of my protest. Bloody hell, it was my house! What was left of it.

"You have to," answered Winnie. "But tell me first, how did you beat me?"

"The advantage of surprise. What's more, I've studied your techniques for two years. Boadicea holds you in the greatest respect. When she was planning to rebel, and setting up the revolutionary cadres, she gave us secret film of your training sessions, and your techniques are now standard, often replacing those of your own instructor, Captain Mellowdrop. So I not only knew your style of fighting, but I'd had special training to practise countering your most innovative moves."

'Techniques'? 'Style'? 'Innovative'? The way I saw it, they simply aimed to do the maximum damage in the minimum amount of time in the most unpleasant way possible. But perhaps I was just having a pre-meet-my-Maker, post-foully-betrayed-by-Maria sulk.

"Besides," went on Shalom, "you've been eating English food for months now."

Winnie smiled.

"Devon cream teas," she murmured. "I dieted at first, but recently picked up bad habits again: Bertie was a real sweet tooth."

"With or without poison!" I muttered, thinking back to the Rasputin affair.

"What?"

"Oh, nothing."

Shalom was looking at Winnie quizzically.

"You could have attacked me when the ceiling caved in."

"I know."

"Is all this because of your old feud with Shade and that unnecessarily bloody Uncluttering on Minerva?"

"Not really. I found out later what they had tried to do to *her*. But a little, maybe."

"Leonardo?"

"Leonardo."

"But one man…"

"…can be enough to prove the whole monstrous lie. When you learn to feel, that is. Then, the imperfections don't seem to matter. Seeing him again made me finally throw off my brainwashing."

Shalom nodded. "It took Boadicea a whole week to open my eyes. And a certain secondary school teacher."

"Not Miss Blubsy!"

"The same."

Winnie chuckled, the first real humour I'd ever heard from her.

"We used to say that she was as good as a press-gang for Boadicea!"

Shalom's smile rapidly disappeared.

"I'm sure you've already guessed what I'm going to do to Shimmer and Shade, since I can't kill them in cold blood. I'll do the same for you."

She had the tone of voice of one suggesting a new recipe for chicken. Still, I began to hope that if she couldn't bring herself to kill Shimmer and Shade then she didn't really intend to kill me. But what if her squeamishness only extended to her own kind?

"Not that easy. I don't want to return to the Department."

"You'll join us?" Shalom sounded really pleased.

"Not that either. I won't fight against all my old friends."

"But…"

"Exactly. You can't allow it. I have too much knowledge. And a complete Mindsweep is the same as killing me."

A small silence.

"You think the Federation could trace you through the Link?" asked Shalom.

"And Retrieve me and Mindsuck me, just as they planned to do with Leonardo. They'd find out the truth about the Forward Machine."

"You've missed out one option."

"There aren't any other options."

"Oh no? What about returning with Leonardo to the sixteenth century?"

"If only I could!" For a moment, there was such yearning in her voice that I shivered with the force of it. "You think I haven't thought about that? But the Federation could still trace me through the Link."

Shalom smiled.

"So you don't know then?"

"What?"

Shalom's smile became bigger.

"What?" repeated Winnie, irritated.

"We know how to remove the Link without destroying the transtemporal chip."

"That's impossible! Bits are embedded in every part of the brain, not just the temporal lobes. Removal is death."

"You're forgetting the Forward Machine."

"I don't… are you saying…?"

"It was one of the first things Boadicea did when she got hold of it. She knew that the moment her plot was discovered she could be traced and followed through the Link. She went to the far future, and had it removed, due to the influence of… someone who said Bertie had once done him a favour. They said they were glad to have been of help, and gave her a pile of self-replicating nanoprobes, and instructions on how to use them. She taught me and others. I can remove your Link, dissolve all traces of it."

Winnie was staring at her, her eyes wide with hope.

"Without the Link, no one could trace me, I could lead a normal life, looking after Leonardo in his final…"

"Exactly. I will have to make him forget he invented a Forward Machine, of course. He spent five years on it, according to what N has said, so we'll have to replace those five years with false memories. Not too difficult, if we stimulate his own mind to generate them. You understand that we can't return those years to him. We have to allow him to invent the Forward Machine, but at the same time we have to take away any memory of it. There are already two time lines interlacing – the one where Leonardo simply painted and studied everything under the sun, and the one where he designed – and built – the Forward Machine. We cannot risk a third one. We can put you back to the day before N and Bertie arrived."

There was another silence, before Shalom spoke again.

"Think about it. Meanwhile…"

She moved across to the two chained prisoners.

"Well, I can't stand round chatting with you two all day, I suppose it's time I pulled my finger out," she announced.

Whereupon she did just that, twisting the little finger of her left hand until it came off completely!

"Not part of the regulation medical kit," she remarked, as out of what turned out to be a hollow sheath she decanted what looked like a mass of tiny electrodes, the ends of which she connected to hidden sockets in her belt buckle.

"In an emergency," she said, "I can use these without removing the finger, but that means I have no fine control over the current. The result is a complete emptying of the mind."

"A Mindsweep," I gasped, for a moment forgetting all about Maria, "that's what you were going to do to me!"

She gave me a tolerant smile.

"You were about to reveal the secret of the Forward Machine," she said. "and a couple of times before that, I thought I'd have to… well, never mind. At that time, I had no other choice. In any case, I was also going to summon a small bomb strike to destroy the house and any papers you might have. Let's just say you were very wise to wait until I was unconscious before revealing everything."

I glowered. The social manners of all my guests left a lot to be desired.

She knelt down in front of the captives.

"I'm pleased to inform you that this is going to hurt," she said.

The two women stared at her with eyes full of hatred and defiance.

"Who wants to be first? No one? Well, a good leader should lead from the front… and," she chuckled, "gentlemen prefer blondes!"

So saying, she stuck the electrodes on Shimmer's temples.

I had to admire the blonde Defender. She didn't flinch, or even try to move her head, knowing it would be useless. And, dishevelled and beaten, she was more beautiful than ever. I almost wanted to rescue her. At least, she'd never pretended to love me. *Oh, Maria! How could you?*

Shalom turned a tiny dial on her belt. Shimmer's eyes dilated, her head jerked and immediately slumped forward.

Shalom, still kneeling in front of her, then attached the remaining electrodes to her own head, and began to calibrate almost invisible controls on her buckle.

Minutes passed, and I noticed that Shalom's eyes were closed.

Had she fainted? I stood up and began to step forward, but Winnie restrained me.

"I think she knows what she's doing," she said.

Shalom remained rigid with concentration, then:

"Pam! Pam pam! Pam pam pam!" she yelled, jabbing at her belt as if trying to squash a frisky ant. Her teeth were bared in a triumphant snarl.

Then she shook her head, opened her eyes, withdrew the electrodes from Shimmer, put them on Shade instead, and the whole process was repeated until, once again:

"Pam! Pam pam! Pam pam pam!"

Finally, she removed the electrodes from her own head, and offered them to me.

"Here," she said, "take a look at this."

I took a step back, fearfully.

"It's all right. It's only playback. I was just knocking out a few memories."

As I was still shaking my head, she gently overcame my resistance by the simple expedient of clamping the electrodes on my own temples, and holding them there with the thumb and two fingers of one vice-like hand. She bent down and turned a knob. There was a kind of hiss, the room disappeared, to be replaced by a reddish haze, and then:

…the pathetic creature is backing away from me, shifty eyes staring with terror, sweat pooling on his low ignoble brow. The Captain, with the aid of the new grunt, is holding me back, but I know that her patience is almost gone, and any minute now…

"I'm going to count to two and then allow my simmering colleague to boil over,"

Oh bliss! My Captain has such a lovely way of putting things! I feel my vagina moist with anticipation…

The base creature exudes fear, the delicious scent of which curls seductively into my nostril.

"All right, all right!" he blubbers. "Bertie disappeared in the Forward Machine or whatever it is you call it!"

I feel a terrible disappointment mixed with the triumph, but I know I'll get another chance. The Captain always lets me break a few legs when we share a mission: she knows how crabby I get when I'm not allowed a decent orgasm.

But the savage has at last admitted what we only suspected: it was the cur Bertie who brought the Forward Machine into our time, and that means it was this snivelling creature who invented it. Now all that remains is…

And then blank. Absolute terrifying nothingness. I yelped in fear, and then the room reappeared, and I saw that Shalom had removed the electrodes, and was calmly stuffing them back into the false finger.

"That," she said, smiling," is the last thing either of them will remember. I wiped out all memory of anything that happened afterwards. They will know, of course, when they recover consciousness, that their memories have been spliced, but they will naturally assume that you then went on to reveal how you built the Forward Machine, and that that was the reason I've excised the memories from that point onwards. They will now be certain that it was indeed you who invented both time machines, and they will redouble, triple, their efforts to capture you and make you talk. The price on your head will be astronomical! Why, Boadicea, or Bertie himself, wouldn't fetch much more! You should feel proud."

Proud! What had she done? Saved me from three bloodthirsty psychopaths (if you include Winnie before her suspiciously sudden 'conversion') only in order to ensure that now a whole horde of them would be after me!

Torn between the desire to hurl myself at her and gouge out her eyes and play conkers with them, and a need to collapse on the floor in a despairing heap, I chose the latter as being the only viable option.

I vaguely heard Winnie and Shalom talking, and then Winnie's voice, as if it came from beyond a line of *Wanted: N, Half-dead or Alive* posters, vultures sitting astride them, stretching beyond the distant cactus-ridden horizon.

"N, I want to ask you something."

I looked up through blurry eyes.

"Why I'm such a success with women?" I said bitterly.

Winnie looked puzzled.

"You, a success?"

"Oh, forget it. What do you want?"

"Shalom says it's safer to let Leonardo remain unconscious, and excise the later memories while he's still out. We can't allow him to stay here, the Paradox would be too great. And it's better this way, not being able to warn him, because he, and we, have no choice in the matter anyway."

I said nothing. I was really getting just a little fed up with Leonardo. First Bertie, now Leonardo. Would I never get top billing? The eternal deuteragonist, if that? 'A History of the World in Two Million Acts. Cast: Nearly Everyone Who Ever Lived or Will Live. Extras: Ants, Cockroaches, N, Platypuses.'

"Does he really love me?"

"What?"

"Does Leonardo love me?"

I was very tempted to say he thinks you stink and can't stand your snoring. But it's such hard work being always bad.

"He took your portrait with him everywhere, kept it till the day he died. He spent five years building that bloody Machine just to come to take you back. Any more silly questions?"

A small silence.

"Slicing me and Bertie into millions of pieces was simply an added bonus," I added. "An early brand of cubism. Artistic licence, you might say."

Winnie ignored that last comment. Women have a habit of doing that. The insides of many a front door are pockmarked with the witty sayings I have hurled after departing ladies. She turned to Shalom.

"In that case, I accept. Please give my apologies to Bertie. I used him, but he tried to be a good husband."

She turned back to me, looking at me contemplatively.

"It's all right," I said. I know when to be noble. "There's no need to say it. You just did what you had to do."

"Actually, I was just wondering how Mabel ever put up with… never mind."

Shalom coughed gently.

"Winnie, we're running out of time. Are you sure you won't join us?"

"I already told you. All I want now is to be with Leonardo in his final years. Afterwards… who knows?"

"Well," said Shalom, turning to me, "and now we come to you. The final loose end."

I didn't like that. I suspected Shalom had a way of doing drastic things to any loose ends she caught loitering at a loose end.

"I'll take Leonardo and Winnie back to Florence in the Time

Space Machine we came in – that's nothing to the journey we took to get here – and leave Shimmer and Shade somewhere near here – do you have any horse troughs or pig pens we can dump them in? – where the Federation can find them and their false information. With Winnie's Link neutralised, they'll assume she died here – I'm going to burn down this house to help give them that impression. Even if they should make a cursory check on the Mona Lisa – they won't, because they know Winnie came to this century – they will assume the Guardians Rectified completely, reinstating the genuine Mona Lisa in her place again."

"One moment! Burn down my house!?"

"Well, it won't be any use to you."

"No use to me?" Was she going to kill me, after all?

"No, you'll be coming to the future with me, too."

My relief lasted about one second.

"Now wait just a minute! I'm not going to any future! You're in the middle of a civil war, for a start! It's full of people like Shimmer and Shade, for another. I like it here. I earn a very good living. I play in the local cricket team. Do you know how much I sell my sperm for?"

Shalom looked a bit disgusted.

"Very well, I could Mindsweep you, or kill you, I suppose, if you prefer."

"I don't want to go to the future. I like it here. I want to stay here."

Shalom sighed. "Even if I didn't do anything, I estimate the next Federation Defender team will be here within two or three days. They might even send Shimmer and Shade again if they Retrieve them in time!"

I was going off her fast!

"This is all your fault! You've made them think I invented the Machine!"

"You were quite happy for everyone else to think it!" Shalom retorted.

"But that did no harm to anybody!"

"We're wasting time. I told you: be Mindswept, killed, or taken to the future: choose!"

"But why?" I wailed.

"Well, for a start, Bertie's invited you."

"Bugger Bertie! This is all his fault. I never want to see him again!"

"Are you sure?"

"I'm sure! I want to stay here and mourn my incomparable Maria!"

Shalom smiled.

"Oh, you do, do you? Why don't you just read this first, and then see if you feel the same?"

She fished out some sheets of paper from that uniform which probably held a kitchen sink somewhere.

"What is it? An organ donation form?"

"It's a school essay."

"A school essay! You're talking about abducting me, and you want me to read a school essay!"

"I wrote it myself."

This was surreal! Had I already been Mindswept without knowing it? A professional killer comes from the future, her mission to save that future at whatever cost – and she brings an old school essay with her!

I spoke very carefully.

"I am very pleased that you still write essays at school. And on paper too. It shows that IT isn't going to take over the world entirely. And I am sure it is a very good essay. Yes, quite sure. Well done."

Of course, my sarcasm was lost on her.

"Actually, the essay didn't get a very high mark. But I brought it, thinking that if I failed it would be a way to let you know what really happened to Bertie, and what the Revolution is all about. It's the story of the Fall. A story every child learns almost by heart from a very early age. How Boadicea the Abominatrix betrayed the principles of the Great Uncluttering. It recounts how one tiny error, and the wrong woman in the wrong place at the wrong time, was able to change galactic history."

I read it.

17: THE ROAD TO DAMASCUS

The nightmare for our people began again, although no one could have known it, when Hemera took her daughter to the pet shop to buy her a Betelgeusian squoggle-catcher for her tenth cloneday. But the last one, it turned out, had been purchased just a few hours before.

Little Maia burst into tears – those special tears that always induced thoughts of either suicide or girlicide in her mother. Even on recycled air, the child's squalling capacity was awesome.

"Are you sure you can't get one?" asked Hemera. She looked the owner straight in the eye. "I could make it worth your while."

The owner, who had not failed to notice the Venusian lava-serpent necklace and the equally priceless Ganymedean shawl, looked round cautiously. They were alone.

"We won't be receiving any more squoggle-catchers for at least a month," she said slowly, "but if you really want an exotic pet… I mean, *really* exotic… then perhaps I can help. Unofficially, of course."

Maia, like everyone else on the Artemis Five trading colony, had learnt the art of negotiation very young. Mother and child looked into each other's identical eyes, and in a single blink the pact was sealed: Maia's tears went into provisional remission, and Hemera nodded to the young woman.

Twenty minutes later, they were in a well-hidden underground warehouse, where the faint peppermint smell of an Andromedan Polypod still lingered. That augured well: the Polypods had built up a fine reputation as audacious starfarers whose contraband goods tended to become collectors' items almost at once. But when she saw the new 'exotic' creature in its cage, Hemera's first impression was hardly positive. It was bipedal, malodorous, and unpleasantly hairy. It looked up when the two women and the girl entered, and began chattering away and gesticulating, and even threw itself on the floor in what in a human would have seemed a supplicating gesture. Maia whooped with delight.

Disinfectant sprinklers couldn't completely suppress a rather unpleasant odour. Hemera wrinkled her nose.

"Don't worry," the owner said reassuringly, "it doesn't usually smell quite so strong. The smell is easily cleared by pouring almost boiling water over it. It makes strange noises when you do this – it clearly finds it unpleasant – but it keeps the smell away, and also makes its skin nice and soft – if a bit wrinkled. But try not to let the water boil completely."

"It's rather ugly, isn't it?"

"Well, it's not very pretty, I admit, but it is extremely affectionate, if treated well."

"Where's it from?"

"You know the Polypods never reveal things like that. But they did mention that it's one of the most primitive creatures they've ever come across, possibly predating even the colonisation of this segment of the galaxy!"

"That would explain its obvious lack of intelligence."

"Ah, but it's not completely unintelligent! Irrational, yes, but not unintelligent. I've had it here for a month or more, and… well, you'll see what I mean if you decide to buy it. Indeed, it's this strangely warped intelligence that would make it such an interesting pet."

"What's it called?"

"The Polypods called it a gollub, but they said they made up that name because they'd never found anything quite like it before."

"Are you sure it's not dangerous? I don't like the way it's looking at us."

"It has little tantrums now and then, but that's no problem; we can throw in a neuro-whip, just in case, which sends a disruptor beam straight at the pain centres."

"Oh, can I try now, Mummy?"

The owner looked doubtful, but a peremptory glance from Hemera resolved her doubts.

"Here, young lady, but only turn the dial just a fraction."

She handed Maia an oblong box with a red dial. The little girl pointed it at the gollub and twisted the dial as far as possible. She jumped up and down in ecstatic delight as the creature shrieked and hurled itself in agony against the bars.

Hemera gently took the neuro-whip away.

"Now you mustn't do that too often, darling," she chided. "You're only to use this thing if the pet's disobedient, or for training. Unless you're really, really bored." She recalled what Maia had done to the Rigan cloud-bat, which had necessitated repainting the whole apartment. Still, little girls would be little girls.

"I'm sure you'd never need to use it," said the pet shop owner, as tactfully as possible. "As I said, this creature's usually quite obedient. In any case, there's an easier, less damaging, way to control it. You see those funny lumps of flesh hanging between its legs? Those two things like dried apricots, the Polypods called them berls. They seem to serve no other purpose than to be violently scratched, but that other thing – I call it a twitcher – has some quite remarkable properties, I can assure you. At the moment, it's true, you can hardly see it, because of your daughter's… um, playful enthusiasm, but it has the quite unique capacity of expanding and retracting. Moreover, I've discovered you only have to stroke it a bit to make the gollub instantly attentive and desirous to please."

"Can it communicate?" Hemera wasn't interested in the ridiculous twitcher.

"It seems to have a rudimentary form of speech. Mainly gibberish, of course. But I've managed to pick out a few sounds that may well be words. What's more, although I know this may sound like gynomorphism, the pathetic fallacy, it sometimes seems to show real, almost human, emotions, although that's clearly impossible. As I've already said, it has a strong desire to please, and will do almost anything for the reward of having its twitcher stroked."

She gave Hemera a significant look. "I might add that it could be much more than just a toy for young girls. Oh yes, it could definitely have other uses. But far be it from me to pre-empt your own discoveries." Her smile really was quite suggestive. Hemera pretended not to have heard: the woman clearly hoped to charge more by making the creature seem more interesting than it really was.

"There's one unfortunate thing I should warn you about." *Ah ha, here comes the candid I-wouldn't-want-to-mislead-you patter.* "When its twitcher has been expanded for some time, a rather unpleasant substance comes out, sometimes with considerable force. It's not dangerous, but it's not pleasant, either."

"Substance?"

"Yes, you know, a bit like what snails and slugs leave behind. Luckily, there are usually warning signs when this is about to happen: the creature breathes much more heavily, its face becomes red and blotchy, its grunting becomes very rapid, and its eyes go funny. The best thing at this stage is to throw very cold water over it, or use the neuro-whip, although it might be better to just let this substance come out, since when it's repeatedly drenched with cold water it tends to become either very morose or even unusually aggressive."

"This… substance won't damage the carpet?"

"Oh no."

Hemera was still hesitating, but she knew Maia had already made up her mind. And the pet shop owner knew it, too.

"A few words on its care. It seems to do well on a liquid diet, alcohol is best, and seems to keep it quite happy. And always – always – make sure it's chained to something in the house. If it escaped… Well, as you know, the authorities are getting stricter all the time. A woman was publicly flogged last month for possessing an inter-phasic Nebulan trunkfish."

"I saw the flogging! It was great fun!" Maia informed them, giggling.

"Maia likes to watch educational programmes," said Hemera.

"Well, I hope you enjoy your new pet. If treated well, it will undoubtedly become a warm, devoted creature, and you'll find there's nothing nicer than to return home in the evening, and have it come bounding up, licking your feet, and jumping up and down in welcome."

The following few days were indeed happy ones, for both mother and child. Maia would take piggyback rides on the new pet, pull hair out of its nostrils and eyelids, put gungy-slugs into its ears, set fire to the strange tuft of hair at the end of its jaw, and treat it as she did all her toys. At first, it was rebellious and prone to gibbering too much, but the neuro-whip and the berl-cruncher (a little device that Maia herself invented) soon solved that small problem, It was the creature's strange twitcher, however, that gave her most delight. She would stroke it until it stuck up, pull it down until tears came to the creature's eyes, then suddenly let go. She liked to paint it, tattoo it, lasso it, and throw Jovian ring snakes over it. Once, she managed to wind it up so tightly that when she let go, the resultant jet brought down a careless fly. Aiming for the opposite effect, she discovered that putting a Scorpius X-1 giant vampire spider near it caused it to disappear almost completely. Sometimes, her friend Aegina, a merry red-haired girl a few years older than her, came round. Aegina, who rarely bothered to wear clothes, had an inexplicably strong effect on the creature: upon seeing her, its twitcher would twang upright almost immediately, without any need to physically wind it up. Both girls found this hilarious, but at the same time, unfortunately, the gollub would get noticeably agitated, and it was necessary to use the neuro-whip or berl-cruncher to calm it down.

If anything, Maia's mother seemed even more pleased with the new acquisition. Her best friend Hestia (they had been cloned in the same lab on the same day) soon noticed a new freshness about her friend's cheeks, a spring in her gait, a mischievous smile playing about her lips. When she pressed Hemera about this, the latter blushed, and said coyly: "Well, the burtee might have other uses, you know."

"Burtee?"

"That's what it seems to call itself."

Hestia insisted on knowing more, so one night, after Maia had gone to bed, Hemera invited her round.

"You just have to experience this," she said, "it's like nothing I've ever felt before."

She was lounging in a chair, idly swinging her feet, while the burtee, with a white cloth tied round the front of its body, was standing at the sink washing up. Every now and then, Hemera snapped her fingers, and it would break off, bend down, lick her feet, and await orders. There were scorch marks on its shoulders, a sign that a certain amount of training with the neuro-whip had been necessary.

"Has the cleaning robot broken down?" asked Hestia, puzzled.

"Oh no! Listen, I can't explain it, but just watching it sweating over the kitchen sink, occasionally kicking it or using the neuro-whip, gives me a most incredible sensation of well-being! Yes, really, I swear I'm not having you on! Just come and sit with me, and see if you feel the same."

It was hard to keep Hestia away after that.

But this innocent contentment was not to last long.

One afternoon, a grim-faced Woman in Black came, searched the house, found the naked burtee whimpering behind the toilet, and briskly clubbed it into unconsciousness. For some strange reason, she stripped and examined both the women and the girl very carefully

(Hemera thought she heard her mutter 'steel in tact,' but that made no sense). After finding out the name of the pet shop, she warned them never to mention the gollub to anyone at all, on pain of an imaginatively protracted death, and took the plaything away, together with Maia's berl-cruncher. A little later, they saw the pet shop go up in flames, and not long after that, a muffled explosion came from the direction where the underground warehouse had been.

⊕

Where had it come from? Were there any others? If there were, there existed the terrifying possibility that the disgusting creatures might once again spread across the Galaxy – after all the bitter centuries spent eliminating them – and usher in a new Dark Age.

Galactic Defender Boadicea Sunsinger, sworn to protect the Federation against the Scum of the Universe and uphold the values of the Great Uncluttering, took off from Artemis Five, with the still unconscious gollub staked out on the cabin floor, and reflected on her good fortune. Without that tip-off a few days before…

Within half a day she caught up with the Andromedan ship, slaughtered the crew, and captured the Captain.

The quivering Polypod Pirate, after she had threatened to inject concentrated marmite into its tentacles, had told a strange story. It had been hiding out with its crew in one of the bomb craters of Old Earth when they had come across some natives who claimed that a strange machine had just appeared one day out of nothing, and that a lone creature had staggered out it, uttered a noise that sounded like 'o sheet!', and promptly collapsed. The creature was so similar to the pictures of prehistoric devils they had seen that they had taken it back to their village planning to sacrifice it to their local goddess. The Captain, who liked to think he was a connoisseur of blood rituals, had gone to watch the sacrifice, and had found the proposed victim so strange that he had immediately sensed profit. The Polypods had snatched the creature from the sacrificial slab, and made off with the antiquated machine as well.

When an order had come through from their contact on Artemis, the gollub had been delivered there.

What now particularly interested Boadicea was the Captain's

comment that 'the creature appeared to have some form of elementary speech'. This was terrifying enough: it implied that somewhere enough Yukhoos had survived over the centuries to maintain some form of social cohesion.

But the real shock had come when the Captain had repeated some of the 'words' he thought he had heard: 'inkland', 'worteh', 'bludiyell', and, above all, 'tymatcheen'.

'Tymatcheen'!

The Black Defender waited only to take a single look at this 'tymatcheen' (it was still in the hold of the pirate ship) and then injected the marmite into the terrified smuggler after all. It immediately spasmed into the Tentacular Death Frenzy which, battle-hardened as she was, still left her breathless with shock. And a pang of guilt: she didn't usually break her word, and the Polypod had clearly had no idea what a Time Machine was, but if it uttered the mere word in certain quarters… Enough people (and alien historians and archaeologists) still studied Ancient English to make it inevitable that sooner or later one of them would have understood the implications.

Although not herself in the Time Division (where the learning of Ancient English, as well as the contemporaneous sub-dialect Bûshian, was obligatory), as a Grade One Defender, Boadicea had a smattering of AE, and was well acquainted with the history of Time Travel. She knew, too, that despite the repeated warnings of the Ultimate Time Guardians, the Federation Council still secretly maintained a Time Travel capability, although they were wise enough not to attempt to make use of it except when their own existence might be at stake.

But this was not a Federation machine!

And it certainly wasn't from the future!

As the ship's robots transferred the artefact – which was vaguely wasp-shaped – into her own Starfighter, she tried to come to terms with what she had stumbled across. Something that had been sought with more fervour than any alchemist had sought the Philosopher's Stone or any Knight the Holy Grail.

A Machine that had travelled Forward in time!

A Machine that would give the United Colonies an immediate advantage over any enemies, even the fanatic war-mongering

Klunkins. A Machine that would even enable them to throw the arrogant Ultimate Time Guardian emissaries out on their supercilious backsides, because for the first time ever they would be open to an attack from the past. She could just see herself announcing her discovery to the Council, and the jealousy on the face of Her Greerness, who only the week before had publicly criticised her for her 'rebellious streak', despite the fact that in some quarters her reputation rivalled that of the almost legendary Defender Winnie Wildflower. Honour and fame beyond her imagining lay ahead.

She looked down with an exultant smile at the yukhoo now finally beginning to recover consciousness at her feet. It represented honours, wealth, and retirement for her. She suppressed a healthy instinct to destroy it at once. She had to deliver it to the Council. After finding out everything she could about the Time Machine.

But there was something to be done even before that. Like so many others, she felt sick whenever she heard about the unnatural goings-on at the highly exclusive Catherine the Great Pleasure Palace on Vega, where it was rumoured a few of these creatures were still bred for obscene uses by certain leaders of more than one Federation planet. Yet a secret part of her had always wondered what it might be like. She mustn't fail to take this opportunity to settle in her own mind once and for all whether the incredible stories were true.

She kicked the yukhoo for a few minutes to put herself in the mood – it certainly was just as exhilarating as she had heard! – and threw off her uniform.

It was maybe five minutes later, according to Boadicea's own version, that behold there suddenly shined round about her a light from Heaven. And a mighty voice said: 'Why persecutest thou us? It is hard for thee to kick against the pricks'.

And that, though at the time she didn't realise it, was the beginning of her metamorphosis into the Abominatrix.

And of the Second Dark Age of the Galaxy.

(At the bottom of the essay, in a neat prim hand, was the following comment: 'You begin well enough (although you should know by now that lava-serpents come from Jupiter, not Venus) but later present the Abominatrix in far too favourable a light. You do not stress enough her essentially despicable nature from the beginning. I have also noticed that you did not spit at her image with sufficient enthusiasm during yesterday's civic indoctrination session. Therefore I require you to present yourself in my study at eight o'clock sharp, with the class cane, and without your knickers. Signed: Frances Blubsy.'

It was shortly after this date that the seventeen-year-old Shalom joined one of the secret revolutionary cadres that Boadicea had set up with the intention of destroying the system from within.

18: A VISIT TO THE FUTURE

During the Trip Forward, Shalom filled me in on a few details.

Leo's Forward Machine is what had saved Bertie and Boadicea, of course. With it, they were able to go into their future, and bring back advanced weaponry, and useful little gadgets like planetary force field shields. They rescued the males in the various Pleasure Palaces (Vega was simply the most notorious) and took them to a wild planet called Charybdis, which became the rebels' stronghold.

There the males simply continued to do what they had been doing before, only this time without whips, torture, and subsequent post-coital sacrifice. They still had a rather full working-day, since there were so few of them. They were expected to be available at least ten hours a day for classes of women to touch and examine as Boadicea's educators attempted to explain and demonstrate old and forgotten quaint customs. Every erection, however, earned merit points, which could be exchanged either for food and drink or an extra hour off.

Apart from this social aspect, a thousand or so more clones were immediately made of each of these males to provide a backup pool of males for the next generation. In addition, they also had to make frequent donations for artificial inseminations in order to fertilize ova and provide future variety. The resulting embryos were still reared in the cloning tubes, unless the mother wanted to be *really* old-fashioned and bear the child herself.

But all this was really planning for the future, since it was, of course, too late to educate most of these males. Bertie, a Caliban among Morlocks, was a prodigy simply through being able to speak and reason (within reason). He was infinitely superior to any other male alive at the time. Hence the legend of a super being which Shimmer and Shade had believed in. Boadicea, an astute politician as well as a military tactician, saw the advantage of this, and put her propaganda machine into full operation, suggesting that even in his own time Bertie had been a superman, and had indeed been sent by Destiny to help them.

Bertie was not averse to this publicity. For a time, apparently, he had pined for Winnie, but was soon equally smitten with Boadicea. I wasn't surprised. He'd have considered the way he'd been clubbed into unconsciousness behind the toilet in Hemera's house and then brutally raped in the Defender's spaceship extremely romantic. As his father used to say, "All Bertie needs is a strong woman."

Knowing, however, that her enemies also had a time travel capability, and that they would almost certainly go Back to try to learn the design of the Forward Machine, Boadicea put it out that Bertie was a hero-king from the *future* (which the Federation couldn't touch), who had been sent to free people from a murderous tyranny. She thereby hoped that no one would notice any connection between this new super hero and the old Time Traveller who had disappeared so mysteriously in the very early days of time travel. And indeed, for a couple of years, that was so. But word got out somehow – maybe Bertie himself in nostalgic mood, or some visitor to old Terra – that the deadly Forward Machine was in fact an ancient artefact, and from there the connection was eventually made with Bertie's disappearance.

"So then, logically, the inventor of the Forward Machine had to be you. Old records were unearthed. But the Federation was never *sure*. How much was history? How much was Boadicea's propaganda put out to mislead them?"

"OK. But why didn't *you* know about Leonardo?"

"Bertie believed you really had built the Machine. So Boadicea, and the rest of us, believed the same."

"But that's impossible! Even he must have realised that if Leonardo was standing in my garden five hundred years out of his time next to a machine he had never seen before, it was more than likely that he'd arrived in said machine."

Then it came to me. As soon as he'd seen Bertie, Leonardo had run at him waving that disgustingly enthusiastic scimitar. On a bright sunny afternoon. All the terrified Bertie would have seen would have been the flashing of a metal blade and maybe glimpses of some wild man wielding it. The idea that it might be Leonardo had clearly never occurred to him – why should it? He assumed I'd invented this new Machine just as he believed I'd invented the other one.

So far, it all made sense. But…

When the Federation made the connection between the new super hero and the old Time Traveller, they sent Agent Wildflower back to Florence to replace the Mona Lisa and keep an eye on Bertie and myself. But if she'd been sent back, it was only because…

Bertie had already reached the future.

But there was only one Machine capable of taking him there: Leonardo's. Bertie couldn't have reached the future if Leonardo hadn't pursued us into the twenty-first century. And the only reason Leonardo would have done that would have been to find the Mona Lisa…

Who at that time hadn't left Florence! Did that mean that Bertie had already come back with a different Mona Lisa?

A Mona Lisa that I couldn't remember because the new reality (with Winnie) had replaced the old one (with the 'real' Mona Lisa)?

Had everything already happened before?

And if once before, why not twice before, a hundred times before? Were we doomed to play the same roles, with variations, for eternity?

"I don't understand," I said to Shalom. "Who the heck was Leonardo cuddling until you lot from the future decided to go back and alter everything? Wenefride from bloody Blackpool? A girl really called Lisa? "

"Even in your physics you know that a particle can be – or appear to be – in two places at once, or a cat both dead and álive, your whole quantum mechanics is based on it, I believe. But when you open Shaw Dinger's Box and find a live cat – well, you say, that's the way the cook made a crumble, and the cat never died: it was, in my reality, only a potential death. But what if someone else is simultaneously opening the box and finding a dead cat?"

"I understand that. Parallel worlds. All nonsense."

"Only half nonsense. What we call history is simply the most powerful of the Time Lines. It doesn't replace the other Lines, it simply occludes them, and sometimes they jut through, like a broken bone. When a Change is Rectified, the Guardians are, as it were, going back to the Line they are used to, the one they want to continue. But the others still exist, or potentially exist, somewhere."

I wasn't convinced, but I turned to another simpler problem.

Here were these people planting moles all over the place and time – Winnie, Shalom, Mary Magdalene, Cain's 'wife' – when it seemed to me that all either the baddies or the goodies had to do was come back, bang me on the head, and take me to the future: one group to beat the shit out of me, the other to soothe my troubled brow.

"I told you, the Guardians," said Shalom, when I asked about this. "They'd have noticed the Ripple. And got very angry."

"But you're taking me to the future now."

"Ah, that's different. The Guardians don't like anyone trying to change history (their history). Which is just what the Black Defenders meant to do by getting the secret of the Forward Machine from you. Our action now is purely a defensive one. By taking you to the future and keeping you safe, we are in fact preventing any alteration to the Time Line that led to the Guardians themselves."

I sensed she was missing something out, covering something up. How come those mysterious Guardians accepted Bertie arriving in the future with a Forward Machine, but wouldn't accept a Federation agent like Shimmer doing the same thing? I certainly wasn't complaining, but…

I thought I had an idea of who was behind all this. To test it out indirectly, I said:

"Who were those two strange (and intensely irritating) scruffs we kept meeting?"

After the briefest of hesitations, she replied: "They've been seen in our time, too. There's a legend about two Jews who heckled Jesus at the Sermon in the Fountain, urging him to 'get real' and later threw a banana skin under his feet on his way to meet the Cavalry, and Jesus, when he got to his feet, fixed them with his glittering eye and said 'Just you wait, you little shits!'

I hadn't seen that incident myself, but then there had been a lot of 'Romans' between me, and Jesus and Bertie – I hadn't wanted to catch their eye. But I did remember the two Sadducees who'd walked away laughing from the Cross. Not laughing now, were they? Had Bertie and I really kept coming across the Wandering Jew doubled?

But no, that was impossible: we'd seen them in the Land of Nod, too, long before Jesus could have cursed them. Unless…

…Unless they hadn't been Sadducees at all, but other Time Travellers! Not having to wait merely till Judgement Day, as the legend had it, but to wait throughout all Time! Jesus hadn't seemed like a vindictive person, but perhaps he hadn't been in the most forgiving of moods on that particular day.

I said, "But Shimmer and Shade seemed rather interested in them…"

"Propaganda warfare. Boadicea put the word out they were really Time Guardians keeping an eye on the activities of the Federation."

"So they're nothing to do with Moroni, then?"

Shalom smiled. "As I said, it appears they were around playing silly tricks at the Crucifixion."

"But…"

It was a sign of our new relaxed relationship that the hand that was now clamped across my mouth was somehow softer and warmer.

"There are certain questions we never ask," she said, "and I would advise you to just accept things as they are."

I had my answer.

I think.

⊕

Before we'd left, there'd been a few things to sort out, of course.

Captain Anderson suffered a slight loss of memory, as did Maria and anybody else (only three or four) who had been aware of Leonardo's stay in my house. How Shalom was able to locate Maria I don't know; I didn't ask her; the wound was too fresh.

We left Shimmer and Shade, as Shalom had suggested, in the pig pen. I was slightly worried about them starving to death, but Shalom said it wouldn't take the Federation more than a few hours to trace their Link and Retrieve them.

And then they would report that, as had been suspected, it was indeed I who built both the Time Machines, but that their memories of my confession of how I designed them had been excised. And since I will no longer be there, the Federation won't bother to go hunting in the past again. And even if they did, they would only find a burnt-out house where the gallant Agent Winnie Wildflower so cruelly perished in the line of duty, her Temporal Link destroyed by the fire. They would also find two hundred unpaid guards. Well, they'd been pretty useless.

⊕

Leonardo and Winnie will be safe in sixteenth-century Florence. He will believe he is with his Mona Lisa. Perhaps he will be.

We dropped them outside Leonardo's old studio. I wanted to get out and take a look for old times' sake, but Shalom wouldn't allow it.

"Ripples," she said, "Ripples."

At the very last, Winnie finally showed some human feeling for someone other than the painter.

"Does Bertie know who I really am?" she asked Shalom.

"No. Boadicea wanted to save him from that. He believes you are still mourning his loss."

"Please thank her for me. N?"

I was too happy to bear grudges.

"Don't worry," I said, "I won't tell him."

She touched my cheek fleetingly.

"Maybe you're not all bad, you know."

And then she was gone. Closing the circle.

I treasure that touch more than all the occasions I had comforted her during Bertie's resuscitations.

I thought it would be only decent to let Bertie Senior know that his son was all right, had indeed done rather well for himself, so before leaving we'd stopped outside his office and broken in through the window. I told him the good news while Shalom tied a rope to his left leg, and another to the enormous desk, then we left him dangling two hundred and fifty floors up to help him assimilate the good news about his son.

And so, finally, we're on our way to join Bertie and Boadicea. Shalom has estimated our journey will take at least a week. This surprised me. Our previous Trips had been almost instantaneous, even when we went as far Back as Cain. But Shalom pointed out that now we were in a Time Space Machine. We were not only travelling in time, we were also travelling in space to Boadicea's rebel planet of Charybdis. And indeed this machine, while having the same basic design as my own (oh, all right then, *Leo's*!), was much larger, and even had bunks for sleeping.

A few hours ago, I looked across at Shalom and couldn't help recalling my happy discovery when I'd been searching inside her uniform for the syringe. Perhaps it was time to test what joys the future held for me.

"I've been wondering," I said, "when we went to the bathroom those two times, why didn't you help me to escape then?"

"Shimmer had the keys and codes to the TSM controls."

"Ah, I see. Of course."

Small silence. I knew she was thinking of the same thing as me.

"And, er, by the way," I added as casually as I could, "that first time, you know, in the house, you didn't…er… take a little peek?"

Shalom, finely-tuned fighting machine, enforcer, super spy, confidante of the possible future ruler of twenty-one planets, blushed. I felt good.

"I've spent all my life working behind enemy lines, I never had the chance to…well…"

"It's OK," I said, smiling to put her at her ease, "you don't need to explain."

She watched the controls for a moment. When she spoke again, her voice was almost timorous. Shalom nervous!

"Could you… could I… just take one more little look? And, maybe…er… just touch it, only for a moment, so that I can tell my friends, you know, show off a little?"

Well, carpe ye rosebuds while the sun shines and all that.

"Shalom," I said graciously, "it's the least I can do after everything you've done for me. Please feel free to ask any time, and when we get to the future tell your friends not to be afraid to do the same."

Life was certainly going to be a bit different from now on.

Yes, I'd lost Maria. And now I thought about it, it did seem odd that she had chosen to leave me on the very day when… I dismissed the thought: mustn't get paranoiac. I would learn to live without her. '*Adequate!*' That from the woman to whom I'd offered every organ of my being! Ha, a billion women would help to salve the pain of that barb! Nearly every one absolutely virginal. Never even seen a man. No experience whatsoever. Unable to compare me with those ridiculously over-endowed sports that had until now blighted my life.

I burst into full-throated song that made Shalom look up in surprise. I gently pushed her head down again. All right, so she was taking liberties, and I would gently chide her afterwards, but… all in good Time, I thought, all in good Time!

Ah, Bertie, dear friend, let me count the ways I love thee! I already imagined myself flinging my arms round my old, my faithful, my pugnaciously pungent Travelling companion, who had made all this possible. A new start, he and I, the best of buddies. I felt sentimental tears welling into my eyes. Bertie was my friend, we would meet up every day and recall over morning (late morning) coffee those incredible adventures we had had, and share our experiences of this brave new world.

Two men of the world.

Practically the only men of the world.

Who the heck needed Cleopatra?

AUTHOR'S NOTE

This novel began years ago as a short time travel story (embryo of the present chapter 12), in itself suggested by Mike Moorcock's marvellous *Behold the Man*. Then I thought of doing a series of such stories – but strictly limited to trips to solve genuine historical mysteries – with the narrator a self-serving amoral creature who always betrays his partner. However, not only must each trip to the past influence the next one, the next one, I decided, must also influence the one before it! But what could possibly connect, for example, Rasputin with Cain with the Nazca Lines with the Roswell 'aliens'? After months of headaches, whisky and despair, I suddenly realised that the key lay in Mona Lisa's mysterious smile and the emergence of a new religion on the other side of the Atlantic...

This is a novel, not a history book, but every care has been taken to ensure that such historical details as are given are completely accurate.

Grief,
by Ed Lark

ED LARK

ISBN 1 905315 02 3 • £6.99

"The clouds were ugly and dark as scabs. I loved Keeku for a moment. A cab drove past me and I pretended it was a horse, swore it was a horse. I chased it down the street telling it to giddy-up. I hated Keeku now, the stupidity of her beautiful neck, the docile barges of her thighs and her mouth with the wet hole in it where the words came out."

GRIEf

reverb

Juan has left his past behind for the seductions of the city and the Crystal Realm – a world of ever-changing fashion, daily plastic surgery, mind-altering drugs and bizarre sex.

He effortlessly climbs the social hierarchy, gaining money and power until the city thrills to his every move – but something is missing from his life, which perhaps only the picaresque troupe of troubadours who are trekking across the desert in search of him can explain.

Grief is both a unique dystopia, or perhaps an interpretation of the present, and a remarkable psychological fantasy, disturbing, witty and moving by turns.

The Group, by Ravinder Chahal

RAVINDER CHAHAL

ISBN 1 905315 01 5 • £7.99

"How far can you really take it? I mean, could you lie to someone, get them hooked? Get them believing in something because they want to, for whatever reasons they have of their own, and then come clean? Would they listen to you then or would they just want to keep believing the lie that they've made their own?"

The Group is a book that talks to people who are successful in an economy that they do not believe in. Aimed at those for whom it is fashionable to be knowing, it tells the story of Khaled, an arch-cynic for whom everyone is a fake or a loser. The only problem is Khaled has done very little himself that he can be proud of and is beginning to bore himself.

Faced with the prospect of drifting through life in obscurity he dreams up a satirical scam to reveal how easily people can be manipulated, and how thin their dreams and aspirations are. But rather than escape The Group, his scam only serves to show how hollow he has become, and how he needs to completely recalibrate his own life.

The Group is a dark and wickedly funny book about people who tell lies and people who believe them.

Light,
by Craig Taylor

ISBN 1 905315 00 7 • £6.99

"Before you know it you've read 100 pages in a sitting. Extremely compelling and delightfully unusual, it would make a wonderful bitter sweet film in the vein of Withnail and I."
Time Out

CRAIG TAYLOR

LIGHT

reverb

Light is a poignant story of love, loss and English summer. After the death of his father and the loss of his job, Ben's reacquaintance with a childhood friend pitches him into a glamorous life among a wealthy, rural set.

In a milieu of infidelity, corruption, cash and unrequited love, the narrator inadvertently achieves artistic fame. Through revelations of long-buried love, mix-ups and malice, an accident occurs and an innocent party takes the blame.

Inspired by the art and media world of the late 1990s, when an idealistic and transient glamour created millions for the elite of the new economy, Light has a strong claim to being the English *Great Gatsby*.

aboutreverb

reverb isn't a traditional publisher. We think of it as a cross between an online community of readers and an independent record label. Why a record label? Because we publish books that have broadly the same 'sound' – contemporary literary fiction with an edge. This edge can be humorous, it can be thought-provoking, but it is something that makes the book stand out from the crowd. We hope that if a reader has enjoyed one **reverb** book then they will enjoy the others.

reverbforwriters

Unless they are already successful, writers tend to get treated pretty badly. At **reverb** we are trying to do things a little differently:

- **Give new writers a chance -** we are committed to publishing 50 new writers over the next five years.
- **Fast but meaningful feedback -** most traditional publishers will leave unsolicited manuscripts on the slush pile for months; many are rejected unread. At **reverb** we promise to give an answer to any writer who follows our submission guidelines *within seven days*. If we do reject the material we will always try and give a constructive critique rather than simply a three-line rejection letter.
- **Working in partnership -** we view writers as talent to be nurtured rather than a commodity to be exploited. We pay high royalty rates and the lion's share of rights sales always goes to the writer.
- **Developing new talent -** we have dedicated a section of the **readreverb.com** site to information and support for new writers. We will also run free workshops in which our writers will share their experience and knowledge to help new authors develop their work.

aboutreverb

reverbforreaders

Without readers there would be no publishing, so we have set up **reverb**review to create interest in all writers, not just the ones that we publish. **reverb**review is a weekly newsletter that contains book reviews, an in-depth look at an iconic author or book and articles from readers on books that have changed their lives. **readreverb.com** contains an archive of **reverb**reviews, features and news stories from the world of books.

reverbforretailers

Independent booksellers are the backbone of the trade, but more often than not get treated like the poor cousin by large publishing companies. At Reverb we are dedicated to supporting the independent trade through offers, marketing material and author visits.

---

reverbreview

At **reverb** we're passionate about hundreds of writers – not just the ones that we publish – which is why we set up **reverb**review.

reverbreview is a regular email newsletter containing book news, reviews and a feature article on the work of a contemporary writer.

Because we are so passionate about the writers that we publish we'll also be giving away ten signed copies of our books to **reverb**review readers every week, plus we'll offer you the chance to attend special events to meet our writers and hear them talk about their work.

For more information please visit **www.readreverb.com**

Printed in the United Kingdom
by Lightning Source UK Ltd.
113327UKS00001B/8